ADVANCE PRAISE

Any new book by Tom Sheehan is cause for celebration in my world. He is, in my opinion, a national treasure, a designation underscored by this latest book of short stories. About these 23 short stories and the characters in them, the author says: "Being in the garden of long shadows is a haven for the memorable, where all the past grows continually in the shade of husk and melon, leaf and bloom, where you recollect faces of friends and foes, mentors, comrades, lovers from the first whisper out of shared darkness. There is no escaping their imprints upon your soul, try as you might, for they come in batches, in singular escapes from wherever they've been hidden, a parade of people, of characters, of the relentless impressions that you own, the ones carved into your mind by some mastery of personality now brought to light in your world, the world of the garden, and often become immediately present for you."

Each short story here is different in tone and tenor. Softly and seamlessly, Sheehan knits together the past, present, and future by blending youth and old age, dreams and nightmares, light and darkness. He paints word pictures like an old master, enticing readers with ghosts of youth, sly humor, exuberant lovers, and heart wrenching tales of heroes and lost souls. He tempers life's wounds and raw hungers with innocence and wonder, allowing readers to laugh, cry, dream and celebrate.

Sheehan's latest book of short stories elevates every day, ordinary people, places and events to the magical through his words. If I had to choose a favorite story here it would be "Born to Wear the Rags of War" because it's an anthem representing everything that's great about the author and the unsung heroes in the country he loves. This book is highly recommended.

-Laurel Johnson

Striking a harmonious balance betwixt poetry and prose, Tom Sheehan's stories are virtuoso concoctions of prosody and narrative power. Sheehan's war stories chronicle the secret histories of those who acted heroically when called to duty, who then returned home to try their best to live quietly as men. His coming-of-age stories touch upon the bittersweet intermingling of the height of youth and beginning of knowledge, often ending in calamity or silent disillusion. But let us not dwell on categorically confusing literary matters, suffice to say Sheehan is the real deal, one of the best writing today, whose legacy will spread out before him like all of Macbeth's tomorrows.

-Steven Hansen, editor, *TQR* stories

Tom Sheehan writes from the heart, with a soul that knows no leash on depth. He lives with a richness, soaks in every ray of sunshine, every raindrop, every glance exchanged and breath shared, each touch a treasure, whether a sparkling gem or a twisted, ravaged angst. We savor his storytelling like a slice of his grandmother's buttered bread, warm from oven, and oh so belly soothing. He is the Master, our Twenty-first century Great American writer.

-Diane Buccheri, publisher, *OCEAN* Magazine

In his latest collection of short stories, *In the Garden of Long Shadows*, Sheehan makes us marvel by capturing yet again the often incomprehensible complexities of human behavior and emotion, in prose so lush and exquisite that a few of these tales might pass as poems in camouflage gear.

-Clare MacQueen, editor, *Serving House Journal*

In the Garden of Long Shadows

Thomas F. Sheehan

Pocol Press
Clifton, VA

POCOL PRESS
Published in the United States of America
by Pocol Press
6023 Pocol Drive
Clifton, VA 20124
www.pocolpress.com

Publisher's Cataloguing-in-Publication

Sheehan, Thomas F., 1928-
    In the garden of long shadows / Thomas F. Sheehan.
    p. cm.
    ISBN: 978-1-929763-58-0
1. Short stories, American. 2. Saugus (Mass.)--Fiction.
3. War stories. I. Title.

    PS3569.H39216 I6 2014

    813.6 --dc23   2014933365

Library of Congress Control Number: 2014933365.

ACKNOWLEDGMENTS

Some of these stories, in present or past versions, have appeared in *Milspeak Memo, Ocean Magazine, MGVersion2Datura, Dew on the Kudzu, Canyon Voices, Nazar Look, Greensilk Journal, Literary Orphans, KY Peripheral Sex Anthology, A Golden Place, Troubadour 21, Muscadine Lines, Open Window Review, Haggard and Hello, The Saugonian, Serving House Journal, Eskimo Pie, Ascent Inspirations, Wilderness House Literary Review* and *Blue Lake Review.*

In the Garden of Long Shadows

Being in the garden of long shadows is a haven for the memorable, where all the past grows continually in the shade of husk and melon, leaf and bloom, where you recollect faces of friends and foes, mentors, comrades, lovers from the first whisper out of shared darkness. There is no escaping their imprints upon your soul, try as you might, for they come in batches, in singular escapes from wherever they've been hidden, a parade of people, of characters, of the relentless impressions that you own, the ones carved into your mind by some mastery of personality now brought to light in your world, the world of the garden, and often become immediately present for you.

Here I labor, in shaded glories, their scent my scent, their dream my dream, their past my past. Their stories unfurl from leaf, from tall husk, from a bloom lost in the wind, in the weather, in the while. The yearning for one more word from anyone of them, one handshake, a passing smile, is endless.

I'd be pleased to make their acquaintance again.

TABLE OF CONTENTS

The Old Man in the Garden of Long Shadows

All things began and ended, Georges Amocine always believed, in shadow, going into or coming out of, cave or womb or thought, place or circumstance notwithstanding. And here he was again, with a semi-darkness beginning, telling him beforehand it was coming.

The shadows had been there forever. At times there were stars with them, and then not, or with horizon glare, and then not. Ragged clouds and alleys and valleys often crawled or frolicked, often atop each other, and all bore shadows. Shadows climbed into trees and down out of them, and leaped from lamp posts and doorways stiff as tunnels, being old hands at darkness, and out of clumps of soft debris holding out in the mind.

Shadows had entity, he vouched, and intensity, and longevity. They were pervasive yet global, submissive but exploitive. They cranked themselves out of mountains and moonscapes and the endless limits of stars. How long he had believed this he did not know, but his bones said so, his mind, and the cool side of his skin.

Shadows were irrepressible, like old hounds about the porch, or old friends when trouble brews. Once they disappeared, they were bound to come back. Dawn or dusk would take care of that; the sun or a dim bulb at the fallow end of day. Perhaps in another endeavor, perhaps on another day, it would be the white light at the end of a tunnel. Despite these beliefs, fear was not foreign to him; he had forgotten more of it than he could remember. Fear would not pile up in him; it never had.

From his seat on the milk crate in the middle of the garden, he looked back toward the house, illumined at the end of the corn row aperture, like the narrowness of his full life, his crowded life. It was a photo coming at him. Black and white, but a photo, alluring but never sophisticated, having an identifiable background, cause and effect faint but colored up like life itself.

He saw Esmel at the window. Oh, girl! Oh, girl! She was watching out for him still, more than fifty years' worth, and her warmth penetrated his entrails, as if magnetized. From that distance she could touch him; always she had had a tactile sense emanating from a core the sun itself would own up to.

She was his only worry; he was adamant about that. There was no

1

other matter for him. How would Esmel handle the stove? Who would shovel her out come winter, the wind beating against the walls, the windows rocking? What had he not done to pave the way? Name a task, he felt himself saying, and shied away from any resolution. Would she again sit in the front seat of the car, knitting in hand, a book closed for rare minutes, a hand like his playing a fly line over the rail of Thunder Bridge, sun in the eyes of two people in love with dawn?

Light refracted someplace within his bodily confines, made angles, caused corners, bounced loose as a kaleidoscope in a child's hands. The world was full of tangents and whispers. They came unannounced, owning silence and dimness all the way in, from wherever it was they came. Speed had never been important, but was obvious.

"The single tick of a second hand," rolled out the voice of his father from its dim yesteryear, "is an echo of history." The shade thrown by the slim hand was known. Finally, doubts and all arguments about that adage dissipated, he agreed he had never known until now what the other old man had meant sitting on the edge of a railroad bridge over the Saugus River, a drop line drifting toward the Atlantic three miles away.

The voice sounded further judgment. "Down the short haul," that other old man used to say, "that's how far. Down the short haul."

Now, here shaded once more, in the midst of leaping corn, he thought of Basho the poet. Involuntarily he smelled the salt air, monstrously sharp, with creditable edges, as it came up the confines of the river, up the reedy and contorted valley, to touch him with memory and saline beauty. One ugly moment on the mud flats as a boy came back to him, the sucking threat at his young feet, and the threat of total immersion of his body a thing to be reckoned with. These images had kept the marsh's beauty on tap for the longest time. He loved the muddy flatlands downriver, without tree or shade, and the rich ocean beyond, bearing the sense of eternal breath, as though it yet waged a long war.

"Down the short haul, that's how far."

Sitting on the milk crate, the tall rows of corn gave him a moment from the heat of the sun, from the high day. Again he wondered about the achievement of shade, where he stood in its measure. When the smallest threat of breeze hurried its hustle he could hear the maize and yellow tassels at their play, the whisper of spider webs, and the silent music of the spheres. On top of it all he swore he could hear the sun's steam pot,

2

hear it hiss away.

The milk crate, an old Hood's Milk crate, scored by fire and ice and earth, by knife or ax, was hard under his rump. Impressions made themselves known on his butt, but were as vague as old scabs or old scars. After all these years, he wondered why he had brought the crate into the middle of his garden, into the middle of the corn. And just a day earlier. Another measurement, he thought, making itself known, as if it were the solution to an equation long looking for an answer. Another sense of shadow, of shading.

With a rigid stab at light, he tried to remember everything at once, the small lore and legends of a gardener, his current posture as crop raiser if not farmer. The radishes were done and pulled in, the peas, the small bed of asparagus, twenty tomato plants with little yield left, the corn now just about ready for a good old fashioned corn boil, the kind they had down New Brunswick way, in Molly's back yard. The iron pot there was almost three feet across, the fire smoky, the grass coming off mustard-colored, the potato fields tilled anew for miles on the sides of rolling hills and the flats of valleys, Molly and Esmel at the picnic table, their hands and mouths busy with the day, winter hiding out miles away up the continent.

The light broke a lightning across his memory, like catalogues of sorts being opened, emptied.

He heard the ghosts of his youth coming on, the smells of the garden making it happen: his grandfather talking, like it was a record being played back, a tape, one of the new CDs they talk about, miracles of miracles: "An old Down East saying, I believe," his grandfather was saying in that high-pitched voice, all the way from the back of the barn on Blackhill Road in Franklin, Maine. "Peas go into the ground on the Fourth of July. Given the climate up here, it seems that some have struggled to meet that deadline, as a few would be ready on occasion, but not until some began to grow an earlier variety of bush pea that was only knee high -- thus less growing, climbing. Some have planted peas as early as March 31-- and as long as the ground wasn't wet they came up. Everett Cocker from Machias would plant them every April 1st for years just for the sake of planting them. He would clear snow off the ground to do it. Sometimes he was lucky, but it was more of a tradition for him. Lettuce, spinach, Swiss chard, kale, turnip, can all go in the ground now," (It was late April then, May breathing easy) "but most people wait.

3

If spring rains keep coming the seed could rot. Sometimes people would plant an early row of potatoes to have new potatoes where the skin is supple and are considered better tasting... Irish cobblers, Khatadin, Kennebec, and such. Strawberries are planted as root clumps or sets and are mulched over in winter and are perennial. They come up each year. They are a bit of work, too; much pruning and eliminating the dead canes. Corn-people usually wait until Memorial Day or a week before because the seeds need warm soil. The old timers would soak the seeds in arsenic to kill the scrabbling crows that try to feed on them. Cucumbers require warm soil like corn. Some plants, like kale, taste better after a fall frost. A lot of times squash, pumpkins and potatoes are picked or dug when the vines dry off. Potato vines wither all brown. Then it is good to leave them in the barn doorway in the sun, to cure and dry the skin a bit before storage, so they will keep and not get wet and rot out on you."

The voices went on. The crooked bar of light shone as if it were loose in the northern sky or way out over the Atlantic in a September storm. It broke like scars or marks of retribution.

Esmel came back to the window, he thought, figuring him to be in deep thought. He waved at her. She waved back, startled, he was willing to bet. He could not stop thinking about the catalogues. The destinies. The days at count. The newest alert, working on its own, he couldn't put his finger on, electrical in nature but microscopic, down the far end of touch. A messenger afoot, like Mercury, wise and winged.

If the shadows were his new movie theater, they held opaqueness, a sepia quality for him. A shade of yellow or copper touch. Tawny. Fulvous. As real as metal. Objective.

At the end of the corn row, below the window in the upper hallway she had just retired from, he saw, still-opaque, old comrade Londo Leuter with the nickel smile you could buy cheap; Londo from Pennsylvania by way of Korea, stripped to the waist, washing out of his helmet, the high mountains a faint backdrop behind him, the radio truck they had called Kumbanchero dug into the hillside with its backside protruding. The name was painted on the bumper alongside HH Co 1stBn 31st RCT. The names and the signs and the sweetness and the innocence bothered him in the midst of the war.

The faint reel moved.

Perhaps that was Chicago's Bob Breda over to the left cleaning his weapon and Stan The Fist Kujawski checking a Walkie-Talkie 300 radio

4

and still committing to memory the names of all the guys he ever served with in the First Cav through WW II and then the 7th Division here as they busted out of Chosen Reservoir and Hungnam and at the end of his tour, with rotation breathing down his neck, digging his holes so deep he never slept but kept digging, thinking about his Japanese wife and the two kids back in Japan and how playing softball in Chicago someday soon would be the dream come true, and over there, leaning on the tailgate of the radio truck, was Billy Pops Podgurski (Oh, Billy, someone out there said, as if ever under breath: Oh, Billy. Oh, Billy, swearing now he could hear the cry) moving at the end of the rows of corn, coming out of the haze, from where he had gone off more than fifty years earlier. Billy Pops gone off into one of the long shadows and never coming out of it, like he had become darkness itself, all black and proper in its memorial tuxedo and all melted into one canister of deep shade you could carry if you had the right handle on it, and he suspected, as he had for a long time, that he had found the handle.

Oh, Pops, you beautiful son of a bitch. Where'd you go? I know you didn't die in Mung-dung-ni. Not there against the tailgate of Kumbanchero, but later, in Connecticut when you came home, but I never saw you again, Pops, and you were maybe a hundred miles away and you began dying then, shriveling up, drying out, you beautiful son of a bitch, so full of laughter even when all things piled up and came down as hurt that day when you got a bad letter and cried in the night like Tex Goode, only Tex lied all the time, a son of a bitch of a pathological Texas liar saying how his wife had died one night and I cried with him in the tent on the side of the hill and a few days later he told some guys from Easy Company that he was shit mad because she wanted more money to fix her teeth and let her go chew dog meat on her own he ended up saying, being the frigging liar he was in the first place, but not like you, Pops, dying on me in my own backyard after all the shit and shinola we went through and I can't even begin to forget the huge smile you wore like the Earth wears the Equator.

Oh, Pops, you beautiful son of a bitch. Where'd you go?

He wondered where Jack Slack had been hiding for those fifty years. "Go into any head in any pub in Albany and my name will be jackknifed on the wall," Slack had promised. He and Esmel had tried, twice, knocking on every door of his old street, Van Schoick Ave., and no

5

forwarding address at all. No evidence he'd ever been there. The one time shadows had lied. "You and Londo wuz a pair of the greatest. I seen 'em come and I seen 'em go in the pine box express. You guys wuz a pair." His old letters echoed now in amongst the corn tassels with the spider web music, the shifting and measuring of shade, the essence of cool skin sneaking under his shirt. "I'll write from my next assignment, when I get out of here, though I'm writing this now directly in the light of tracer bullets. Ha ha!! I'm in for the long haul, you know. I'm RA all the way! Try the walls in all the men's rooms in Albany. They'll all know me, me and Ernie Gatti. We wuz a pair too. We just got rations and Ernie's skunk drunk in the back of the cook's tent. The old man'd shoot him if he saw him, but he'll be straight and narrow in the morning. Old RA himself."

Verbatim, even from the shadows, came his message to a veteran's site: In my search for Jack Slack I've enlisted (free) detectives who are veterans, newspaper people, and have called/talked to 171 John R. Slack numbers found in White Pages or left a message. I've been offered Slack Family histories, dinners if we get by (assuming Jack is with me), and all have been cordial. But I have to share the following with all the searchers out there: Here's a morsel for you, from one of my free calls I do on the computer looking for Jack. Got a woman answering the phone, someplace out West during a host of random calls, and follows the conversation and what went with it: 'Ma'am, I'm calling from Boston and I'm looking for a John R. Slack who served in Korea in 1951.' Great noise, exuberance, yelling to her husband: "Daddy, daddy, there's one of the guys from Korea on the phone." Chair-moving sounds in the background, the sound of a book dropping on the floor, some other unintelligible menial and muffled racket. I thought of a walker in use, crutches, a cane, had awful pictures in the back of my head. The guy comes on: "Slack." The voice hard and steady and not like the pictures in my mind. "John R. Slack?" "Yup" "You in Korea in '51?" "Yup." "You there in '52, too?" "Yup." "You in the 31st Regiment?" "Shit, no. I was in the Marines." "Oh, shoot. I thought I had you." Lots of noise on the other end, part of a hacking cough. "Hey, Mary, whaddya think of this sonofabitch! Here I've been telling you for forty-five years of married life that there's only one of me in the whole world, and now this strange sonofabitch from out of nowhere is trying to tell me that there is two of me." We talked a good thirty minutes on the phone, at times hilarious, at times sad, some old pals really missing, and on parting he said, "I hope you find your pal, Georgie, and let me know if he's as good lookin' as me." As one newspaperwoman said, "It's not always the destination, is it?" She's a great help but can't get an assignment out of her editor because "that war" is old news, is a good guess. Pro Patria.

And suddenly old Pete Leone had a piece of a shadow all to himself. The first time Pete Leone crossed in front of him, back at Fort Devens in 1950 with the 278th Regiment up from Elizabethton, Tennessee, he had seen the grace of carriage saying here in fatigue uniform of floppy pockets and customized drabness of dull green was an athlete, saying he was cocky, saying he was countable in spite of the first attributes he'd come away with. Later, in Korea, they had crossed paths a number of times, Pete riding the gun carriage of a 155 Howitzer down the MSR near Chorwon, an hour later bringing him along to chow by going right to the head of the chow line, like he was a frigging general; Pete busting their balls as he elbowed his way right up to the front of the chow line to the First Cook, saying, "Charlie, this is a pal of mine. He's a writer too, so give him extras or he'll make numb nuts out of you some day. You can never get away from the black and white, Charlie. Never. It can haunt you until the day you drop and there ain't a hell of a lot you can do about it. The book on you will follow you to the grave, Charlie, every last goddamn line written about you. Every goddamn word, curse or not, plaudit be damned too. You think you got secrets, Charlie. Even your mother will find out what you've been hiding all these years." Pete's laughter ran the length of the disarmed chow line, feet shuffling to an unknown tune of hurry up and wait, mess kits dangling in anticipation, the air based with metallic elements stretching out every sound, every note, and the quick laughter to be noted as though out of place.

Charlie had waxed purple. Popovers he hadn't seen since Anthony's Restaurant back home, in the neighboring city of Lynn, fell on his mess kit, fried chicken he might never get again in-country, mashed potatoes thick and white as snow, Pete all the time cajoling each of the cooks and attendants in the serving line, drawing allusions, looking back at Charlie every now and then as if punctuation was being rendered, giving advice, smiling and nodding at him all the while. "Hey, Zebra, old buddy, new corporal, this here's the real new Hemingway, if he ever gets to cut back on his vocab. This is Zebra, Georgie, whose letters are priceless, not his but the ones from his pappy back in Elizabethton,

Tennessee, home of the angels of the written word. Ain't that right, Zebra? Ain't that old man of yours the new coming of Will Rogers or more like Rod Jenkins of the 278th than old Rod himself, still at the still, still carrying the same load of bricks on the back of his truck, the stuff stuffed down inside the bricks and the straw?"

Then, as now, Pete's eyes were Italian gray stone and lit up, his hair black and severe in its trim, his jaw with the merest sense of slack cut into it. Later, on a visit to Pete's home high on a hill in McKees Rocks, Pennsylvania, his wife Barbara put out the same spread for them, right down to the goddamn mess kits she scrounged at an Army-Navy store after reading an old letter for the tenth time. A lady like Esmel. Shadow of shadows.

On the milk crate, seeing it all clearly, he knew everything in the whole world had aged except for the very moment of the pictures; the pictures were as sweet as they were then even in the midst of the horrors of the war that most people had forgotten. He felt funny thinking of it that way, but it was true. It ran through him like a delicious train, pistons popping, steam belching, thrusting, knocking down walls. Sweetness and war, and not seeming to push against each other with much effort, yet co-existing, sharing the shadows if nothing else. There was sweetness to the irony, sweetness of and by itself, hanging out in its own shadow in among all the other shadows.

Oh, Christ, the old wounds could gather yet a storm. Oh, that damn yetness.

Then the phone had rung one night and Frankie Mitman's voice came out of a longer shadow. "I can't find your house. I'm at the White Hen and I can't find your house." You can't beat that for timing and irony, can you? He gets all the way here to Saugus from Bethlehem via Korea and he's not three blocks away and can't find the house. This gymnastic kid, purveyor of Polish goodies, who knew the reality and the scourge of the two-way Steelers linebacker, Chuck Bednarick, right out of Bethlehem High School with him, hard rock as hard rock can get. But Frankie's voice is breaking up, sounds dry and the beer is loose and cool and another shadow's coming out of the long night, and it's Frankie coming up the trail as he's coming down and Ralphie Moore is almost sitting on the point of Frankie's bayonet and he's driving him up the hill as the 17th is replacing the 31st somewhere in the Iron Triangle.

"I'll come down tonight and tell you about it," he says, and prods

8

old Ralphie up the hill. Ralphie is noted as not carrying a weapon and not wearing a steel helmet and that is fishy enough in itself. It sort of broadcast what it meant; that Ralphie had taken a trip on his own and didn't get to where he wanted to go, which was the Great Lakes and the Mississippi River where he had worked on boats since he was eleven years old and once there could hide out forever.

Of course, shadows demand light. The pronouncement comes easy.

The light shook in his eyes again, a stream of light, now a straight arrow of light, a beatific beauty, a laser punch. It went to the back of his head. It lit up the far ways. Something caught itself in his throat. His fingers tingled, his arms. Behind his eyes both shadow and light had sudden places of combat before he settled down. The old tasty breath came back, the reserves touched upon and counted. The movies. The catalogues. The shadows.

His lungs eased.

A sweetness, he fathomed, had been fully released.

It was sixty years old, the sweetness, the bitter sweetness, the testament of time, a yellow busty sweater looming in front of him in a morning high school study hall and his groaning with a morning erection that would cause laughter if he stood in front of the class. The sweetness tasted like the South Side of Breda's or Kujawski's Chicago. Or his own North Shore, crowding in on Rockport or Gloucester. Or the edge of a small lake near North Barnstead, New Hampshire and cool on the face. Cool on the face, on the arms, in under the edge of his shirt, talking to him about Leon Bellargeron or Eddie Lampack, surely there, off to one side.

It smelled like he was thirteen or fourteen and one war was long over and there'd never be another. Or it was the same full-blown sweetness that he once was, later on, when Esmel on a steep night heavy of passion had said her mouth was cursed by his sweetness. "I labor to remember all other things but not your sweetness." That's how she said it, her smile in a curving and wicked radiance reflecting again in his eyes.

Oh, she owned him forever, the lady in the window in that house in the shade. She owned him forever and ever.

Then he remembered why he had brought the milk crate into the heart of his garden a full day earlier. All of sixty years had gone by and he recalled his grandfather's other words of warning: "Old Sam Parker went sitting on the crapper. That's where Mildred found him, straight up like he was frozen to the damn seat. On the crapper, and his pecker stiffly upright."

Not fair to Esmel, if I went that way. Not fair at all. My drawers down around my ankles, me stiff as a board. God forbid the scene!

Almost Insular

A series of strange bubbles of unknown origin broke the water only 25 or 30 feet from Jasper Henry, resting in a fog bank in his kayak on a morning trip on the Atlantic Ocean. An excellent swimmer and kayaker, his vest strapped in place, he was a mere mile from his home in Nahant, a Massachusetts peninsula running into the ocean from Lynn. At first floated in the thought of a sea turtle, the bubbles were so large, like balloons had let go their breath below the surface. But he suddenly became aware of a huge presence below him, a huge presence, one he had never imagined, shadowy but solid, seen but not seen, spelling displacement to the core.

He was leery, World War II in high profile, his brother Jim off in the South Pacific, on that other body of water, and treachery possibly afoot in his homeland. He was 13, but his mind loaded with imagination at every vector made him a reader, a romantic, and a slight adventurer who could still make a fist. He had seen a movie a week earlier where a troop of Boy Scouts had made the difference, thwarting off danger, saving the innocents. He loved the movie, took it into his dreams, saw scenes over and over again in his half sleep, and could see the puffy cheeks of the young leader, Jackie Cooper, boy movie star. It was high adventure for Jasper Henry.

And he had heard about German U-boats on the prowl on the coastal Atlantic, the east coast.

With a decision as quick as his paddle, Jasper Henry drove himself against the fog bank, heard more bubbles popping up behind him, followed by a whoosh of noise coming from underwater, and small waves touching like hands and fingers on the sides of his kayak. He made a low profile, shifted his paddle, and drew it onto his craft and kept it motionless. Holding his breath, letting all curiosity find silence, sitting at the very edge of the gray fogbank, he felt a mysterious and different wetness on his arms. He was not alone in the waters off Nahant.

Afraid to breathe, to move, he kept the profile log-low on the water, heard the final bubbles break the surface, saw a hand paw at the water and a strange head appear, a head with an apparatus on it, like a diver's helmet. The apparatus and the hands moved toward the shore, halted, looked about, seemed to stare past him and the kayak, continued on.

Jasper kept his frame low, log-low. The figure of a man eventually stood up in shallow water, took off the apparatus, walked onto land's edge, found a large stone, stuck it into the skull of the apparatus with difficulty, walked back into deep water, dove, and came back up without the apparatus. He stumbled back to the shore, started a search for something, found it and withdrew a black bag from under a pile of stones. Quickly he dressed in clothes taken from the bag, put the clothes he wore into the bag and carefully buried it under a pile of rocks. He walked onto Nahant proper, took a turn, climbed a rocky path, and set off as though the morning had called him out for a seaside walk.

Jasper, with his heart beating, disbelief and fear pounding his senses, paddled ferociously, beached his kayak, ran up on the other side of a big rock, and saw nothing of the stranger.

The swimmer, the man up from the depths of the ocean, was nowhere in sight.

Then panic hit him like a fever. He heard his brother Jimmy say, "Don't let him get away from you, Jazz, I'm counting on you." He ran down the first street and there in the front yard of Donnie Brougham's house was Donnie's bike, the new Western Flyer with handlebars a yard wide. He grabbed it on the fly and took off.

Ten minutes later he still had no sight of the man, blond hair, blue shirt, black pants, and black sneakers. Nobody walked this end of the road. The fog had not crossed onto Nahant proper. The diner at the beach was lit up as usual, the police cruiser parked outside with several other cars. He put the bike beside the diner and through the window he saw Officer Rogalski getting his morning coffee from Perly Gates who owned the diner, two fishermen having a small breakfast at a window table and two older ladies having coffee and rolls, and the blond man in a blue shirt, black pants, and, he was willing to bet, wearing black sneakers.

Jasper kept hearing his brother's voice, so he walked in and said to Officer Tim Rogalski, "Hi, Tim. How are you this morning? Foggy, huh?"

"Well, Jasper, were you out there today at the point?"

"Oh, no, Tim. I just wanted to tell you something."

The blond man shifted in his seat at the counter, turning his head slowly, pretending to look around the room.

Jasper said, "I have to tell you, Tim, that I borrowed Donnie Brougham's new Western Flyer bike, not a week old and it was right out

12

on the lawn in front of his house where he left it. Can you imagine that? Right out on the middle of the lawn." His hands were on his hips as though a teacher was expressing concern about a student to another teacher.

"Gonna teach him a lesson, huh, Jasper? Good idea. His father's got more money that he can count, so Donnie's got to learn from someone else. Might as well be you." He looked up at Perly Gates and said, "Kid's ahead of the game already, ain't he, Perly?"

The door opened into the small diner and another man walked in, slapped the blond stranger on the back, and said, "Hi, Greg, I told you I'd make it. The walk on the beach was great, all the way from over in Swampscott. How was yours? And the eggs smell great or is it the bacon?"

He sat beside the blond, pointed at the blond's plate and said to Perly, "I'll have that, but doubled, if you don't mind. Another coffee for the officer, too, if he wants one. My walk was just great. I feel like celebrating."

Rogalski said, "Thanks, mister," and to Gates, nodded his head and added. "Might as well while I'm here. It'll come in handy. I've got to do some coast-watching later today. We've had reports, pretty firm ones, that German U-boats or submarines have been spotted off Nantucket and up in Maine. Nahant's not far from either place. When we hear those kinds of reports, we think about spies being set ashore, so I've got to keep a sharp eye." He rubbed his hand on Jasper's head, and offered him a salute. "Keep it up, Jasper, I'll be watching you."

"I might as well go out with you, Tim," Jasper said, "and take another spin back to Donnie's house, see if he calls you before I get back there. I bet he does, or his father does."

Rogalski winked at Gates and the policeman and the boy on the watch left the diner together.

Jasper wheeled around a corner on the bike, came back to the house a few doors from the diner, a garrison being repaired, scrap lumber in odd piles around the yard. From a seat on a carpenter's horse he had a view of the whole street where five cars sat against the curbing and the small parking lot across the street where four cars were parked. Beyond the small lot ran a narrow section of the beach, and beyond that the Atlantic ran all the way to the horizon. A ship dotted the very fringe, the Atlantic as calm as the morning kitchen at home until his father walked

13

in, the day already loading him down, his mother doing her best to smile, cheer on the day for him, and worry about Jimmy on some open sandy beach in another ocean.

Wondering if he'd be able to see a car if the blond got into it, thinking the other man might not have walked all the way from Swampscott, all along King's Beach and then the whole causeway onto Nahant, he thought about his options, how best to see and record any plate registration numbers. If they were up to no good, he'd have to record it somehow. Could he remember the numbers of one plate? Of more than one plate? His breath, as with each problem appearing, came heavy again.

At some point, not sure when it began, his stomach hurt, a small throb of uneasiness making news. He could hear his father say, "At least it's not my heart, which is not down that low." His mother would smile to make him feel easy, as if she had laughed at his small twist of humor.

Jimmy's voice came back, secretly, but with a nervous edge to it. "Don't let them get away with anything, Jazz." He always loved how his big brother called him Jazz, the only one in the family, the only one on the whole island of Nahant.

In the solace of that thought, the nub of a carpenter's pencil slipped its dark slabby lead into his awareness. It was hardly two inches long. He leaned down to pick it up even as he looked at the cars, counted them, tried to read the numbers. He couldn't read them all, and guessed that he could never remember them all.

Jimmy, from way off, his voice thin and weary, simply said, "Think, Jazz. Think."

The weariness in Jimmy's voice made hum jump and hustle.

He grabbed a piece of clean scrap wood, dry, almost off-white in color, and in a second act picked up a dozen or so used nails, leaped on the Western Flyer, hoped Donnie or his father had not called the cops, crossed the road, did a few wheelies in the lot, and at the end of the lot, close to beach sand and the ocean, he printed the number of each car's plate on the board. He made the trip four times, did four wheelies, and checked the numbers one last time. They were complete, correct, all Massachusetts plates.

Down the causeway in its slow curve into Lynn, he rode back towards the diner to get the numbers of the cars parked on the street. Up a slight rise he drove the bike, pushing hard on the pedals, found another

14

site to study the cars, and waited for the men to exit the diner. With a nod to himself, he was glad he had also noted each number by location, in the lot and on the street, and by relative positions.

The last time he had seen Donnie Brougham, they had a fight about some movie. He could not remember what it was about, who won. But Donnie would call the cops if he had seen him take the bike. Behind a high bush he stashed the bike, returned his watch, remembered the smell of bacon and eggs in Perly's place, heard his stomach acknowledge the aroma, wondered how his father had been this morning, how his mother was doing.

The two men, the swimmer and the walker, came out of the diner and he decided to note the walker as "W" and the swimmer as "S" whenever he recorded any comments about them. He studied them as they stood away from the diner about a dozen feet. W looked up and down the street and across the parking lot and along the beach. Jasper somehow knew he was looking for Rogalski, who was not in sight. The man wore a thin summery jacket that carried an emblem he was not able to figure out, some golf club emblem he assumed. He wore a pair of pants that sure looked to be suit pants like his father's, but were not walking pants, not beach pants. And he too wore sneakers, the kind S had on. He looked down at his own sneakers, black high tops, and a buck a pair from the Converse Rubber in Malden.

Then, right there on the sidewalk as if they were out in front of their own house, like they belonged someplace, W in a secret move handed S something from his pocket, shook his hand, and walked up the street, climbed into a Chevy, backed up, turned around, and headed off down the causeway towards Lynn, slowly, easily, as though he might be counting the waves of the new tide, looking at the early women walkers. Jasper checked off the Chevy plate number with a W.

S, also looking around, perhaps also searching for sight of Officer Rogalski, crossed the road and entered the parking lot where he sat down in a Packard two-door car with a hood as long as the Erie Canal. His uncle Owen had the same 1939 model, the same long hood with the same threat of power under the hood. Once he said he ran it up to Portland, Maine on a few stretches at 90 miles an hour ... 90 miles an hour!

Jasper marked the registration numbers with an S, realized he should do some more reading about U-boats on the coast, and suddenly remembered he had seen a few likely magazines in Easy Eddie's

15

Barbershop but hadn't given them much attention, his father sitting there, drumming his fingers on his knee like he was counting the hairs falling off a head. That'd be easy too, sneaking looks at Easy Eddie's magazines, or else he'd look in Santry's Drugstore and slip behind the door with a few other magazines off their rack, fill in the threats of German U-boats, here and all along the eastern coast. Vaguely he recalled a U-boat once was suspected of being in the Gulf of Mexico, just beyond New Orleans. It made him shiver, and he felt the sting in his stomach start anew. Rogalski's comments in the diner might have carried too much information.

The Chevy was long out of sight, and the Packard, once that engine got warmed up, could be out of state in an hour or two. He didn't know which way to turn, who to turn to. It would not be Rogalski who'd fake interest, drink coffee, rest, but remember other tales Jasper had told, and snuff it off like one of his butts right into the gutter. Nor would his father help, too angry early in the day, too tired at night, his mother at such times too busy making up for all other things in the house.

He wished Jimmy was here. Then, as if coming from an intolerable distance and bouncing off a clean rock of Nahant, like a bugle call or a razor's edge, he heard Jimmy say, "Don't let them get away from you, Jazz. I'm counting on you." When he added, "We're all counting on you," that did it.

All the things he thought he should do started to fall into order, and a small joy of being in control began to find some appreciation. The glow was short-lived when he saw the Packard start up, move down the parking lot to the far end, and stop in a new spot. S stood up outside the car, took off his shirt and put on a short-sleeved summer shirt, as though he was preparing for a walk.

Jasper panicked. He thought that S would go back to the rocky landing place, look for his stowed gear, destroy it or get rid of it in some manner. He had to beat him to it.

Without looking back, he retrieved Donnie's Western Flyer, flew out a back yard and raced away toward the rocky point without S seeing him.

Or he hoped so.

He resisted the urge again to look back. The pedals came up hard against his feet, his thighs felt the thrust coming back into them, and then found and matched it with his own power. The sound made by a '39

16

Packard was comparable to his energy, he believed for a moment, as he drove hard over a hill and saw the whole Atlantic out there, the one small ship on the horizon. He wondered if a U-boat's periscope watched the ship as he did, saw it better than a dot on the horizon, saw it as an easy kill. The movie "whoosh" of a released torpedo sounded in his head, he saw the light of an explosion on a thin, thin horizon where the world fell away.

Staying away from Donnie was important; he'd mess up everything and every which way. Donnie and his father would run with it, their mouths blabbing like babies, terror running out of their mouths so all Nahant would go all abuzz, explode … and miss what was important.

He drove harder, ditched the bike down between two slabs of sea-worn stone, and scampered down the rocks. In a few minutes he had the hiding place located and recovered what was hidden there. It was a black bag, smooth and oily to the touch and made him think of the table covering on his mother's kitchen table, the red and white squares leaping into his mind like a strange checkerboard, how water would run right off the edge.

Not daring to take time to look into the bag, he grabbed it tightly, climbed between rugged rocks to keep his profile and silhouette as indistinct as possible, and found the bike where he'd left it.

His stomach hurt once more, now tingles of pain as though needles were loose in him, flashing their points around with little care, no care. Down two lawns he rode, off the street, keeping out of sight, and suddenly saw S turn a corner ahead of him, on a casual walk. Jasper ducked behind hedges, flattened the bike, lay down with the oily black bag still in his hands. His breath was heavy and fearfully noisy as he tried to hold it in place.

S was coming down the street leisurely, as though he was a neighbor from the other end of town or over from Lynn or Swampscott for a morning constitutional, the sun only part way up in the sky, the sky a perfect blue on a day coming perfect … for a U-boat spy checking out Nahant, perhaps trying to cover his tracks, or retrieving the buried black bag.

Jasper wondered why S'd dare come back. Was there something in the bag he had forgotten? Didn't dare leave behind for discovery? Would slap him in jail in a minute? If he waited and it was found by someone that someone might think it had fallen from a boat or ship, to be claimed

17

by the finder, carried off to be lost forever in the heart of the country, in the heart of America.

Or point fingers where fingers should be pointed.

S passed him as he hid behind the hedges thick as grandma's oatmeal, heart pounding all the while. He waited until the blond was out of sight around a corner, jumped on the bike with the bundle and headed down toward the beach. On the way, behind his own house, he hid the bundle inside the tool shed, tossing it onto the small shelf above the door.

Meanwhile, the Packard bothered him. A few Halloween tricks came across his mind, and one of them loomed as a definite possibility for immobilizing the vehicle. He decided against stuffing a potato into the end of the muffler or pulling spark plug wires from the engine. A dozen other pranks rode his memory from past nights of the holiday.

The few wheelies he performed in the parking lot attracted attention only for a while, and when he rested he rested beside the long-hooded Packard and with utmost caution, alert to anybody who could see him if they wanted to, stuck two slivers of wood into the air stems of the tires on one side, and loosely tossed the nails from the construction site around the area. It might spend some of S's time to think about nails in the tires. It was the easy part of the equation of "how and fixed."

Air began to escape its tight compression and leaked until the tires were flat and the Packard settled lower on the ocean side of the lot.

S was not in sight as he gazed back toward the rocky point, so he sped back on another street, came to the rear of Donnie Brougham's house and saw Donnie in front talking to his father, and saw the cruiser come to a stop out front. Rogalski slid from the cruiser, just as Jasper walked from behind the house.

There was instant yelling from father and son and Rogalski did not say a word until Jasper reached them. "Hello, Jasper," he said, "how you doing today?"

"Oh. I'm fine, Mister Rogalski. I just came up from the point and saw Donnie's new bike back there near the shed and was telling myself how great it looks. I love those wide handlebars."

Rogalski said, "I had a report his bike was stolen, but I guess that was a mistake." He turned to Donnie and asked, "Didn't you say you left it out front, right on the lawn last night. Donnie. Is that correct?"

"Well, maybe I forgot. I sure won't leave it around anymore." His father walked off in a huff. Donnie ran to get his bike and Rogalski said,

18

"Where you headed, Jasper, home or down the beach? I'll give you a ride if you want one."

"Can I ride in the front seat?"

"Sure can," Rogalski said, slipping into the cruiser. Jasper went in the rider's door.

Before the cruiser came to a stop, Jasper spotted the Packard leaning on the whole left side in the lot, but he said nothing to the policeman who paid no attention to the vehicle.

He wanted to get to Easy Eddie's Barbershop or Santry's Drug Store, catch up on U-boat information. He caught the edge of something he had forgotten, but it didn't surface. Worries crowded him that all he had seen wasn't real, wasn't dangerous. Maybe it was a test of home defenses, alertness, the home guard as it was. Rogalski always seemed kind of sleepy at the switch.

During the day, S went off after he had seen the condition of the car, walked back toward Lynn and returned a few hours later on a bicycle with a bicycle pump across the handlebars. When the tires were fixed, he placed the bicycle and the pump in the trunk and drove off down the causeway, towards all America.

It was the last Jasper saw of the Packard, but he knew the sound of the engine, could pick it out of a dozen different cars.

After 9 PM he went to bed at his father's insistence, knowing he'd be unable to sleep: he hadn't warned anybody yet: not his parents, not Rogalski, not anybody. Not even the FBI. He sat up in bed at that. The thought sat there in his mind, fermenting, thinking of what he could say. How to phrase it.

Past midnight he heard an automobile. The tappets said it was a Chevy. Nobody on his street came home at this hour, though a few families did have one, and Pete and Jerry Milburn each drove one. The car turned around down the street and slowly passed his house again, and he could imagine S or W checking him out, the oily black bag discovered and taken away.

"Oh, Jimmy," he said, "will playing cops and robbers bring trouble home? I remember Dad always saying, 'I know you'll never bring trouble into the house. Was he talking about something like this?'"

The next night it was the Packard he heard, the thrusting purr of the engine. He couldn't imagine how big the engine was beneath that long hood. It was well after midnight as the Packard went cruising down a few streets, but not his street. Could he take that as a bit of security? Was he clear of them as their suspect who had taken the black bag? That made him laugh in the back of his throat, but not loud enough for anybody to hear. There was no one he could tell what he knew about S and W.

Just Jimmy, but so far away it made him cry.

The newspaper the next day carried a report of U-boats off the coast of Maine and New Hampshire and one report of a woman being caught as she came up on the beach in Maine in an inflatable craft and she carried a large sum of American money. Police whisked her away before newspaper people could even talk to her or take her picture. She might have slid into the middle of the country if one man had not been on watch for the country, an old WW I veteran, his eye on the horizon, the beach, and odd entrants to his neighborhood.

Jasper read the story when his pal Barry Reese left it on his doorstep. Barry had two brothers in the war, one in Germany and one in the Pacific. Not yet 6 in the morning, they chatted a while about last letters and known places their brothers had been.

Jasper read parts of the story to Barry who replied, "If I caught someone like that I'd bash their brains in with a baseball bat, even if it was a woman." He could do it, too, Jasper knew, as Barry was the best hitter on the island, picking right up where his brother Buddy left off when he joined the Marines.

Barry said, "My dad watches the whole coast line some days from the second floor back porch. Mom thinks he's sleeping, but he's got his bird glasses in his hands all the time."

Jasper said, "My father just gets mad all the time, like he never sleeps."

"Maybe he just want to be out there with Jimmy and can't. That makes some guys mad. Ever think of it that way?"

Jasper said, "Maybe. I hope so," then he said, "'member that triple Buddy hit in that last game? How sweet was his swing, huh?"

Then Buddy reported, "Rogalski says he's the best he's ever seen from here to Gloucester, and he's seen 'em all."

It had all gone around and come back again.

Maybe Rogalski was the chance for him.

The fog was in again, sliding in with a soft breeze, and sat on the grass as well as the rocks at the end of Nahant. Jasper felt a minute chill touch him. The sea was making noise, too, the swells coming ashore, washing sand, washing rocks, running out of breath on the beach, the ranks of waves eternally deep. Boat motors had begun to hum their morning music. Road traffic was steady on the causeway. The gulls were quiet, some other birds as noisy as ever, and chipmunks and squirrels played tag along the stone wall and in the trees and he could hear their chatter snappy as popcorn.

He heard Jimmy, too. "It's time to step up to the plate, Jazz, Your turn at bat. Pick a good one. Right in your wheelhouse. Give it your best shot. Slap it silly, Jazz."

In bed that night, he chose Rogalski, "He didn't snitch on me to Donnie or his father, but it has to be on my terms," he kept saying, making an oath of it. He had checked the black bag in darkness, just making sure it was still there, untouched, unopened by him. He wondered again why he had not opened it. The thought of secret explosives thumped at him, or sticks of dynamite to cripple some special target, shut down a bridge, a tunnel, the subway. That kind of surprise was too much for him; let the police take care of that.

The radio in the house was on continually as his mother listened to war news all day, especially about the Pacific campaigns. She kept shining Jimmy's pictures on the mantel above the fireplace, his First Lieutenant's bars of gold as shiny as a new coin, his smile handsome enough to wilt a dozen hearts. His patience at building model planes was unequalled, and when one was finished, like a P38 or a British Spitfire with expended .22 caliber shells added like supercharger exhausts on each side of the balsa-covered and camouflaged fuselage, it made him want to fly. His heart would soar when Jimmy wound up the elastic band motor, stood tall on a high rock and commissioned each model to flight and to the sea. Off they'd go, in a nice steady wind, the propeller striking for more air, pulling the nimble little craft until the moment of death came, and it dove out of the sky and into the Atlantic. Once or twice they had tears, measuring the work put into the craft, or thinking about the pilot, the war on top of everybody … and Jimmy's turn not far away.

So, trying to bolster his confidence, he thought again and again what he'd say to Rogalski. When it was all settled he realized he'd have to admit a few lies he had already told the officer … and be prepared to face the consequences.

Rogalski, coffee in hand, came out of the diner and approached the cruiser, Jasper leaning against the trunk of the vehicle. "Tim," he said, his voice as deep as it ever had been, his eyes downcast, "I need to talk to you on some very important matter. Nobody can hear us. It has to be a secret for now."

The officer, a sly smile on his face, said, "Jasper, I know all about you sneaking out of the house to go on your kayak rides ever since you got Jimmy's room downstairs and your folks never knowing. I used to do the same thing when I was your age."

"Oh, I heard all about you as a kid, Tim. Everybody knows, but this is real different. This includes something about Jimmy out there fighting the Japanese on some crazy island nobody's ever heard about, and the other guys who are fighting in Europe."

He took a deep breath and added, "This is life and death of someone somewhere I just know it. I heard you about your coast watch. I've seen you doing that, some early mornings, some evenings."

He took another breath and said, "I saw something, Tim, I was afraid to tell anybody. I didn't even tell my parents, but I saw something you should know about or the FBI or whoever."

Rogalski looked into the boy's eyes, took his own breath, and replied, "No more crap in it. Not a single word."

"I have proof, Tim, in my tool shed. I saw a man with a crazy thing on his head come out of the water near the Point after lots of bubbles came up first. He came on shore, took the thing off his head, found a big rock and went back in the water and dove and came up without it. Then he looked for a package, which was a black bag buried under some rocks, changed his clothes and put his wet clothes in the bag and buried it. I have the bag in my tool shed. Like I said."

"Let's go look at it."

"There's more, Tim, lots more."

Rogalski nodded again, and then shook his head. "What else?. Is it going to get better?"

"I hoped it wouldn't be like this, Tim. There's a lot more. Remember that morning in the diner when I told you I stole Donnie's new bike, and one guy there said he walked from Swampscott and felt so good he told Perly he'd buy you another coffee?"

"I remember."

"Well, the fellow that he met in the diner is one of them. The other one, blond hair, blue shirt, black pants, black sneakers, is the one that

22

came up from the water with that thing on his head."

"My God, Jasper, you're making me a little upset with all this made-up drama."

"Tim, when I prove this is all real to someone and you were the first to think it was all a joke, you'll be laughed at. I'll tell Jimmy when he comes home and he'll tell all his buddies."

"Is that all of it?" Rogalski said.

"He came up out of a submarine. I can show you where he dumped the thing on his head."

"Now that has got to be the end of it. You're getting way ahead of me."

From his back pocket, Jasper pulled out the piece of wood with the registration numbers on it, explained about all the cars listed, showed him which two cars were directly involved, showed him the Massachusetts plate numbers, described the vehicles, drew Rogalski's memory to the '39 Packard. A pal had one just like it, and the one in the parking lot came quickly to mind. He explained the S and W marks.

"Is that it, Jasper? I think you're starting to convince me it's worth checking."

"There's some more, Tim. The Chevy has gone past my house on a couple of nights and I've heard the Packard on the other streets, and I've seen S walking by and I hid from him. When I flattened his tires on the Packard, he knew someone was on to him. He went off and came back with a bike pump and pumped up the tires. If Jimmy was here, he'd go after him right away."

"Let's go look at what's in that bag." It was like Rogalski had joined the ranks.

"I'd be afraid of that, Tim, those guys getting near my house. If I could tell Jimmy somehow someway he'd get real upset."

"Okay, you go home, keep watch. I'll be off in a couple of hours, and I'll keep patrolling, then after dark I'll sneak over your place come in the back side and meet you in the tool shed. Is that a deal?" Then, as though he had gained a whole lot of smarts and odd information since he had last talked to him, he asked Jasper, "You still use the window from Jimmy's old room to sneak out of the house?" It was like the cop had known everything there was to know except how to catch spies.

"Yes," Jasper said, put in his place a bit, "as long as you don't tell anybody and swear to it."

23

It was the first time Jasper Henry ever shook hands with Patrolman Tim Rogalski. The closest was an occasional pat on the head.

The round-faced and usually lazy policeman had made some secret arrangements other than what he had with young Jasper Henry's parents. He had a friend invite them to a secret home showing of new paintings by a noted Nahant artist ... out of the house ... out of the way, "and keep them as late as you can."

And at the far end of the causeway, sitting outside a restaurant at the Lynn shore circle, another close friend watched every Chevy and Packard that came into the rotary and headed down the causeway to Nahant. Both these arrangements were with Rogalski's high school pals, still as tight-fisted as ever, and tight-mouthed. Except for the one watching traffic.

Near 10:30 he telephoned the Henry home where Rogalski waited his call. "The Chevy's coming." He repeated the plate number. "It's one of the two cars you're interested in, Tim. I'll watch for the Packard. Good luck, whatever it is." He hung up the public phone and went back to his Ford pick-up truck. It was 10:45 on a thick, dark night, overcast and rain predicted.

Rogalski and Jasper, at the receipt of the phone call, had slipped out of the house and into the tool shed. Jasper told him to touch the black bag on the shelf. He touched it with his fingertips and advised, "It's waterproofed alright, and thick. I bet it was heavy."

Jasper heard the Chevy tappets coming across the darkness. He didn't know where the car was, but it was somewhere on the next street, on the backside of the Henry property.

"That's the Chevy, Tim. That's it." His excitement was almost visible, and Rogalski said, "I sure hope I didn't make a mistake here, Jasper, but we better not get cornered in here. We'll go behind your father's woodpile. I'm betting they don't dare carry guns, but I have mine."

They'd talk about it afterward, how the voices, even in whispers, came to them on the clear night air, the voices of S and W, most all of it in English, and all of it pretty audible.

W was talking, with near a curse in his voice, "You should have taken the *dumm* bag with you." One word was clearly German. "You have me deeper in this than I was supposed to be. All I want is my money

24

and to be done with this. If U-509 is sunk because of this, they'll kill us. Cousin Hans is a crew member. I haven't seen him in a couple of years, my last trip to Spain. It's all getting worse because of a *dumm* kid." The German dialect came again on the one word, as if it was a pet word. He must have stepped on the rake Jasper had forgotten on the lawn. The curse was cut short, as if he had stuffed his fist in his mouth.

It was S's turn, and he said, "The parents of the family are out. If the boy's here, he's got to be alone, asleep. We get the bag, take care of him, and get off this stupid island."

W said, in a paraphrase, "This dumm island."

S, seeming conscious of their voices carrying in the night, said in a new whisper lower than before, "He must have hidden it. If he told the parents the police and the federal men would be all over the place. So he must have hidden it. Let's first look in the shed. The door's open. Perhaps it's in there."

One of them stepped on a shovel, or stubbed his toes. "Gott damm," he grunted, pain in his voice, his reserves beginning to break down. *"Es ist alles wegen dieser dummen Jungen."*

Somehow, Jasper Henry knew he was being cursed. He tried to remember it. He had to tell Jimmy when he came home, not yet knowing it meant, "It's all because of that stupid boy."

The pair of agents entered the tool shed, half as big as a garage, and pulled the door closed behind them and began a quiet search, now and then a tool touching another tool, a saw blade clattering upon a hammer or rake handle popping on a shovel handle.

None of it was alarming in tone, but it provided some cover noise for Rogalski who grabbed a three-foot piece of 2x6 Jasper's father used to keep the woodpile aligned and to prevent it from falling onto the neat grass.

"Shhh," he whispered and held his finger against his mouth, stepped from behind the pile silent as an Indian, and reached the shed without making a sound.

When he jammed one end into the ground as forcefully and as silently as he could, he slammed it with noise and great force against the door and quickly sat on its incline. It jammed tightly against the door … and all hell broke loose inside … and out.

Rogalski fired his pistol in the air three times, three loud bangs that cruelly invaded sleeping Nahant.

25

Most of the neighborhood and much of the island heard the gunshots and also heard Rogalski screaming in the darkness. "Call the police! Rogalski here on the Henry property in trouble. Officer needs assistance! Call the FBI, hurry! Hurry! Rogalski needs help. Officer needs assistance."

The shots sounded like an invasion was taking place.

But it really wasn't and wasn't going to come this time by way of the U-509, because of Jasper Henry and Tim Rogalski, insular coast watchers.

Jasper's mother was in the kitchen and did not see the official looking uniformed man get out of an official looking somber gray vehicle. He was a Marine captain, his brass shining like a whole new day along with all the ribbons and medals on his chest ... and a yellow telegram envelope in his hand as he looked once at the address on the mailbox and then again and started up the walk in a very serious but slow stride.

A neighbor, who had moved in only a year earlier, held her breath. Mr. Henry, she knew, was at work and his wife was in the kitchen most likely. She wondered if pain ever ceased hanging on to people, or crowding them, and she didn't know where young Jasper was.

But he was at the window of his room, saying again and again, "*Es ist alles wegen dieser dummen Jungen.*" He knew it by heart and also knew he'd have to give up his room too, as previous connections had allowed his new captain brother to deliver his wounded-in-action telegram to his parents.

26

Lover, Not Yet Lover
(a Memorial and a Fantasy)

And so it was, plain and simple, a necessary thing to do, an oath moving in one's self at the beginning of resolve, a slow upward presence, a climbing of spirit, so that he saw it coming as if from a field of mist caught out atop a pasture, the morning young, dew spread and spent under the sun exerting itself always, and with it all he saw the outcome, how it would come down the line swift as a memory in some far place where he was out of this habit range, this wide place he might have called home grounds except it was not solicitous at the time, and that memory, as stark as it might be at the finish of its appearance, would come like that same mist off the grass, at first as conceivable, then as probable, and finally, with a conscious note of thanksgiving, come whole and moving and it would be her in a final presence in the same place, in his heart and not his mind, in his heart and not behind his eyes where he thought he'd see it again and again, in his heart and not in his hands the way he'd recall her at odd moments of the night with a twist and a turn and a sigh, but sleep now a dread enemy, sleep an impossibility, sleep that came of wretched evasion and long mourning, and just as always she'd be visible in a new haven, looking at him, her chin in hand, blue eyes as wide as ever, and sending him that continual message, only to have it waylaid by someone other than either one of them, another body in her place, a new touch, a new taste, a woman of thought, a woman possible, perhaps around the corner, perhaps at the next cup of tea, perhaps a pair of eyes he'd know would be her eyes in the second place of their coming, and he'd roll over and hate himself and cry his poor soul to sleep.

Where it all began and might end had come upon him as surprise comes to any alert soul, her illness an unaccustomed turn, a brevity of concern at first, a slight indication of some small piece not working, the way it happens in ordinary door chimes, the least of importance, for the knock would follow and the entrance conducted and the gaiety loosed once more, or then, more thorny, as in a clock where a spring might be caught unawares or a notch filled with debris or a gear snagged, and time, by the minute, would go its way, or an hour, to the end of the month where some due would get undone, unfinished, lost.

He'd know his loss more than separation, more than death.

She had the last words saved up for a delivery meticulous and persuasive: "Do not stop what you are doing; do not chase after me in any hurry; and in all loyalty and bound by this promise, find someone to talk to, to read to, to release to."

He brought himself back to a new day where it would begin for him, coming that ordinary way, in a soft hour of evening as the sun tipped its hat goodnight at the kitchen window and across the room in a friend's house he could see her acknowledging again one of her last days, in that special way she had of salutation, reminding him how everybody on God's hard earth loved her, the patients whose cries she could hug, the nurse orderlies that she trumpeted to all and sundry, how they had come from devastation and nothing to hope for, unto this place of hope, agreeing with her that all should be pain free and exalted in their dignity, even as all those days dwindled into sobs few heard but her at the door of the room, at the end of the hall, with the last step from the inside of that huge place to the outside, the evening blessing her tired moves, her muscles, her spirit looking for nourishment for the day to follow, for surely repetition was the sin there.

He knew how it would happen.

It began for him, across a room in that friend's home where people mixed in merriment and talk of another loss and celebration, the babble and groundswell moving in slight waves keeping all corners alive not with the same words but with the same intents … the look, the approach, the answer, the assent without a sound, agreement working the fields of the bodies in the large room, in the field of his body, that new pair of eyes saying all the things he might want to hear, putting aside judgments and comparisons, putting aside the cause of the initial attraction, because her eyes were running with the words he could not hear but understood, the way semaphore flags at the lip of an aircraft carrier can spell its position and its acceptance to a pilot winging his way home, out of gas, praying for the lap of safety, the parts all together for maybe the last time in this life.

Later, the stub of afternoon coming spent, the one with the announcing eyes would point out the window to three children of the neighborhood playing in a side lawn of a neat house whose red bricks had taken on a dusky red hue the sun has some days in late summer, whose hedges were trimmed by a barber with comb and scissors, and whose windows must have been dressed by a quaint old lady who had asked for one more turn at decoration to carry her name and her last thought caught

28

up in a deciding of colors.

This mere stranger for the moment, who had come from across the room at the beginning of her place in all of this, with her own loss, stared at the children, a light falling across her face, across the lenses of her eyes in the way those children ought to be seen, in a choice part of the inner eye, a roll call brought to bear with their histories coming on, the schools of their growing years assembled piecemeal in the new fiction as though they were now promised, or had been promised long before these new parents had come on the scene to make their wishes, to say their prayers, to offer their thanksgivings.

Her voice had a mysterious quality in it, a dream coming alive. "Let's make them ours." She said it with soft passion, with an eye on their clocks, and with solemn promise, as if it had already happened, that mini-adoption, that quick attachment. "Let's watch them whenever we can, as obliged we would be, enjoy their goodness ahead, their coming small sadness, see them leap up and onward, and hold them dear as we ought in the silence of our hearts. That is the most of love I can muster."

She was, for the moment, at half-truths that did not last long.

The words that followed might have been spoken before, by her of the past.

"Let's be in love again, each of us, with all possibilities for as long as we can." She took his hand and held it close and in another moment he knew she'd move his hand upon the promise.

The nights would say their names and it would be enough to hear soft syllables once known as though they'd echo forever.

And so the way it was supposed to happen, it did, love advancing the soul's illumination of inner light, the mass of it coming at once, at first an illusion so beautiful it was previously unimagined, and then, after his wanton sleep was beset and circulated with toss and turn and turmoil, and with a side glance at once mistrusted but leaving a hard dent in his memory, she moved from the covey of her own shadow into the scan of his horizon, and remains in that one spot, that totally owned place by herself, a grace emanating from that aura unseen as music but the tempo and the unbidden language coming along with it, the rhythm of a woman who moves with ease into the depth of a man where she assimilates, absorbs, animates by a motion so subtle to this day it still overpowers him.

She moved like the appreciation of a mountain morning hovering over a lake, a mist slow in ascension to translate into an unseen level allowing iridescence to appear in a painting his eyes said existed solely for his vision, no other person seeing what he was seeing; and in its climbing into a nothing that did exist for his wonder and awe, knowing from the inception she was a dream come alive for him, this woman, a mere mist at first, coming alive, a smile wide as horizons, coming alive, a voice saying she was real, coming alive, its tone so meticulous and full of clarity it struck him with lightning delivery, the first word coming alive his name, the very first sound saying she was thinking of him and beset with the energies and want littering his days and nights, never letting go, truths hanging on past dear life.

His name came softly in the night, on the breath of a woman moving the way only a woman moves, a languorous length of her, a gloried broadness, a hip salutation as much sign as her signature, into his mind waiting for the word, the gesture, the hand sending its touch on a linen full of sound but so silken and smooth as though his name carried there first, the manner of passage broadcast from soul to soul, the elegant length of her reduced, brought closer, a loop in its coming, a grasp, a homing brought to bear his all in a grip only her kind owned.

He said her name, and it rose pious, devout, an unseen feather on unseen air but letting off a whisper of promise where imagination is king, but her grasp essential.

Then he heard her voice as from the far end of a tunnel, or the top of a mountain so distant it was out of sight, the soft syllables advancing on him the way balm dissolves worry.

It was necessary now, the time for it to happen, and he moved a ways and looked behind him and saw how far he had come in his loneliness, and there was silence he could not comprehend, which made him think of being a distant star looking back here and saw himself less than he was and knew the difference, knowing nothing of time, only of manner --- how it happened, not why, not where, but knowing the form of it.

It was her.

The Town Without Butter

It happened in the town that had no butter, a town in the foothills of the Rockies where little popcorn was sold and nearly every person was thin. Most people living there liked to run, out on the flats or on the slow inclines. On a snappy dawn some of them ran marathon distances without breaking a sweat. If butter was in town, the butter packers brought it, illegally.

Pearl Trimm came into the square from her morning run, five miles out and back, and saw three men standing beside the bank looking suspicious. It wasn't that they were fat or just overweight, but they looked like unhappy bankers. Pearl had an idea of what they were up to, conspiring some way to repeal the butter law or trying to skirt it: butter was not allowed across the town border. The three men, a bit hefty, were in charge of the three banks in town.

Pearl ran over to them wearing a yellow running shirt, blue shorts and a blue sweatband across her forehead. Five feet eight inches tall, she weighed 121 pounds, with a blazing red hair ponytail in a white ribbon. The morning sun fit into her smile, shaping her mouth, lighting her eyes. Her skin was unflawed by any minor imperfection and her eyes promised music and dancing were comfortable in her soul.

She put her hands on her hips, the stance of a nineteen-year-older.

"Hey, guys, you still trying to slip that butter thing through the town meeting? It'll never work. I know they've been on to guys like you since butter was ousted fifty years ago. Why try to get it back? We're better off with butter gone. Toast is great with mom's extrawnerry jam." The kidding was in her voice. From the corner of her eye she saw Banker Caldwell snap his belt up a notch. It was not a harmless gesture, she realized. Once he had been trim, long before he started worrying about losses, balances, business in general. She thought he at one time had probably been a good looking man.

"Butter's a way of life in some towns. Why not here?" Banker Bramstock got in his two cents worth. Once he'd been a sprinter, lean and mean at that. He made a hideous liar out of such talk at the moment, being the widest of the three men. His eyes were caves of forgotten dreams, the plump cheeks stealing too much from them.

"A way of death, you mean," Pearl retorted. "Statistics will show we're all better off without butter. It's a paralyzer. On potatoes. Corn.

31

Toast. Pasta. Especially popcorn, the way theaters had buckets of it. At a dime a whack, too."

Now she noticed Banker Caldwell's mouth was practically drooling. "I trust there's no contraband coming into town, gentlemen. No side orders of butter slipping through with the green things like asparagus, spinach, really fresh green beans with lots of pepper, a little salt thrown to the wind. No pats and slabs and bars and tubs like they used to have. Lord, we were little more than a piggery in those days."

Pearl patted her midsection. She noticed it did not go unnoticed by any of the men, all old enough to be her father, or Banker Caldwell to be her grandfather.

For a moment Bankers Caldwell and Coldbit were near apoplexy over the illegal menu sported on them. "I was up at Pure's Pass this morning. I noticed strange tracks in the ground. I'm suspicious. Likely they're from some butter packers who made the trek over the mountain with a load."

Each man looked at his toes and then into each other's eyes before looking into hers. Distance grew in their eyes as well as long planning, with a bit of discernible suspicion, she thought.

Banker Coldbit's sweet tooth was often a half pound of butter and a loaf of hot bread. At the moment his jaw was caught at a strange angle of gnashing a stubborn morsel of food, probably a greasy remnant. He managed to say, "You're so thin it should be no problem to you. You have no worries. Why do butter packers bother you?" He coughed once on his own words and added, "If those tracks 'were' from butter packers. Butter packers indeed!" His proud head was like a snotty colt suddenly knowing he could run like the wind.

Pearl said, "Butter packers don't bother me. Butter does. Wise people got rid of it long ago. We've been blessed since. We're thin, healthy, and we can run down day's end. We've got a fifty-year head start on fat."

Banker Coldbit replied, "But each man should have his own choice, whether to run or not, whether to butter or not butter his bread, his toast, his popcorn, his waffles before he puts on maple syrup. Ought to be law." His eyes were red and a thin drool ran from the corners of his lips. In his thick neck the esophagus sent its contractions with a known taste. Banker Bramstock had to put out a hand to support Banker Coldbit, to keep him from falling over from a butter tantrum.

"Hey, Pearl," yelled a voice from across the square, "Archie caught some butter packers this morning, in Simms' barn. Had more'n a thousand pounds of grease in their packs. The grease valise, huh!" His laugh set off the next statement. "They plain out rented mules from Stafford's Stable on t'other side. Believe it?"

"What's Archie going to do with it?" Pearl yelled back, her eye on the three bankers, standing at quick attention, fully aware that Pearl had questioned the fate of the illegal butter and not the butter packers. A mere sign of the times; in butter-free Saxford butter packers were treated, when caught, like minor celebrities, like the loop-the-loop drivers in old Charlestown near Boston doing the Bunker Hill loop in speeding cars and daring the police to hinder, never mind stop, their reckless rides.

"Having a bonfire tonight down t'the lake, to celebrate this holiday. He's going to burn every ounce of it before it gets passed off t'the children. You know how Archie is."

Knowledge of Archie, town sheriff and butter chaser nonpareil, hung itself in the air. The three bankers, faces saddened, wallets obviously to be thinner before Archie's fire went out, looked at Pearl Trimm.

"Did you report the butter packers, Pearl?" Even if he had been handsome at one time, before the butter packers had gotten to him, Banker Caldwell could muster a mean sneer.

"That's not my job, and you know it. That's Archie's job. I don't like butter. I'm against butter. The three of you are my strongest argument. Look at you! What woman would ever want to be with you, slobbed with butter, your whole life sliding away from you, the skids greased unto eternity? Snuggling with you must be like trying to catch a greased pig like they do over in Sherman at the October Fair."

A subtle snap of her hip accompanied the plain disgust on her face. She turned from them and walked off a dozen steps, her svelte shape in the running togs about as beautiful as any of them could remember. Stopping, turning, she said, "If you only could remember what it was like before butter, you'd gladly give up some of your money, some of your stature, some of your fat." Her departure across the square was sylph-like, silken, sleek, and carried heavy chains linked near-mythically into the long past of each banker.

Banker Coldbit said to his counterparts in a whisper, "I'm tired of losing my money having butter packed over the mountain and having it

33

burned up for some silly celebration. We get a proficient crew or turn to something else. I cannot have my bread with jam or my green beans without butter. It's an effrontery to the select. Not so much the masses, but the select. It's due men of our stature. We are the backbone of the community."

But stature had nothing at all to do with the eventual repeal of the butter law, not in Saxford. And it was Pearl Trimm herself, a few years later, who got the repeal started.

Saxford, then on a metropolitan water source, had deactivated the old standpipe at Pure's Pass and had built a park at the base of the iron-plated tower. Rust was the sole climber of that old skyline marker homebound Saxfordians could see from twenty miles away. And it was here that Pearl Trimm, four years married, used to bring her twin boys to play and where she showed them the route of the butter packers, how it came up from near Stafford's Stables on the downside. Pearl could point out fifty places where their ineptness trapped them, by Archie or one of his butter-packing deputies angling on their trail.

One day one of Pearl's twins, Angus and not McDermott, fell into an abandoned pipe near the standpipe. It did not look good for the boy. The entire rescue attempt was in serious doubt, for the pipe had been inserted down through a hole in solid rock an old timer remembered had taken weeks to drill. Someone suggested dropping a rope down the pipe but they were concerned about accidental strangulation. The boy was stuck, down about thirty feet. He could be heard crying for his mother.

In the gathering crowd was a midget from the carnival soon to arrive in town. The diminutive one's name was Silas Aberhorn and he volunteered to be lowered down the pipe headfirst to save the boy. "All I ask," he said, "is that you coat me with something slippery so I don't get caught myself."

Alert Pearl Trimm Averguard, most anxious mother, yelled to the crowd. "Any butter packers here?"

Five hands were raised. One belonged to Pearl's father. "My load's under the trash barrel." He sprinted to the edge of the park where the barrel squatted in the standpipe shadow. Turning the barrel like a bottle cap, he spun it off the screw-threaded base and pulled a large pack from below. Archie and his butter packing deputies shook their heads in disbelief, missing that hiding place. The crowd began to cheer.

Pearl hugged her father.

34

Silas Aberhorn, stopped well short of normal growth, greased with butter and more slippery than any pig ever, went head first down into that narrow pipe to retrieve Angus Johanne Averguard from his certain death below the standpipe at Pure's Pass. It was one memorable day before another memorable day in the history of Saxford.

The next evening Pearl stood at the special Town Meeting and said, "I make a motion that we do away with the butter law." Blond and curly-haired Angus Johanne Averguard sat on one side of his mother and redheaded McDermott Cleston Averguard sat on the other side. They held hands behind their mother's back as she spoke.

A near silence loomed in the air.

In the back of the auditorium Robert Bruce Trimm was whispering, telling Archie and his deputies a few things they had never known.

New legends had already begun about Saxford's butter packers.

Delicate April on Hodd's Mountain

Oliver Kettering remembered almost everything. And judgments came of that memory. So it was that two coincidental things happened within seconds of each other as he sat on his porch: April, the sweetest month to him for close to 80 years, was into a third most memorable day, and his youngest granddaughter, Holly Gatersby, had come down off Hodd's Mountain in a sour mood. Showing attitude in her face and in a most determined walk, she went past her grandfather, without waving a salute, right to Fleet's General Store. The Kettering patriarch, on the porch of the small house he had righted from a barn more than a half century earlier, two wives ago, six boys and girls and six good hounds ago, noted the rigor of her walk. "The girl's only 17," he said to himself in polar judgment, remembering 17 like it was last night right after the evening meal. Like then, Delicate April was touching him with her ten delicious fingers. He was sure April would never let go her grip on him.

He hoped that somehow April's ten good fingers would also touch Holly Gatersby before the day was out.

"It's a damn shame if they ain't doin' just that," he continued in his communal prayers, the thick white beard reacting to a breeze more than his jaw at self-talk, the hazel eyes catching early sun and making them live as lit kindling. His half left leg was thrown up on a barrel top, haphazard, bent. Every time he threw that leg up on railing or barrelhead, Oliver Kettering swore he could see Brutus the mule snapping back at him the fiercest of kicks. A dozen or so neighbors, in a hurry, had come to his rescue a good fifteen years back. Once he swore he remembered every face of theirs; now he wasn't so sure he could pull all into one scene again.

In quick summary Oliver acknowledged most folks around about were kin of his, from one strain or another, and mostly friendly otherwise. He understood his own "otherwise" as being poor advice that he'd tossed from his present spot in the world, the sole chair on the generally-proclaimed Judgment Porch where he sat at the moment. Oliver, as all Hodd's Mountain knew, was a curious mixture himself…he neither looked like he was near 80 (seemingly half that age) though he oftentimes acted like 80… in proof he thought it had to be 30 years or more since people stopped calling him Ollie, sort of an extension of respect of what he had become the whole length of The Chawtenauga, advisor of all and such as he preferred to call it.

And Holly, true to one strain he knew as well as the book, was capable of going in one of two directions. Like her father Luden Gatersby, she could be idle, shiftless and sorry most of her life, like Luden a damn scarecrow of what he could have been; or, like her sister Marvel Alice Gatersby, she could, one illustrious day, haul up her damn britches and damn well get to work gettin' out of a rut. Marvel Alice, after her britches hauling, hard work, daring, dreaming, was three years into college, the first girl off Hodd's Mountain to do so in the best part of a hundred years. Though he loved Marvel Alice and her attitudes, he knew he loved Holly just as much; yet that thought caused him serious argument; did he love Holly a bit more because she needed more loving, and more security? He savored those thoughts in his usual fashion, fully and consequentially.

Then, in further adjudication, he said another prayer for her... Holly now mostly blessed in haymow adventures. Quickly he counted on his fingers his diverse intentions, marking with her name the deep sweep between thumb and index finger each time passing through that valley. Delicate April, as ever, coming around every year with sweet hope, touched him again and he prayed once more that its most decent enterprise and selection would include this grandchild of his at an obvious precipice of life, a place where he had been a time or two.

And so, absorption came on him again. A tremor in the bent leg, the hoisted leg, brought Brutus back in a hurry, and he spoke to nobody in particular, a sense of sharing accosting him, as he said: "Damned if I can't smell old Brutus' field work leather comin' back from its winter stash. And I can see the old cinches, reins and checkreins hangin' in the barn the last time I hung them up for good, seein' them over these late years slowly givin' way to dryness and crackin'. Every time I go in the barn, Old Plow, I swear on Eternity I can smell you." In his mind, in all about him, came a cessation of all other images and thoughts as Brutus came home again. "You ain't none lettin' go either." A furrow, as straight as a rifle shot across the back acres, from a long day past, fled its neatness through his mind.

Holly, in sudden realization, came back just as quickly in the mix of images; he could picture her down the road somewhere drying on the vine, ageing, missing the richness and true goodness of late years, her hair thinning, lips curling, thoughts dimming. "Oh," he thought aloud, "what a mixture of hope and disillusion abounds." It felt as though Brutus had kicked him again.

Then, from the mid-section of Old Smoky, the line of rock edging the road to Mt. Albion, his friend April sent down the smell of new maples afloat in the universe, and also the hidden horror of an old accident. His first wife, Therese Fablon Kennesy, came back in a rush, and he swore in another instance that he knew the same perfumed scent she had set adrift specifically at him one night at a dance almost 70 years ago. So drifted was that scent it clung to him for her whole life. It was a special life until the wagon, with her and their first daughter Ida Ells, had gone down off that Mt. Albion road, straight onto a pile of boulders and the inevitable and unaccountable smithereens. Life then, for a bit, had rushed about like a headless chicken, and he had gone everywhere for every reason until his soul had quieted down. Sanity had led to preservation, he swore.

Oliver's bad leg gave off one small ache of memory, and Holly's determined gait, so it said to him, was one of anger, and he judged it to be dead against her now-and-then boyfriend, Angus Hollerfield. Angus, handsome as handsome comes, more man than boy, knew all the paths and all the valleys of The Chawtenauga... and traveled them, as word went, usually after dark from forked leg to forked leg. One path led directly to Holly's barn on the side of Mt. Albion, and most other paths had their own same conclusions, moonlight notwithstanding. With a sense of wisdom, and long practice at life's endless war, Oliver could damn near orchestrate the illuminated arguments rising out of gray matter and understandable hungers put in place at Creation itself.

In one memorable night on the Judgment Porch he had argued with great gusto against Merle Preblum whose daughter Alice Colber, named for her uncle Al, had apparently been dishonored in a neighbor's barn. "Goddamn shame, Merle, you forget your manners and memory what you exercised in and out of a barn or two in your own time. The boy was coltish, not forsakin' anything at all, and that girl a fair mare in her own right. They been right-minded for a good dozen years now. More power

38

to 'em both, that lesson in humanity and all its cravin's."

Oliver had sprung that same argument on Holly a time or two, or one interpretation of it, to make his point, to give her self-reflection something shiny to look at for a change.

"Way in the past, girl," he had said, "perhaps 10 or 15 thousand years ago, or perhaps longer than that of which I ain't sure, you can make up your own mind to whatever, someone kin to us back down the road, made up his mind about somethin' and set the pattern and path for us, all of us. Makin' us like we are, he did, and they ain't much we can do about that decision of his and why it comes down to us. So just picture someone in your friend's family, over the hill there, or off in another cave or another valley makin' a decision that came down to your friend and they ain't a helluva lot he can do either about that old grandpap of his a few hundred steps back down on the ladder of Creation. Locked up in the blood, it is, tighter than the front door on the hive out there back of here."

Holly, as most kids off Hodd's Mountain, or for that matter anywhere in this here universe of looking up and looking back, paid little heed to words from an elder where sauces and hungers were involved. "He's such a liar, Gramp. Out and out, a liar from the first word. Never once said he snapped another pair of bloomers like he ought to have said. Ownin' up is important to people. And he didn't spend a breath on it. Just holdin' onto the goodies like he couldn't ever let go."

The blush of her pure pink was as healthy as the old gent could imagine it. "Girl, you can imagine him in your image or in his image, but you don't get both, and don't try to make his image be your image. It don't work that way. Never has, never will, believe me. You can go down to the river to pray for all of that, or up on the mountain in the mornin' glory, but it ain't comin' to you on any silver platter, no matter how hard you pray. Best thing is to let him do the prayin'. That's the secret in all of this here houndin' us. He gets to do the thing best needed. Sooner or later, the way he combs his hair, how he holds his head, the path shows itself."

Now, obviously on this sweet April morning, it appeared the frisky colt had run an odd course. "I best warn that boy of eternal loss," he said half aloud, knowing April, in its most fierce grasp hardly ever lets go, and granddaughter Holly had as many good parts to her as anybody on Hodd's Mountain.

In a sudden vision he saw the silhouette of Angus' widowed mother, Best Pearl, and knew a slow, subtle ache of another sort. As part

39

of the same vision, he could almost frame up the picture of a long-past forebear, Cro-Magnon or whatever name had been given him by people who invented such names, moving from cave to cave with more than one kind of fire with him or about him. The picture tickled the hell out of Oliver; Brutus and the ugly kick, and all the old leather work, made a hasty departure when he saw a saber-toothed tiger sitting beside a cave opening in the face of a dark cliff, licking at bone remnants, drooling. Time, so twisted upon itself, marched in the abrupt darkness across that imagined cliff. All Oliver Kettering's genes, some thinking they were deeply hidden and nearly lost, gave thanks in a rush.

Best Pearl, upon hearing a caution come from him as they sat in her kitchen, said, without a bit of hesitation, "Oliver, you know well as I do, there is barns and then there is barns. They do make memory, I swear. We knowed 'em and they know them, and like you always said, 'It all makes the world one whirlin' place of addiction,' and bless me so for sweet addiction." She added a shyly spoken but clearly heard, "Oh, yes. My! My!"

She herself was a late mother, and now at 50 or thereabouts, prime and robust, a light within emanating, hair as blond as a bottle would allow it on short order for a special occasion, set tasks in a row. With near effortless moves she primped her hair, ran a cloth over the shiny blue-checkered oil cloth on her kitchen table, righted and smoothed out her apron with the sweep of one hand, and just as casually let an elbow touch the old man of the mountain… less some degree of work still in the till, as he often said.

"There is one way we can square those kids away, Oliver," she volunteered. Immediately he somehow felt the old Cro-Magnon spirit moving in the woman. She tickled him right down to his funny bone, the hair shaping, the apron primping, the forgotten light hustled from some back acreage, the Cro-Magnon woman at her best. He figured whatever she had in mind was right as rain, and would have some prominence to it and a damned lot of years of refinin'.

"You just didn't all of a sudden come up with that notion, did you? Or you been spendin' some of the moonlight workin' part time at it?"

"Oliver, I must admit, for only you to know, that I been that way ever since I seen you and Hustice Helen in the back of a wagonload of hay some time past. Never was any sinnin' there either. Oh, my, no. No sinnin' there, just naturalin'. And you never fooled me none with the philosopher stuff, knowin' you're a man all the way from the very beginnin' you're always talkin' about."

In a queenly and outright manner she practically knighted him as she added, "You're the mountain itself, Oliver, and I swear my boy is trackin' the route you laid out so long ago over half of Hodd's Mountain. That kind of talk is endless, you know, once it gets hold of by some hereabouts... and you can imagine where I'm pointin'." Her nod was down the road from them, at the Town Pulpit, Bernadette Mabel. "She does swear by some things as being gospel good."

Part of Oliver's recall went skittering down the ways and valleys and over hills and hummocks long gone into mist. But a stubborn way held at some things so precious they seemed on their own not wanting to part. His smile was not an old man's smile, nor was that smile one of boast.

"So what kind of an idea you been spinnin' about in that pretty head?"

At last, he was thinkin', things are gettin' kicked out in the open. He affirmed within himself, It's time enough. Too much seed gone to pot.

So he said openly, "You thinkin' we been wastin' time and those young ones showin' us a thing or two about time itself?" The old mountain was straining in him; it was bound to break loose in a landslide sooner than later. As he took in all signatures of any sort in the room, any leftover ownership marks that might have been dropped in passing, a line of her hip movement, subtle as tea smell in the back of the kitchen, eased its way from wherever it had been tucked away and made itself known again.

It was contagion and he believed in contagion.

"It's easy, Oliver. You up and promise to marry me, do it all over again. We party, make speeches, get holden onto one another, and then you just up and back out of it all, like you went and changed your mind without a single fuss. Ought to slight hell out of that boy of mine. Make him somethin' miserable 'bout his mother gettin' stood so."

He thought about it for the shortest spell. The picture of a Cro-Magnon man came back to him in all his raw glory. As if in a partnership with that older man of the mountains, he then said, "Whyn't we make like I'm tryin' on seducin' you, getting' you into your own bed and lettin' him

41

catch up to us." It really wasn't a question he had proposed. "Now that might scare the hell out of him, him bein' the really worryin' type boy we hope he is. That might put the thunder under him, shake his outlook all to hell and then some."

"Oliver," she replied, the mouth ajar with her words and a move at false surprise, "You do get past yourself sometimes for a man your age. I have to admit the thought's been there more'n once since his nibs last took a belt out of me and got himself killed too on that bad turn of the road, like he was bein' served up one more time for all his shenanigans and such. There's always been a good connection since we both lost folk on that crazy road up there. I think it's been cookin' for a long time."

It was little more than a week later, and the stage was set.

The routine on Angus was decoded and duly noted, for Saturday was usually a night for Holly; a walk uphill for him, a new go at heaven for her, or a good shot at it. The maples and the early blossoms, the richness of new grass, the spill of a decent moon so soon after a few chilled nights the week earlier, said romance was well afoot, and the whole of Hodd's Mountain echoed with possibilities, with encounters promised as sweet as could be dreamed.

Best Pearl had put on her long flannel nightgown, where pink flowers roamed at will, where the long folds allowed all beauty its hideouts. On her head the knot of hair, newly golden, was loosed and tossed for best of measures. In her mind, little was left for chance; the house spruced from corner to corner, as well as herself. Signs of loneliness she had borne for endless nights were put aside, like the screen magazine at least three years old but radiant with a picture of one handsome dog of a movie star; and the tired, worn, nearly obliterated .45 Elvis record of new love was finally dropped into the waste bucket. But she was perfumed for the fare-the-well of all else she owned.

Scenes, she knew, were being set. A sudden glimpse of how movies were made came to her and just as quickly disappeared with an in-taken breath.

Oliver Kettering, the old man of the mountain, performer yet, waited down on the corner of Fleet's General Store with some of the old bucks, passing time and tobacco and old stories between one another.

"Damn thing I noticed, Oliver," Malcolm Brisbee said, "that you got yoreself pretty clean shaved for a Saturday night with the old boys. You ain't one bit losin' that bait on me; you got sonethin' goin' on we don't know about, like you'd let us know just as many times you did before." He raised his hands in bounden salute and waved them at the sky and whatever else. "I think we gonna run you for president, Oliver, or raise some damn fine stature for you at the end of the valley, some that all the old folks from here to the end of The Chawtenauga can take heed."

"It's what I'm ever tryin' to fathom, Malcolm, this boundless bit carryin' on in us since Creation did its thing, and we ain't got it figured out which way is really right and really wrong. Beats me at times all to dazzle, it does, lookin' at it from all sides." Oliver looked down the road toward Best Pearl's house square and neat against the barn behind it. The image of a man of the caves came back to him in clear luster. "We look at things two ways or more every time out, seems to me, and I'm not lettin' myself out of any argument here."

"Oliver, you cut the furrow a little deep for me every now and then, and I suppose this here is another one of them now and thens, you figurin' you're still asittin' on the mighty porch of deliverance and all us here at your feet waitin' on judgment. But if you're talkin' about men and lady things, ain't no way to hide it in mystery talk... it's damn well mysterious all by its lonesome. When there's honest couplin' 'tween folks, I can't think there's two ways of lookin' at that, no matter what age we're at."

"That's strictly the point I'm makin', Malcolm. Honest couplin' for the moment or for some kind of promise? The future counts itself on what's goin' on now."

"Hell, Oliver, none of us knows what's around the corner, never mind plannin' on what we don't know's goin' to be there. It ain't logical for me, not enough to change my appetite for supper, that's for sure." He laughed his way out of the whole argument, coughed once and nodded as Oliver Kettering, the old man who ought to have a stature raised up for him, walked off from the group of old timers and headed toward Best Pearl's house still neat as a straight furrow against the barn at the other end of town.

The confrontation came in Best Pearl's kitchen, not in her bedroom.

But Best Pearl's essence had assailed Oliver from the moment he entered her small house at the edge of town. He could not stay away from her in her loose gown where all promise seemed to leap about as she moved around, lovingly, coyly, proud. They gabbed a bit. Stopped gabbing. Closed a bit. Came together a bit. Oliver's right hand, hidden in the deep folds, was at anointment when Angus stormed into the room from outside the house.

The young Lothario of Hodd's Mountain screamed at Oliver, who turned and said, "Only as far as you go with my granddaughter, same distance, and not makin' her any decent promise. Is that enough for you? Is that a truce? Or do I let your mother speak her piece right now?"

Best Pearl's arms were still locked around Oliver's neck.

Angus, before bolting in defeat, said, "All right, Old Man."

And Best Pearl added "All right, Old Man," perfectly happy with all considerations, though not in perfect mimicry of her son's words.

A Tender Grave

Nyall Alden, standing on a Pine River bank, was bent on reflection, from long ago and recent happenings, fixing only on the important, yet his mind was filled with this place and it would be difficult to nudge it aside in his thoughts. At first appreciation came the unimaginable silence that sat all about him, and then, as he listened past that silence, past the core of it, came the music of the place, a low music of ownership he knew was not deeded to many of his friends.

Of course, none of them had Hagen Dolphin as an uncle.

It was at an upstream pool of the Pine River, his fifth or sixth trip here and him barely twelve years old, and the glade behind him softened the morning. Air filled with the slow burst of bird calls, invitations and neglect at one and the same time, letting all earth unfold itself from a dark curl of night and a hard winter still in mind. It was then that Nyall Alden first became aware of how his uncle, Hagen Dolphin, fit himself into a new day.

The reach and stretch of his uncle was minimal, slow, and embraced a grace Nyall did not know immediately that he had seen before in the tall mailman. All his own short past must have rushed at him then, where, from thick brush still a short way further upstream, he had paused to hear the morning say hello and became aware of his uncle's being wholly attentive to his surroundings, as if to let go would cause him severe loss. He saw, through the leaves, one step of the man, one leg, halt midair as though silence had set up a strict demand, as if he were hearing earth music other people could not catch, and obeying it.

For that moment the forest silence kept its place.

Even for a twelve-year old boy, Nyall knew he was at the first act of something new, and the silence would resonate for years on end, pieces of it falling into neat little quarters in his mind, small rooms he could find when he had to.

Yet at the same time, Nyall never knew how it was happening to him, but he was learning things; not in leaps and bounds but in an old fashioned way where they entered your mind, found those little places to anchor and settle in, forever. He could close his eyes and hear them speaking their pieces, making him sit up and take notice in a split second. Oh, he knew early to listen to the quiet and to the babbling mouth of the river, how it whispered and gabbed through the leaves as he neared it, the shine of it frequently coming into sight as if a mirror with its own sound was being held up by an invisible hand – and he knew whose mighty arm that hand was on. The whole face of the forest, and all its grins and grimaces, was there for his putting away after he came to know each one. The treasure grew in him, the angles of the sun on leaves and water and the accompanying shine that sometimes only lasted a mere second. If he stayed in place it would not come back until the next day, and at almost the exact same hour, all letting him know that life was passing on, pieces going by he had to grasp to keep as his own. In a soft, unobtrusive way, he knew he was learning.

No matter where he would be in the forest, going to or from the river, the river was always at his mind with its music and freedom, moving to wherever it was headed, the next bend, the next pool, the heady ocean beside Portsmouth. It rushed on some days in some seasons, and crawled on others, like an old man on a last walk of the day, at the end of a perfectly lovely day, and the end of his world just around the corner. The measurements made and satisfactions gleaned settled on him early, though none of it had a voice or a name or demanded to be put down on a piece of paper.

There was a time he thought of how images and memories sat in Hagen's mind, and how over a lifetime he could squeeze them out until there was no more squeezing to be done. He and all he knew would be diminished and then they'd be gone.

From that long ago morning the early May breeze yet bore an edge on his skin, an edge that called for a collar, and it in turn touched coolly at Nyall's fingers itching for the fly line to send quick messages to his lead finger. He hungered for memory and return. He wanted to rush to the water, to cast a soft floating line and the subtlest lure, to start working the stream, but he was held back by another presence.

Overhead, in a mass of thick greenness, hidden away in the rich tapestry, a squirrel chatted and an unidentified bird sent off small alarms. That day he knew he could not read the signs presented to him the way his uncle could. Nyall did not know what the squirrel chatted about and only supposed the bird was noisy at nest protection. He also did not know that Hagen Dolphin had been in love for forty years with a girl he had not even kissed. He did not really know this uncle who seemed so visible in knowing. The deliberate foot of his uncle, halted in mid-air, posed a further moment before releasing its hold to settle lightly on the mix of

46

moss and old leaves. The silence continued.

On that sharp morning long ago, Nyall realized he had not before seen his uncle in such a posture, though he did know that the man had deep heed of what was about him, what floated near at hand, and what spoke from afar on the wings of day. Nyall had always supposed, in his short term, that fishing was the most important element in his uncle's life.

Now, years later, other thoughts had made deep impressions. He remembered so much and so little about his uncle who, lanky, a minor stretch at his beltline, carried himself with a sense of well-being, making him at peace with the world, in tune with its rhythm. That comfort radiated as smoothly as good earth growth. He had seen it at berry picking and worm digging and grub discovery under one rock and not another, in the way some men know tools.

Hagen Dolphin, bachelor uncle, was a letter carrier of narrow boundaries and particular interests. For more than forty years of route delivery in his hometown of Saugus, a mere dozen miles from Boston and a half dozen from the Atlantic, he collected Indian arrowheads and spear heads and ax heads found on his daily paths. He was a tall man of robust frame, and in the beginning of his career, before trucks and wheeled carriers, the mail bag was often loaded with found rocks. Sometimes his feet hurt, but the job was laden with discovery. He had trade-offs... on his free days, much of all good weekends of spring through early fall, and twice or three times every year for a week's vacation at a time, he fished for the phantom trout in the Pine River at Ossipee, New Hampshire. Many times his only company was a nephew, his sister Myra's boy, Nyall Alden. Many times Hagen would hang on the edge of a promising pool for hours, alone with contemplation, promise, and rare sounds and usual silence, all mere as contentment. Nyall, never knowing otherwise, thought the immobility to be brought on by Hagen's foot problem.

That morning of surprises, in a surprise statement uttered by the uncle, brought the two of them into the closest encounter. "Here," Hagen had said a few minutes after he'd been discovered by his nephew in the odd position, "is true Eden, the most distant place my mind can tolerate for the eternal stay of a simple man who has spent much of his life in this same spot, in a physical and a mental state. I've loved it here before you and will do so after you move on in your own life. I was made for this," at which he gestured about him, "and for this place."

The last statement hit Nyall like a promise or a threat of

47

magnitude, exactly which one he was unsure of. Only later could he exact the truth of it as a promise, with a threat sitting right behind it.

To reveal a measure of Hagen, it is sufficient to know that he had been in love with classmate Marleah Mitchum once for two weeks of his freshman year in high school. He soon fell out of love, later saw her swimming nude at Lily Pond when a junior in high school with half a dozen girlfriends, and loved her for the next fifty odd years. Oh, how he loved the ghost of her, the grace she released in swimming, the soft arch from the diving board leaping down inside him deeper than he would ever feel, the flesh and sylph-work and utter loveliness carried by one person. She belonged solely to him.

Never would he give that up. For hours he could speculate on her person, her affability, her acceptance of him as his own person. All possibilities came to mind, just as there never was any doubt in his mind that each day of his mail rounds presented a chance of finding an Indian relic. It would promise a remarkable connection for him to those who had ambled through Saugus long in the past, who had touched seriously the article or relic that came into his hand hundreds of years later. The details mesmerized him and locked him up for hours in new adventures, high romances, and so he accepted his place in this world with Marleah Mitchum. She presented a chance for a similar connection; one day she'd be as dreamed.

Few people, of course, knew about the long love affair, and a few rare times did Hagen drop her name by accident. For Nyall it was a soft word in the midnight darkness of a Pine River campsite, and only then did Nyall discover what longevity meant. He seized and kept his uncle's secret, believing he alone shared with the man who could spin half a day away beside the simplest pool of the river, locked into whatever dreams such pools give off, the promise outreaching the catch, the dream outreaching the promise. And Nyall came to know the man fully, the man who loved from an untouched distance for so long. He learned simplicity, truth, endurance, and love at a scale no one else could teach.

Once, and only once, Myra asked Hagen if he was ever going to get married. Common knowledge said that lots of people wanted to ask the question of the likable mailman, but a certain reserve and the private perspective he carried, like ammunition not yet fused, kept such people away from the subject. The minute the words escaped Myra's lips she knew they were a mistake, for her brother looked away in the deliberate manner he brought silence to odd moments. Locked in deep thought, he came back with a terse statement: "Well, I have my stones. For somebody like me that's enough to make a stand on." She never asked him again, and he never offered any hope on the subject.

As for "his stones" all the while, from long before Nyall's first trip to the Pine River, the collection of Hagen's Indian artifacts grew, by odd degrees and by odd and curious happenstance, to become a significantly magnificent collection. Hagen carried history with him, like a gunslinger ready to shoot, needing no excuse for spinning tales of Tontoquon and Montowampate and Sagamore James and the last remnants of their tribe that finally succumbed at Round Hill in a desperate winter. Hagen found at Round Hill a wide assortment of arrow heads and spear heads and heavy ax heads, in most cases discovered as precious ground litter. Now and then he kicked them loose in new or old gardens along lanes and shortcuts over easy acres, between plots or houses or at the end of streets. Some of the relics were partly immersed in walkways where the sun illuminated an identifiable shape. The triangulate pattern leaped into his eyes.

On his routes around town people, usually postal patrons he serviced, delivered into his hands their solitary findings, accepting the light and goodness in Hagen's eyes as sufficient reward, for he was often toasted as "one of the good guys that come by regularly." Once, with permission from old Dalton Scaller, who shared a bottle of beer with him, he chipped an ax head from Scaller's stone wall fronting on Central Street, Scaller celebrating the final release with a second bottle of beer for his mailman. "Don't mind me, Hagen, as I'm celebrating history coming into your hand, and I'm right here watching it unfold. Yes, sir, I say amen to that." Late in Hagen's collective activity, numerous organizations maneuvered in line for its bequest. Speculation about its final resting place ran around town in the rumor mill.

Nyall's first trip north was an accidental event when a measles epidemic hit his Little League team and Hagen told Myra he could take him fishing up in New Hampshire for a week, to keep him away from teammates, playmates and all those afflicted in the old home town. On that trip, and succeeding ones, Nyall found a love that bloomed on both ends, fishing and his bachelor uncle. In time they supplanted baseball and football in the boy's mind and activities, and girls for a while, but not fully successful there.

Myra was impressed by that first trip when five more of Nyall's teammates came down with the measles, and she realized her family had been graced with a savior. She never refused a request for Nyall to go on upcoming fishing trips, joy settling about her as trip preparations were made, supplies being gathered and packed, and her back yard become a haven for Nyall's young friends who came together to see the careful proceedings. There was up for exhibit the art of packing, the matter of bait and food preservation, the conglomerate of tackle box and creel and rods and reels, the outstanding promise of adventure and its far reach coming home to dreamy-eyed and envious kids in a quiet back yard. They eyed the Coleman lanterns as figureheads for outdoors and for camping, and the large cast iron grill at least half an inch thick having the yield of a kitchen stove, the black icon. Some of them found it hard to believe how much space the small bundle of a tightly packed tent yielded when unrolled in the woods. Hagen, once on a Friday afternoon, unfolded the pack and erected the tent in the back yard, satisfying their curiosity.

Only one time, in all those trips, did the pair return to the yard directly after leaving to retrieve a forgotten item, the black grill they had left behind, a black iron patch on the edge of the paved driveway. And Myra was amazed to see the neighborhood kids, who a short while earlier had dispersed with sadness about them, gather anew in the yard as if a clarion call had gone out to them... the adventurers are back. Hagen is here (or there)... Nyall has returned. There was a loveable reaction from Hagen, who Myra knew had read the sudden renewed pleasure of Nyall's pals and managed to spend another hour in discussing the situation with them, and how not to forget things that were important.

"You must know," he said to them, "that this small black piece of hard iron extends the kitchen all the way into the deepest woods, as if your mothers were there getting the big breakfast for you. On this flat surface come morning we will find mounds of golden eggs and great kielbasa and tongue-twisting bacon and dark toast that are fit for kings of the woods, like Mark Twain was spinning out a yarn for you right off Tom's and Huck's own river. And at night, after a day on the stream amid the birds calling across your back and foxes yelping and a deer in flight over the glade behind you, the trout roll over on their backsides and draw the attention of every animal in the forest, and you feed your keen eye and your ravenous appetite."

On the river the magic continued, Nyall often seeing his uncle from

50

a distance, at the favorite pool for hours on end, waiting out a strike on his line, biding all his time and energy. He became aware that his uncle enjoyed a serene peace on God's earth.

And, as a curious follow-up, Nyall went on town forays to find information about Marleah Mitchum, just in case the topic ever came up, and he was sure that it would. That information came from many sources, in whispers, in short dissertations, lest the mailman find out he had been gossiped on. Evidence said curtly that he was not a man to speak about too freely, lest it get back to him. "Don't you dare say a word about that girl to him, young man, else he'll skin me alive. That's one true man, believe me so."

From several sources he found all about Marleah, how abusive her first marriage was, and how her short second marriage seemed to cut vitality out of her life, and Hagen was determined that she'd never be aware of his love for her. There was a time, Nyall found out, that Hagen, on substitute routes when another carrier was ill, had to deliver Marleah's mail. She never knew he passed by her door. All of that hit with the wallop of a hammer the extremely saddened nephew. He wanted to know everything. How would his uncle share it, if it came up as a subject? Did he know what was said around town? How would Hagen deflect it or disguise it, who had never admitted to a secret and never requited love.

Hagen, we know, reflected on particular moments and memories on the river, and could go back to them in startling recall, yet now and then the more special moments came back in alarming clarity, as if some part of an old day had hung around just to be repeated, loping in from a nearby haven where it had lain in echo all the time since its becoming. It might feel as if the day was vacuumed off and a warm replacement sidled up to him and covered him warm as an old afghan.

It was about those times Nyall loved to hear, with his uncle's words slyly coming out of the woodwork of the forest, down from a near limb, or from a clutch of leaves ready to burst in April's first trip north in the year, all as if holding him a prisoner: ...This is a place to be forever, when the bird calls are choir-like, the foxes call their young, a fish breaks the water right behind you in a teasing moment, when your soul joins another soul that has stood at this same spot before you even got here, before you even thought of getting here, coming to this exact place, like an Indian on a food hunt, winter threatening or spring breaking its neck behind him and he knew a peace was also at hand, perhaps that he could

51

in some way know my presence here, even long after he departs the site.

So, the flame-lit moments beside the campfire were branded special. Hagen said, on numerous occasions, the way lessons are learned and shared, a whole schoolhouse of instructions: "Fishing is a state of mind. Don't frighten the trout with your cast shadow." And he'd chuckle at that, like it was an inside joke playing with the words, and then he'd go on. "Traveling downstream, when you're lost, is as good as any map ever made." And he'd naturally move on to what he had wanted to say in the beginning, making connections he felt were worth making, like roots were at work and he was responsible for them; "Make all your thoughts kind. Be partial to goodness and it never hurts when you remember those thoughts. If someone is special, keep them safely in place. Work inspires work. Love inspires love. When you put them together you touch a winner."

A host of these echoes kept returning to Nyall from the river way, from beside the pool, from the glade and the glen back of it… the words Hagen left for him, handles on them, graspable, understandable, instructive, a way of going on. He kept seeing his uncle's face and his eyes and his mouth moving and saying truths lasting forever in this world. They would go on as long as he himself lasted; he would carry them all his time, he affirmed. That final oath landed inside him like a bomb.

One night, at the campsite, the moon a good companion, Nyall finally dared to ask what had long bothered him, even though he felt like nothing less than an intruder. He asked his uncle about Marleah. Straight out, he said, "Tell me about her, Uncle."

"About who?"

"Marleah. I have heard you say her name at night, at midnight, here by the river, and only here." He knew that last part was a definitive qualification, an out, a release if the old man wanted to use it. At the same time Nyall realized that a sense of maturity was striking for good ground in all his matter. He could almost measure it, coming as it did with such a rush of wisdom, education still afoot.

Hagen Dolphin, his eyes wandering off into the abounding darkness, accepting the chill it could possess on an early May evening, not at all thinking ill of an inquisitive nephew whom he loved with another passion, let it finally all fall away from him.

"I loved her totally, exclusively, without a moment's doubt, for just about all my life. I still do. I never dated her. I never touched her. I never

52

kissed her. But I love her, have loved her, as she has never been loved in this life. I have been happy with that. Know that I knew her best here, always at best, the purest best. That's important in all this mix. She parts brush and limb for me getting to the stream, shows me the underside of golden trout, accompanies me over hill to the pool, and back again, fills my creel, shares every cup of coffee I've had on this river, morning, evening, and at midnight when I can't sleep thinking about her, hearing her laughter beside the pool, see her dive off the board the way I saw her dive once so electric and so rewarding it has never left my mind. There's a part of continuity that, if it comes to you, you have to grab it and run with it. It's your ball, and your ballgame. Like I said, make all your thoughts kind, be partial to goodness. And she has been good to me."

As if to extend his talk, or perhaps to surround it with some good earth, as he often said, he added, "This place has been good to me, to us. We've taken care of it as it has taken care of us. The warden stopped me one day as I was starting back home, many years ago. I was barely out on the logging path and there he was, at the side of the path, smiling. I asked if he wanted to see my catch, for we had a strict limit at the time. He said, 'No, I know you do it right. I've been behind you many times on your trips and know you're one man who leaves the place cleaner than he finds it. It's been like following the wake of a boat all these years, never catching up and I thought it's time we got to know each other.' I know he saw the bag of trash in the back of the car. There was a time we buried everything, and then times changed and we had to carry out all our trash. He knew I was up to that and wanted to say thank you without really saying so. But we shook hands."

That handful of trust had gone a long way. As had all the lessons.

When the faithful mailman fell from a ladder while painting his little cottage, a neighbor raced to his aid, calling for help. Hagen was unconscious, and the ambulance came and rushed him to the hospital. Nyall was at work on a summer job. It was the year of his high school graduation.

Hagen was 79 years old, Nyall was 18, and they were the best pals and buddies that ever were. They had fished for over a dozen years the lovely tract of the Pine River. All their neighbors, and most of the townsfolk, knew of the true kinship; some friends of Nyall's had grown up in the presence of it.

53

The small hospital was a drear place, with occasional beds in hallways, lacking room for all their patients. Doctors and nurses scurried about seemingly oblivious of those in the hallways, as if their numbers were already counted, placed among the near dead, soon to be gone. Hagen Dolphin was a hallway patient and Nyall could hardly stand the visits. But he went daily, usually in the evening when the job was finished for the day. Never once did he think of going off alone to the Pine River for a weekend of fishing... he'd never gone there without his uncle. It would be a sacrilegious trip.

When Hagen died from problems induced by the fall, the family agreed to have him buried at the local cemetery, at the far end abutting a stream where room was becoming scarce. It was a problem area, and twice on earlier occasions, when rains were fierce for days at a time, the banks of the small stream flushed with the rush of water, several caskets were found water-borne and deposited downstream a ways. The outcry was ferocious, but it was decreed an act of God and casually put aside.

The burial of his uncle in such a place was the most unsettling event in Nyall's short life. He could not escape something nagging and digging at him, and it would not leave him. Like an awed commission, it had descended upon him, demanding attention.

He told himself he had to remember what his uncle had said about approach, how it had to come early into play in order for all other things to be realized, to come to fruitful existence, to be at hand. He wondered would this arm his new desires and ideas, the network of thoughts and feelings some days seemed to be rushing through him with abandon, or direction. Perplexity, he found, could surface so quickly, and confound him. Only when he heard the words and the tones of that other voice in his mind did odd lines come to straighten themselves, find a way out. How did Hagen approach things? "The approach is most important," he had said. "Like the way you can approach trout in a stream or pool or death or starvation or out and out misery a day at a time." He never said again, after that one admission at the night campfire, how it was to love a woman, revere a woman, keep a woman, and at a distance and forever. That had gone back to being a private matter, all the way.

For all he had learned from his uncle, Hagen Dolphin, Nyall Alden was aware that it wasn't fully settled. There was another step to take in the matter. The weights and fist of justice hung out for the grabbing, had handles for his clutch at them. All of it had fallen on him, like a gift or a

54

commission; as yet he could not give it a proper name, so he did not try. But it pre-empted any other thought.

Thus it happened, as darkness started to settle one evening, as recall pounded at him, Nyall loaded his car and drove into the cemetery, the domino stones and monuments shaking loose the light in quick departure, and the shadows coming back faster than ever. In the trees the slight wind talked back, partly at the disturbance, partly at the visitation. The young man unloaded his equipment and supplies, and then drove the car out of the cemetery and parked it a half mile away, beside Charlie's Hay and Grain near the railroad tracks. Back to the site he went and erected a black poly sheet on two poles around the grave site and began digging. In front of him the poly sheet served as a backdrop to anybody in the cemetery, hiding his activities.

Both happiness and excitement clutched at him, transgressor, servant of the dead, memorizer of the living, nephew. Some half hour later he saw a vehicle enter the cemetery at the far end, the lights bouncing where the road sat awash in remnant pavement, the lights bouncing with duress. He was nervous about being discovered, but highly suspected it to be a police cruiser, at this hour, with a uniformed lover at the wheel on a late date. The car drove along the far and low end, near the stream bank. It stopped, the headlights went out, like crows across his vision. The gossip in school pummeled down on him: and satisfied him and his minor fright of being found out. It was, as all kids in school knew, a cop with a lover, most likely a woman just off her shift as a waitress. The young cop's name (he hoped him young, rather than an older, married one), and his friend's name had already bounced through the school lunch line like an extra burger was at hand, a hot potato of a burger.

After the departure of the cruiser, which had stayed no more than 20 or so minutes in place, near as it could get to heaven in such a short time, Nyall exhumed his uncle's body after serious and laborious work, wrapped him in a canvas, filled the hole in, put grass sod pieces back in place, and retrieved his car. He loaded the body and all the gear in the car and drove away from the site. Soon, the clouds now darker in the sky, a mere owl for company, he walked back in and restored as much order as he could, leaving all things as neat as possible, hoping that wandering eyes would not see the disrupted ground.

The next day, beneath a sparkling sun, solitude and satisfaction coming as close to utter happiness as he could ever imagine for himself, but knowing there was another level to reach, he drove one hundred miles to the Pine River, into the ruined Deer Lodge site, and then almost a mile further on an old and narrow logger's path. Leaves and branches slapped music against the car windows and the roof top, and his antenna snapped back and forth keen as drumsticks. A rabbit, posed stock still in the middle of the path, as if daring to be run over, finally skittered off quick as a rocket. Beside his window a colorful bird leaped, with blue appearing as a flash of light and yielding sudden darkness.

The feeling he had felt the day before in the cemetery was back on him, finding room to grow down in his gut, and sending off a warmth that filled the whole of the vehicle. Beads of sweat ran on his face and on the back of his neck, but the ease and contentment came upon him with a deeper sense, something owed and penetrating and completely tolerable. He knew he was sharing it with Hagen, supposedly still wrapped in one position in the trunk, but who was probably ahead of him, at the edge of the pool or a short ways back, summoning him, picking and choosing, marking the spot.

In the favorite glade he buried Hagen Dolphin, just back of the Pine River pool where he had spent most of his lonely fishing hours, though with company. Never in his life had Nyall been so happy, hearing the hush come back at him from the glen and the glade and the upstream rush of white waters and the almighty clutch of the forest, the tree-borne whispers that Hagen Dolphin left for his grasping and for his memory. And all the while the twin beings of the river grabbed at his heart.

It was a kind of heaven unfolded for him, to be carried from that place to every place he would come into in all his days. Silence and sound came to him as one. A cooper hawk slashed down through the trees. An ache hit on the air as a squirrel, or the road rabbit, went aloft in commotion, leafy branches touched and swayed en route. A breath of air hit him as if someone had issued a sweet message. From a midpoint of the pool, from elegance and serenity themselves, a trout with a startling speckled underside leaped for a mayfly, the way trout had leaped for years on end, a momentary panic amid the silence.

Continuity shone or glittered or moved all around him and the last shovelfuls of earth fell atop the man who already was moving in his own way, with his same dear company.

56

Nyall easily recalled the first time he asked Hagen if such a love was worth it, was it enough for a man, and Hagen had replied, "Well, I have my stones."

Now that gentle man had his river, and his girl, both of them for good, and perhaps the stones bore no further value in the mix.

Temporarily Unemployed

Brenda Beal, "Worth a feel," she'd said a thousand times since Jack had dumped her and two kids, without a car, without a washing machine, without a refrigerator that worked, without all the money from her bank account, owing two months' rent and the electricity and heating bills including the A/C bill (but he took the A/C because it was new and worked better than he did on his best day): all of this too soon revealed in their marriage. Little Jackie was her reminder of the night in the back seat of Jack's father's car, at the lake, under the moon, in a soft breeze the Atlantic sent in over Nahant and Lynn beaches. And Jenny carried the memory of a three week hiatus after Jackie was born.

She worked two and three jobs a week, paid half for child care, the rest to barely live on, to eke out the future, as her mother used to say. Then, one of the sitters fell down the stairs at the subway and was suing the transit company, and another got pregnant, which found Brenda with her arms wide open for help, having to quit two jobs, sneak around on the third at odd hours, the kids back in the apartment alone for a few hours, giving her constant headaches.

That's when Curly from the oil company, making a delivery, said to her, "You know how beautiful you are, Brenda. I could write this bill off on my own if I could come by sometime and see you, when the kids are asleep, of course."

She fed him first (spaghetti with a great sauce was her specialty), gave him a few glasses of wine, said to herself, "What the hell," and took him to bed. Curly was a nice guy and when he was fired a season and a half later, she did him favors for a few weeks, but then he got a new job, had to move, got a new girl who was cold, she figured, and was gone, like he had evaporated.

The meter reader for the electric company was too old, the mailman too young, and the building super too afraid of his wife to make an overture. She took a late night job as waitress at a club that stayed open beyond legal hours, and made lots of tips allowing a few quick feels by stupid louts who could not speak their own mind in the presence of a sexy lady. It made her wonder what they were like at home. "No sexy lady there," she was apt to say.

The club was shut down after a police raid, and one cop let her go out the back door when she slipped her phone number and address into his hand. She saw him a dozen times in a dozen weeks, always on a Friday evening. He paid her rent for the three months. She liked him, but he was almost getting re-acquainted with his separated wife and kids all the time, and finally did. He never rang her bell again and she never made a line-up at the police station.

A friend owned a beauty shop and had her do some work, and she worked as a night watchman at a few places, when she could get someone to keep an eye on the kids at the apartment, all these late jobs with proper paperwork, for she had the idea of collecting unemployment benefits sometime down the line. But she had always sworn that she'd never take that route.

Some things held her back, though she was insistent that paperwork, all paperwork, had to be completed, authorized and reported.

Then, when the kids got sick, one and then the other, in quick succession as though they had been drinking from the same cup, using the same spoon, things really fell apart.

It all crumbled in on her, and she found herself, one sad day, standing in line at the State Employment Security Office. The fellow at the counter at the head of her line was an overgrown giant of a man, soft in his voice, polite to the near extreme, and an Irish redness in his cheeks. Brenda noticed that he treated one and all with a certain amount of regard and respect. She heard some obvious regulars call him "Jimmy Boy," which did not bother him at all, for his smile was always there.

His voice was warm and pleasant, as he sat behind the counter with her paperwork in his hands. "You still at the same address, Brenda?"

"Yes, I am."

"Looking for work? Ready for work?"

"Anyplace and every place I can. With two kids it's tough, but I'm not a quitter."

He smiled a wide smile in return. It made her feel warm. "I don't have anything listed here that's applicable to you. You keep looking and we'll give you what's coming to you based on your records. That sound okay with you?"

His smile was authentic.

She gave him the biggest smile she could. She felt it to be as wide as the horizon at Nahant Beach on a grand morning, Europe pushing the Atlantic all the way.

He nodded and they finished the application. She was 12 weeks on unemployment. She thought she was in heaven.

An alarm sounded when she received a notice in the mail that her benefits would soon be running out. Before she knew it, she was Jim's line at the office. "You only have a few weeks left, Brenda. You keep looking for work and I'll be able to grant you some extension of benefits, if they fit the case." She swore, later on, that Jimmy winked at her.

Two weeks later he granted her another two week extension, And again a few weeks later.

"You still at the same address?" he said.

"Yes."

"You still looking for work?"

"Yes."

He stamped her paperwork for two more weeks. She could have kissed him.

The next time, the threat of discontinued benefits as alive as ever, Jim's boss was standing behind him, arms folded, scowling, a motionless little black mustache sitting on his upper lip like a black marker had been snapped across his face. He looked like that bum Hitler, smoky and unreal, but threatening her all the way, like he'd send her off to some stupid prison or concentration camp. She tried to pull up the word "gulag," but couldn't do it. It seemed too far away; too implausible. "Hell," she muttered, "that war's already more than 50 years away."

"You still at the same address?" Jim said.

The boss turned away when she stared at him, like she had found the classroom stoolie right there in the back row all the time.

"You ready for work?" Jim said.

"Yes," she said and unbuttoned the lone button on her thin black raincoat.

She was stark naked, all the way up and all the way down, beautiful all over and whispered, "Do you like spaghetti with the best ever sauce?"

And he whispered in turn, "With red wine?"

"Yes," she whispered, "a good dago red."

"Your benefits are extended two more weeks, Mrs. Beal," Jim said, and the stamp came down on the lone document in front of him with the full authority of the whole Commonwealth.

Jimmy smiled the horizon smile, the red Irish smile.

Brenda Beal, in anticipation, squeezed her legs as tightly as she could.

She affirmed all over again, "There's nothing like it, Jimbo."

Secrets of Sawyer's Icehouse

Long before the Japanese planes took off from their aircraft carriers hiding on the broad Pacific, most of the world already awake to one kind of a storm or another, Sawyer's Icehouse on the Cliff Road side of Lily Pond was a haven for returning icemen each winter, for hockey players needing a break from games that often lasted for a whole weekend day, and for midnight lovers getting out of a bitter north wind and breaking the frigid barrier in one manner or another.

As it was, the icehouse was used by skaters and swimmers for romantic interludes, in seasonal appreciation.

Frank Parkinson, who also had a key to the mostly secret clubhouse on Henshit Mountain, kept the icehouse availability in his back pocket. Once he told a confidant (trusting him only as far as he could toss him), "I know where one gent hides the key to his place on the pond. If it ever comes down to a quick move, I have a place to take the lady."

Frank never spoke of a female acquaintance other than "the lady" no matter who he was talking to. Never was a name mentioned. And he'd never let on it was the icehouse he was talking about, letting his pal think it was one of the two dozen summer camps crimped about the edge of the pond. Little did any of them know that in a matter of a few years after the war out on that same wide and sandy Pacific and parts of the Atlantic, with most of Europe thrown in for kicks, they'd be jacking the camps up with cement blocks or poured foundations, winterizing them, and bringing their war-worn brides to babyhood, which brought one town wag to say, "It's like Halloween all year over there at Lily Pond, with all that bumping going on in the night."

He might not have been far off the mark. It was paradise for a time in the late '40s. Only the knots or the knotholes knew the difference. Scars as well as sutures made the trip home from the far places of the ignited globe. When Sawyer's burned down after the war, most of the secrets went with it … except those that survived in special ways.

At Harry Bamford's Rathole, the only pool, billiard and bowling emporium in Saugus, Frank was a connoisseur of the first table in the establishment, meaning he had first dibs in a tie for game-break. And the local ladies loved him, mostly, as it turned out, in a secret way. Frankie never breathed a word about one of them. Today, in Valhalla, in the armory of the war gods and occasional lovers along the way, he is as quiet as a frog on a lily pad. The big bite on a girl's reputation, as far as he was concerned, might come from any direction, but never his.

Frank told his late date that night: "This is the place where Dick McDonald got himself about 200 stitches when the big ice saw went wild. Here's where we push the ice blocks onto the ramp from the pond, then a saw, a huge band saw, cuts them in neat blocks for storage until summer. Well, it went wild and loose, that old saw, getting Dick on his arms, his legs, across a chunk of chest. 'Just think,' Dick told me the night he left for the army, 'I could have lost my pecker in the whole shooting match. Where the hell would that have put me in all of this?' Isn't that some kind of situation to find yourself in?"

She crumbled as he entered her. "God, Frankie," she screamed, an octave even the thick walls did not hold all the way, "I'm glad it didn't happen happen happening to you you you." She never knew she climaxed again and again and again in the middle of the Sahara Desert, in the middle, too, of the Panzers and German infantry after sand storms and Egypt's sun god at his fiercest. Frankie took her on a world tour, right in the ranks with him, and never once said her name, awake or dreaming, the night full of her to an astounding reality, more than one comrade, the observant kind that might be found in some ranks, noticed Frankie's honeymoon kind of smile on odd mornings.

Her name, it must be told from this end, was Millie, and one night, a whole war later, parked alongside the pond in the dark shadows at the side of Sawyer's, Millie said to her boyfriend of a year or so, "I heard there are a ton of stories connected with this icehouse." Nothing secretive would ever pass her lips, no old tale, no fresh memory, nothing.

"Oh, Millie, I'd guess there are. I worked here as a kid. If you whisper in there, it will never come out through those walls filled with sawdust more than a foot thick. Part of the insulation to keep the ice solid through the summer." His hand, under her skirt, was at the crux of the matter, silken as a spider web, gentle as suds, and she was positive she loved him.

"Like secrets locked home forever?" fell from her open mouth, but her eyes were squeezed shut, keeping an image in its proper place.

She hadn't seen Frank alone since he'd come home, wrapped into a bunch of scars and memories and silent announcements she never could understand. Her father, in a conciliatory manner, said, "Frank's not the same kid that went away to save the world, Millie. He barely saved himself, and I don't know how far that will go for him. They say he went through three kinds of hell out there if there was one. I know guys who said Africa has three kinds of faces she wears."

With parts of France and Germany still locked in his own mind, he knew a bit of Frank's journey past himself. He sometimes admitted sharing was the hardest part because it brought guilt and amazement about his own salvation, if he could call it that. At the edge of every image and thought came faces of lost comrades barely recognizable because they only came back in pieces, never whole except for the names. He'd admit later on that the names also went on by, all in their own time.

"He won't even talk to me, Dad. Never says a word other than 'Hi' and on his way."

"He has too much baggage, Millie. I believe he really thinks the world of you, but doesn't want to bring too much of the baggage with him and drop it in your lap. Obviously, it's never going to leave him. Some of the old guys down at the hall say he just walks out when they begin to hash out stories about their war and where they've been, and no telling where and how far when they all get together."

"I could handle that, Dad," Millie said.

Her father coughed and started a bit in place before he replied, "Your mother couldn't, Millie, not that she didn't try. It was just too much of my baggage. I can say that now, looking back, but I couldn't then. It was just too much for her."

Europe, for him, was a horrible little animal with ragged nails that clawed at him for almost thirty years.

Millie, as she had for half a dozen years, tried hard to see her mother's face, but it was lost in a series of quick images. Frankie's face was clearest, even from the darkness of Sawyer's Icehouse the night she and Frankie celebrated love and war; and departure, as it proved. A return to a moment of true passion never found any promise in her mind, though she dwelled for memorable dark hours recreating it.

By then Millie was a nurse working at Massachusetts General Hospital, loving her work, once in a while coming across a patient who had been in Egypt during the war. She found them fascinating, realizing she had a connection at hand, but none of them knew Frank until one afternoon when a strange reunion happened on her floor.

Three young ladies had come to visit one patient. Young, all beautiful to the extreme, dressed like models off the pages of a ladies magazine, they were vibrant, noisy, talkative, bringing the patient whose name was Reggie almost to tears. He laughed so hard that Millie, who had seen his chart earlier, feared stitches would loosen and mess up his surgery. Then she heard one of them say, "Was it Sawyer's Icehouse, Reggie? We've heard some stories about that place."

"So much history went down in that old icehouse," Reggie said, "they ought to write a book about it, but the stories would have to come back from elsewhere, not from inside. There must have been a pact somewhere along the line. Nobody I know has ever let a secret out of there."

That 'nothing ever said' was a huge revelation.

Something grasped him even as he spoke, feeling he was in dangerous territory. A ghost or some kind of providence was upon him, possibly a formidable robed judge whose territory included Sawyer's ice house.

Reggie, it seemed, might have been on the verge of hidden information, but abruptly shut that route off when the nurse entered the room. There was a command in order when he saw her, her face red as if she had been the subject of the immediate conversation. There was also a familiarity about her face, a part of his past, a bit of Saugus. It came home in a hurry.

Reggie said, "I was never in the place, but I heard the usual romantic bits. It was like any place on the pond where you might take a girlfriend."

Reggie looked at Millie and knew they had shared something. The feeling swept through him. The visiting girls were quiet, alert that they were in the middle of an exchange, though nothing was said.

Secrets always have a way of escape.

At the other end of the icehouse the night Millie and Frankie had parted, Reggie's sister Francie sat astride Herbie Williams, pounding him into total submission, and when she said, "Good luck in the war, Herbie," he said, "I'm never going to die out there, Francie, but I might die right here."

All the connections had been made at the icehouse, one way or another.

Francie had told Reggie and he now told Millie when his visitors left the hospital that day, the sudden compulsion coming over him that he should get closer to her, that they ought to share a part of the past. Millie

65

married Reggie well after his release from the hospital, the ice house connections still moving.

Thereafter, in the scheme of events, Frankie, drinking as ever to escape some of the past, was found at the end of Lily Pond one morning, where he had passed his last night in the open, the war still with him, with nothing else except the freezing cold, which also had taken hold. From where he was found, the icehouse was only a couple of hundred feet away.

When the war was over, Francie married Herbie and they had 52 great years until he fell down the stairs one day after getting several trays of ice cubes from the freezer in the cellar. She had never forgotten the night at the icehouse. Not for a minute. Some girls find it that way.

And some guys.

Reggie and Millie moved away from town, some place out there on the broad Earth. Few people had heard from them until they came to Herbie's funeral on a terrible winter day. Millie wanted to visit Frankie's gravesite but the weather was too bad, snow falling, the wind icy and brittle in its attack on the veterans' section, the pond a white expanding promise, and Sawyer's icehouse, all the old boards and beams and sawdust and secrets, long gone to ashes, then to dust, then to weeds and brush.

Millie had the longest memory of all. And like most of the players, she kept it for her own.

66

Mushawie off the Hill

Jimmy Mac, on the second floor porch of his Smith Road house and the early sun barely creasing the edge of Baker Hill, looked over the top of the box scores, the Sox winning their fifth in a row, and saw, for the first time in he'd later guess to be about eight years, Mushawie just coming to the bottom of the Cinder Path. Coming off Baker Hill. He couldn't remember Mushawie being off the hill. My God! Jimmy, said to himself. Nobody saw Mushawie unless he wanted them to see him, him socked away in the back of the Delmere property where he'd been since VJ Day in '45. Now and then, and always after dark and often after Tate had closed his little Variety Store on Western Ave, Mushawie would come to the back door, and with meager pennies and odd coin get tobacco, a couple of cans of soup, some real day-old bread old man Tate'd hold for him like it was barely suited for the birds, once in a great while a bar of soap. Mushawie never bought a razor, matches, tools, or containers of any sort. Tate was sure of that. Now and then a hill denizen would mention his long-handled spade had disappeared from the back yard, or his hoe or his rake "had just got up and walked off the damn hill." People counted off such losses as contributions.

"Jeezus, Martha," Jimmy Mac said, urging his wife out of the hallway and onto the porch. He hurled his 135-pound body up out of the wicker rocker as if he'd come off a launching pad. "That's him," he said loudly, surprise rampant in his voice. "That's Mushawie. That's him. Jeezus, Martha, he must be sick or something. I can't remember the last time I saw him. I can't remember him ever being off the hill. I never saw him off the hill! I wonder if he got burned out, if he got the bum's rush finally from the Delmere clan. The old man would have a friggin' bird." Jimmy's arms were thin, his face was thin and coppery, and energy appeared to leak out of him as if he had enough for the next guy.

Martha McLaughlin had never seen Mushawie. Twenty years married to the widower Jimmy Mac, and she had never seen this empty-looking man, clothes obviously dirty though his khaki shirt was buttoned at the collar, his pants tucked into dark socks. She could remember Jimmy saying that the man she had never seen, who lived in a shack on the hill, used to blouse his pant legs all the time. "That reaffirms military to me," Jimmy had added. She knew she'd remember that word, the pictures coming with it. Jimmy was loyal to anything to do with the army, the navy, the marine corps, the coast guard, World War II, Korea, veterans organizations, old vets he could pick out at the shopping mall, the way the light folded down and back in their eyes, the way they held their heads in a crowd of any sort, perimeter checking, ears cocked like a .45.

They watched the man Mushawie come off Cinder Path the way some people come off a roller coaster, trying to gain his legs back, looking around, detecting places, things, almost as if he were looking for the enemy, or for friends. Jimmy had told her years ago about the strange man who came up the hill one day, walked to the back of the Delmere property, found the old chicken house way in the back end of a mess of apple trees, and took up his lodgings. It was VJ-Day, 1945, the silence at last coming across the vast oceans of the world, coming to rest on quaint streets, hushed dales, secret cul de sacs, and the quietly agonized farms across America. Plenty of veterans were soon loose in the world, some of them guaranteed never to go home again, keeping company with the dead, with their lost comrades, with the unreported.

Mushawie walked down the edge of Smith Road cautiously. Martha said, "Tell me what happened up there when Mr. Delmere found him."

Jimmy had his eye on Mushawie, looking for signs, looking for a single sign, and could find none. "The old man, he was with the 69th in France in the First World War, got a dose of gas for his troubles, goes up there one day and there's a Purple Heart on a ribbon hanging on the door of the chicken coop, which had really undergone a few quick changes, two windows had been added, a tin flue was coming out the side wall, some ground turned over like there's going to be a garden if there's time for it."

"What did he do?"

"Old man Delmere?"

"Yes, the owner."

"He just pointed to the Purple Heart hanging on the ribbon on a nail on the door of his old chicken coop and said, 'Is this yours?' Said Mushawie just nodded. The old man asked his name, he said, 'Mushawie.' Not another word. Went back to his family, did Delmere, sat them all down at his dining room table, every last one of them, grand kids and all, said, 'If I go out from this life and anyone of you so much as says a bad word to that man, I'll goddamn come back in the middle of the night and haunt you. That old shack is his house for as long as he wants, for his lifetime if need be. You all swear by that this very minute, on my blood, on my screwed up lungs, on my soul, so help you god.' Never was another word said. The old man was gone in two-three years, and none of them, 'til this latest ramble about houses coming up there, saying or doing anything, yet some of the young ones starting a sneak attack from what I hear."

"Look," Martha said, leaning against the screen of the porch, "he's sitting down on the curbstone. I bet you're right, Jimmy. He's probably sick. You better go down there."

Jimmy was going down the front walk and Harry Matthers came out of his house two doors away. "See what I see, Jimmy?"

"I got a sinking feeling he's sick, Harry. Let's check him out."

"You okay, Mushawie," Jimmy said, as he and Harry Matthers stood a few feet away from Mushawie. Jimmy first noticed how time itself really had folded itself down in the backside of Mushawie's eyes, the palest green he could remember, and distance knocking itself further away. A ring of bites circled one ear looking nearly savage in their redness, and more bites were on Mushawie's hands, as if the black flies had hung resolutely back on the sides of Baker Hill from spring's onslaught, or the green horseflies had come up from Rumney's Marsh. A few prominent black spots behind Mushawie's lips announced serious dental lapses had occurred. His nose was thick and wide at its bottom, his forehead wide, his hair was full and still as black as night itself. The brows above the distance-seeking eyes were hemp-thick, the cheekbones like new shellac in a drying stage. The hands clasped on his knees were huge hands. If he walked out of a teepee he could have been home, if he swung a quiver and bow across his shoulder, Jimmy McLaughlin would not have been surprised. The man from the backside of Baker Hill looked to be about seventy-five years old, and he looked tired, a sense of loss or displacement evident about him. If it were steaming out of him it could not be more noticeable.

"Are you okay, Mushawie?" Jimmy shivered and put a hand out to touch the shoulder of the strange man who had pinned the Purple Heart on a chicken coop door so many years before.

Mushawie, his head still up as if he were standing in the ranks, said, "My name is Clinton Baker Thurstbody, my serial number is 11270952." His voice was droning and his eyes began to float. He repeated the name and serial number half a dozen times, the voice thick, phlegmy, and dull in its monotone. Perhaps a day or two earlier he had shaved, showing depressions below the lacquer-like cheeks.

Mushawie's words hit Jimmy McLaughlin right in the middle of his gut, like a sledgehammer had come home from way out in space, like Lucifer's hammer. Whack! Bam! Whack! The Been-there Done-that buzz came on him. Years before, the slight German corporal had leered at him every time he'd asked a question, his eyes yellow, his teeth full of food not yet fully chewed, morsels at the corners of his lips, sort of bragging how good he had it, living like a king, good food all the time, America on its way down to her goddamn knees just like the Poles and the Slavs and the Danes and the Norwegians and soon the stubborn Brits holding on for nothing at all. All of it came back in one resounding rush that slammed him in the gut again. Jimmy Mac put his hand out for Harry Matthers.

"Jeezus, Jimmy, not you too!" He spun and yelled to Martha on the second floor porch. "Martha, quick, call the goddamn ambulance. Call the medics. Call the fire department." He heard a door slam in the neighborhood, then a second door. He sat Jimmy Mac down on the curbing. Mushawie said it again, "My name is Clinton Baker Thurstbody, my serial number is 11270952." This time he added, "United States Marine Corps."

Martha rode to the hospital with Harry Matthers. Jimmy Mac rode with Mushawie, both on their backs. Jimmy came home with Martha and Harry a few hours later, flabbergasted at what had hit him. One doctor said it was too much recall all at once. That night, just after midnight, the man known for years as Mushawie died peacefully in his sleep. And Harry Matthers and Jimmy McLaughlin set about to recover the life of Clinton Baker Thurstbody, USMC.

It did not take too long. Through the long arms of the Legion and the VFW magazines the story unfolded. Clinton Baker Thurstbody had come out of the University of Iowa when the war started, joined the Marine Corps, ended up in Naval Flight School, chose to be a Marine fighter pilot, and shot down five Japanese planes on his very first day in combat in the South Pacific. Twenty-two Japanese planes fell from his shooting accuracy, until the day he did not come back from his flight out over a small group of islands whose occupancy was still being contested.

70

His wingman said small arms ground fire had claimed him and he had bailed out. Five months later, with the aid of a Japanese soldier who knew the end was coming, he had slipped away from a prisoner of war compound and was picked up at sea by a Navy submarine that had surfaced at dusk. Captain Thurstbody had been awarded a host of medals, shipped home in June 19, 1945, the same day that Marine ground forces were forcing Japanese troops back toward the cliff lines of Okinawa where many leaped to their deaths rather than be captured. Not long thereafter the big bombs went off.

Official reports, eventually surfacing in Saugus, said that Captain Clinton Thurstbody was last seen when he flew (commandeered was the word whispered at an aside) a Navy fighter from Pensacola and took it due south, out over the Gulf of Mexico, not to be seen again. He was written off as missing while on routine flight assignment, a last fateful and justifiable task the base commander could do in accounting for "one helluva pilot."

Now, even after a small fire had started at the old chicken coop and had been beaten back by neighbors, even as the coop has begun its journey into eventful dust, even with the threat of that whole side of Baker Hill being smothered in new houses or condominiums and the apple orchard being leveled by Cal Delmere's grandchildren, each August 10th for a whole lot of years, a group of veterans have gathered there and remembered a man who ran away from it all, from what he had trouble remembering in the first place, and where he had found solace, they had hoped, in a rude hillside home, back of the apple trees on Baker Hill.

Caught in a Cave

He saw the fire flicking up through the trees in the distance, with a vertical shape in the middle of flames, and wondered what it was. He did not know how long the fire had been going. His view was through a channel of sorts, a mini-tunnel, perhaps crawling space allowed, but iron bars set into the rock beyond the window. The window had a screen attached to it, and both parts of the window could be operated by him, on the inside, as if he was responsible for selecting the appropriate use; let in fresh air, let out stale smells, keep warmth in when necessary, keep out the cold.

As though it was a one-room, one-window apartment.

But he was in a cave or old mine on the side of a mountain in the Tetons. A prisoner he was and he knew his firefighting buddies from Squadron 9, were out there fighting the fire. He did not know who or what had hit him, or brought him to this place. Looking around, he saw quick evidence of a previous tenant. Another prisoner? Someone else had been here before him. Scratching was on the walls, endless scratching, words, symbols, "my name is ..." was deleted at its completion, probably by some heavy tool. Who had that prisoner been? Where was he now? Or she? Did he or she write it?

Stanton Knauber could not remember how long he had been here in this place, but all his firefighting equipment, from helmet to boots and all the raiment and tools in between, had been stripped from him. He wore his service dungarees, but had on a shirt he did not recognize, green, wooly, warm to the touch. It was buttoned almost to the neck. He had not donned it himself, had not set those buttons in place, and could not remember the hands that did so.

Looking around the place he was in, he saw the thunder box of a toilet in a far corner, a cot with mattress on one wall he had woken up on after what seemed like a heavy sleep. Something stirred in his memory that he had eaten, had been given food and drink, had slept deeply.

He remembered a sound he had heard, and looked overhead where a hole appeared in the semi-darkness. That's where the food had come from, at the end of a rope, on a tray hitched at four corners.

He had eaten, and then slept. Nothing told him when that was. How long ago? A day? Two days? He had no idea.

But he had slept. He had eaten and he had slept. Time was now an illusion for him, to him. He shook his head, and then grabbed his chin in doubt, in question of all things.

And found he was clean-shaven.

Did that just happen? Was he here only less than time let him think, like a matter only of a few hours? But that did not calculate with the disappearance of his firefighting garb and equipment, his long sleep that his body told him he had had.

He had eaten ... and then slept. Slept soundly, with no memory of that sleep but what his body was telling him ... and the clean chin, sideburns neatly trimmed, no stubble in the touch. That all said he had been shaved by other hands. There was a remnant smell of soap or lotion about him, faint, thin as the razor must have been that shaved him clean.

He had shaved himself, the last he remembered, on the morning before the call came in to load up the two choppers and head out to help fight a major fire in the Tetons. The fire was up-range of them and up-wind. Then memory struck at him, feeling the helicopter begin a crazy spin, the pilot yelling out they were in trouble, the smash coming in horror, Roberts right behind him, the new kid on the crew, flying over his head and smashing into the pilot's back and getting tossed free into the path of the still moving blades. The impact knocked him back again; the horrendous, tearing, rending sounds, the single scream that was still in his mind. Was that scream his own scream?

Now here. In providential hands? In whose hands? Why? How could he sleep in the midst of all this?

A noise came from above him. The tinny sound came down the shaft and the rope, in someone's hands, lowered another tray of food. He took the food off the tray and the rope pulled the tray back up through the small shaft. No voice was heard. Not a sound made other than rope being hauled up, the tray hitting the side of the shaft once in a while. When he looked up the shaft only darkness came back at him.

In the view from the window, a stream of morning light, the far drift of smoke rose between peaks of the Tetons.

He studied the food. It was a breakfast meal; coffee in a mug, two fried eggs, bacon cooked crisply, dark toast, a clump of jam or jelly on one side of the plate ... a meal he had ordered a hundred times at roadside diners, a diner menu fit for thousands of orders.

On the edge of the cot he sat, looking at the meal, inhaling the aromas now salient about him, appetite energized by them.

73

It flashed on him that he would eat and then sleep. The thought came fully and with possibilities attached to it; he could be getting drugged by some addition to the food. A Mickey Finn for Stan Knauber, firefighter, downed flier, prisoner.

It made him laugh for the first time.

It would be payment and reward. For him or his captor? For both?

The argument loosed other thoughts. How did his captor get him in here? How did the cot get here? How did he get shaved? There had to be an entrance.

He went searching and found nothing after studying cracks in the wall, depressions slight and pronounced, tapping endlessly for different sounds, echoes, revelations. Nothing came free to him. And it was then that his mind took another turn and went absurd on him.

It brought another laugh into his throat; keep humor about you, his grandfather had espoused on numerous occasions, and he in a classroom once more.

He thought of the unnatural, the spiritual, and the supernatural. Some relative of Big Foot? Of Sasquatch? Of some alien creature doing a study of man, and him the prime object? It was the beginning of a wild flow of possibilities.

He let his mind go even as he slipped pieces of the breakfast meal past the open window to a place just this side of the five iron bars. It only took a few minutes, and several chipmunks were at the food, then a squirrel, then a bird that made several trips to clutch food in its mouth and carry it off. In that manner the meal was devoured in 20 minutes. The revelation inspired more possibilities, all leaning to escape from this prison in the midst of the Tetons. He wondered how he could use this revelation.

Thirst, meanwhile had risen in him, and he studied the drink that had come down to him with the meal. It smelled like orange juice, looked like orange juice. He smelled it again. It seemed fresh, as if recently squeezed, and he saw pulp in the mix to affirm its freshness. No evidence of foreign matter appeared in the container, a rugged black mug with a thick handle.

He drank the juice in slow sips, enjoying the freshness.

He woke later, assuming he had slept for hours. Through the window he saw skies red with flame, but all else was dark of night.

The drug was in the drink.

He'd prepare himself for further adventures.

Outside, the fire he believed was eventually out, for he saw no flames or smoke in the sky, and the leaves had run themselves into colorful autumn, and then winter came upon the land. He had determined a number of facts: every 4th day the drink was drugged, drugs came in some element of food in the second or third day following the drugged drink. Now and then small creatures like chipmunks showed evidence of being drugged as they literally dragged themselves from the barred space where he shoved particles of food.

He managed to make a rod about three feet long which he used to push bodies off the edge of the barred space, and hid the tool in the cot from which he had fashioned it. It had been what was needed when a squirrel, gouging on some of the food, fell helplessly in place and he had to push it off the edge, out of sight.

It had been some months that he was a prisoner, he calculated, seeing the seasons change and his daily markings on the wall, and those in themselves not proof positive of elapsed time because he had no idea how many times a drug had knocked him useless for more than a day ... or had shrunk time.

Oh, how he'd love to talk to someone, anyone, like one of the guys from the Squadron. Even inattentive Gibson would be received with gratitude, though he was more interested in gaining some kind of fame from his firefighting life that would shove his book onto the Times Book Pages or be mentioned in the Great Books Project. Gibby wrote everything down on his endless supply of pads, every comment, every situation, but never asked a question, never explained his interpretations. What a gift it would be to hear that mute voice. Or Shocky the eater who'd eat even the leavings of a meal belonging to someone else and never gain a pound, and often quoted his aunt who raised him, saying, "I'd rather pay your board, Shocky, than feed you."

From all that he suspected he was really getting lonely and a bit stir crazy, though he fought those outcomes by dwelling on the facts that he had found out or determined, caused to become available to him in one way or another. They formed his balance point, "keeping me sane," he'd say aloud whenever doubt tried inserting its stiletto.

And if the person or persons that held him captive had studied him enough to know what he had gained, about himself as well as his situation, his surroundings, would they have found what they were really looking for? As a laboratory object, had he showed anything promising, intelligent, surprising?

Once, opening the window to get some fresh air, to let out a bit of sour smell, the freezing temperature rushed at him. He had to shut the window in a hurry, but that set him thinking about grassy sidewalks and grass growing in the smallest cracks and working its infinitesimal but powerful way. Grass and weeds came up through the slightest niche available in concrete itself, in cement structures, in paved roads.

An idea came to light.

At his next meal he poured the "drink of the day" as close to the root of the bars where they were sunk into the rock and held in place with some kind of material he could not recognize … but all he wanted was a porous finding, a little hole hopefully leading to the foot of the bar, a defect in the material. The liquid made its quick way into some kind of depression. He tried it several times in the worst of the weather, the temperature clutching at him as he opened the window, the drink finding its lowest spot, to feed his dreams.

A few days later he noticed a slight crack at the base of one bar, and a few pieces of the unknown cementing material that had been forced loose. The weather warmed up for a few days, and dove again. But in the meantime he poured more liquid into the evident small break, then into two breaks now showing. More flakes and pieces had appeared on the flat surface from the minute upheaval of the cementing material.

He was encouraged; and there still was no light or voice or condition imposed from above, from what he now called Tin Pan Alley. He laughed every time he heard a tinkle from the tray, and was thirsty enough at times and so compelled to drink and come to know again the singular feeling of waking up after a deep sleep.

But there had been not a single known invasion of his person or his tenancy other than a mysterious occasional shave, or finding himself washed and cleaned, privates and all, and never a clue to the point of entry. Once in a while he thought of a miraculous passage through the stone, as if some being had been transposed or transmuted, though he was not satisfied by that possibility. Yet he swore he heard strange words in his head, similar to echoes, soft annunciation of words that he could not grasp, as if the creature that passed through solid rock was in the cave talking to him, the way one might hear a foreign language spoken slowly, like a tutor expressing a language sample to a student, real but not

76

understood.

He felt the accumulation of many possibilities coming into his intelligence, bearing the promise of reality.

And thus the wonders of imprisonment came to him in manifold ways; he had never been asked of anything, forced into anything, known any loss from his person, but he had been imprisoned for months, bare of knowledge, of reality. The desire to see spring outside leaped up in him, the pastel of the early summons of the year that came like a slow mirage over the landscape he saw daily, yet hoping all the time he could break loose some of the bars beyond the window. The idea of escape stayed alive in his mind in its deep secret.

The day came when he dared to work on one of the bars where the material had cracked, loosened up, spilled onto the surface. He made sure each day that such residue was collected and scattered so as not to be seen by his captor. Around the room he scattered it, not much but noticeable when collected in one spot as it was at the base of the window bars.

A surge of joy hit him when the bar moved in place as he twisted it; and the more he twisted the bar the more it came loose and more cementing material fell from the overhead joint onto the flat surface. The rush of emotion nearly overcame him until he realized he was still a prisoner, still had to find his way out of the cell of rock. But the bar came looser in his hand and was surprised when he was able to force it upward into what must be free space. In this revelation he was able to free the bar and draw it inward: thus, he had a weapon in his hands, a steel bar more than two feet long, a formidable weapon for any prisoner.

At that moment he heard the metallic tingle of the tray and knew his lunch was being lowered through the hole in the top of the cell. His gaze went to the wall where he had collected the count of his days and summarized his induced sleeps, and figured today was drug day … his drink would put him to sleep and he would have a visitor while he slept.

With emotion working on him, he poured the drink into the recess where the bar had been, then ate and placed the empty dishes on the tray and laid down. He tried to count the minutes, but too much time passed and more than an hour elapsed while he was flat on the bunk as if asleep. The new weapon, though, was right beside him, out of sight under one arm nearest the wall. But his hand was close to one end of the bar, like a finger on a trigger.

In the midst of his feigned sleep, in the stillness he knew to be nighttime, he heard a distant rumble, the way one might hear a freight train in the night rolling across a line of rails cut into the broad face of a mountain. The air about him, in seconds, was fresher and he sensed a wave of it passing over him, touching the hairs on his arms, touching the side of his neck. The coolness sat down on him. Then he was aware of a heavier, deeper rumbling, heard the roll of a weighted mass passing from one point to another ... and a section of the wall, the section containing much of his markings, slid away from its place and moved back into some other space. That space was beyond the parameters of his cell seemed a vast opening like the mountain had opened up.

Perfume came then, the real perfume of a real woman, a natural, heady, irresistible aroma possessed of beauty, promise, and a moment that brought to him a quick urgency. He heard her feet move softly as if in slippers. He heard the rustle of silk or some such fabric he had not heard for a long time, longer than his imprisonment. It was being carried on the air as much as the woman herself.

He could not strike a woman, which revolted him, though his hand had closed on the end of the bar. Through squinting eyes, careful to not move his lashes, he saw her. She was as beautiful as the mystery she evoked, holding him prisoner, washing him, feeding him, care as much as he needed, except for freedom. She was his age, golden-haired like he was, red lips, kissable even in this prison. His fingers relaxed on the bar.

She saw him move, turned quickly and started to depart. He had her by the hand and held tightly. She cried and said, "Don't hurt me, please. I'm having your baby."

She broke free of his grip, spun away quickly and headed to the hole in the wall, which lead into a long, well-lit tunnel.

He leaped off the cot as she snapped a switch on the wall. She slipped through the opening. The section of the wall began to close behind her. He slipped the bar between the sliding section and the firm wall from which it had slid away as if electrically controlled, on rollers, or tracks, or some kind of unseen device. The bar prevented the section from closing, and he forced the bar solidly into the slight aperture.

Too much had come upon him in the instant of her declaration of having his child. She was a lovely creature, he recalled, and then he recalled the hazy, fuzzy unknown reason for contentment after a drugged sleep. It was a mysterious feeling that overpowered him, and wondrous at the same time. But a quick survey of circumstances told him he had to get out of there if he had any chance.

At the bars of the window he found another bar that could be jammed into an overhead space, and with some effort, broke it free. He crawled into the new opening and with some difficulty managed to slide and squirm along the opening and dropped off the end into a cluster of brush and trees. He could see the far mountain through a clear space. From his imprisoned cell had seen spring through that space as it lit up the mountain.

Spring was bursting all around him as he made his way down an incline. It was difficult without boots on his feet, or a shoe of some kind. As soon as he had put a fair distance between him and the cell location, through a ravine and up another incline, he pulled a strip of bark from a tree and made soles for his feet. They stayed in place when bound with twine fashioned from grass. In the matter of three hours he had to make new soles a half dozen times until he came across an old road winding downhill, tire tracks evidence of recent travel.

He headed downhill and spotted a log cabin set off the road. The cabin was empty, but somewhat lived-in, and he found a pair of sneakers that fit him well. There were two cans of food on a cabinet shelf and he ate both of them right from the can, Spam and tuna fish, each with a taste that did not bother him. A third can without a label, along with a G.I. can opener he found stuffed in a pocket of a jacket hanging on the wall.

He set out again, still going downhill.

He had to get someplace civilized, had to get help. For God's sake, he was going to be a father.

When he heard the whine of an engine coming from the forest behind him, he ducked off the trail. A closed Jeep passed by him and he was unable to see who was driving, concerned that it might be the mother of his child-to-be, or someone connected to her and the prison.

Two other vehicles came on the road and he hid from each one, wanting to pick who would first see him, get help for him. He wondered how his parents were handling the situation, his brother, his sister. How could he tell them? What could he tell them? For God's sake, I'm going to be a father, was all he could say.

At the top of one rise in the road, he saw the roofs and chimneys on several structures ahead of him. Down in a valley a stream raced by, water high near the banks, a full rush of spring melt on its way downhill, down toward the middle of the continent, and the Gulf of Mexico at the end of the run. To him now, as it had been for so long, everything was distant, unreachable for the most part, but perhaps that would change soon.

It was a small mountain village. A store stood on one corner of an intersection, and a garage and gas station with a single pump sat across from the store. A diner was open on another corner with light traffic of pick-ups and SUVs coming and going, customers gabbing and jawing in and out, hands and arms waving, like talk was taking place. Words were being said, stressed, expressed, punctuated. When he got to the diner, he mixed in with an SUV full of fishermen, the roof loaded with rods carried openly on a special rack. He seemed to be one of the crowd.

In the diner, coffee and bacon riding the air topmost, bustling and business on the move, he grasped at conversations. It was the sound of voices that drew him, not the meaning of words. It was enunciation and pronunciation mixed with mountain talk, lingo, slang peculiar to the region, human voices at the daily trade.

But one booth of two men and a woman caught at him, as if he had been zeroed in on. "She's as beautiful as a girl can wish for," said the woman, "but she can be weird from all that I've heard. Believes in UFOs, space travel, thinks aliens are here already. Thelma Trotter told me she wants a child in the worst way, but doesn't ever want to go near a man. Says she hates to be mauled by men. I heard she's tried several times to adopt, as a single mother, but no takers for her on that account. Like it's a losing cause. Like there'll never be a chance."

"What's her father say?" one of the men said. "Must be strange for him in his position as sheriff, and a miner to boot with some serious questions. People keep saying that he's hidden a good strike for years, saving everything for the girl. Why'd he call her Avonna anyway? I never heard that name before. Have you?"

The other two both shook their heads.

The girl gasped a surprise. "Don't look now, but there she is, right outside. Came in that black Jeep parked right behind her. I have to admit she's an absolute knockout. You agree?"

There was no audible answer, but a firm nodding of heads, eyes displaced for a time.

Stanton Knauber wanted to announce his name when a man in another booth, said, "You hear anything more about that missing

80

firefighter from the Squadron 9? Hell, he's been gone too long now. I heard a few of the guys in the squad figure he got burnt up. Something horrible the way one of them was decapitated. Hell, the stories making the rounds say that the guy who leased the copters to the Squadron had been using parts from copter wrecks in Viet Nam, parts that had a shelf life and didn't make the fit."

There was no answer from the booth.

Knauber looked out the window, saw her at the black Jeep, talking to an older man he assumed to be her father because the man hugged her before he drove off in another black Jeep.

It had to be proclaimed sometime: her father was in league with her; and her with child. His child. He caught the words before he nearly said them aloud.

Knauber stared at her through the wide window. She was extraordinarily beautiful, hair like dawn to a pilgrim out and about the dark world, shapely though some of the evidence was not immediately seen. It was tucked away in mountain clothes that help in bad weather, at mountain heights, but never at serving up beauty. Much of her was still hidden on a glorious spring day ... the interminable puzzle of a strange woman, a beautiful woman, one who took his breath away despite the circumstances, the cave, the cause of it all, whatever it was, or whatever it had become.

Dizziness leaped upon him. He began imagining striking scenes, or parts of striking scenes: What had happened? When? He knew the where. How many times? "Oh," he said almost aloud in the mountain diner, "I'll never drink orange juice again." He didn't know if it was a cry or a promise. He paused, looked at his captor again, his striking captor, as though he was still in the cave, and said, "Never again."

A few customers looked at him with question, then looked away from an ordinary man in an ordinary diner, egg and coffee and burnt toast aromas mixing in the air, the glorious morning making other demands.

When he looked out the window again, she was gone. The black Jeep was gone.

The day was moving on, into its place in the week, carrying him with it. He wanted to say, "Time doesn't stand still," but it did not issue from his mouth. Instead he said, "What'll I do now?" It came as an inaudible mutter. Probably the way he talked to himself in the cave, he thought.

81

The money that had been in his pocket when he set out in the helicopter, how many days ago? weeks? was still there, his wallet intact, small change in a pocket. He had to call home, call the Squadron, call somebody.

Say something. Make an announcement. He was alive. He had a child coming. He'd be home. Sometime.

The fire had to be out. How many beside the kid Roberts had been killed?

He'd not call his parents directly. The shock might knock them down. Had they accepted his disappearance? He'd call his sister and have her make a visit to the old house, tell them about him as they sat around the kitchen table, telling the old stories, introduce a new one, tell little brother Charlie he was okay. Tell them he was going to be a father. Would that make up for the long disappearance?

He'd go back home sometime. But he'd go up the mountain first. Find another entrance. Make his way back in. Be face to face with her. Be company for each other.

Wait out her time, Avonna's time, his child's time.

Oh, the Wounds He Wore, Death His Neighbor (Jimmy the Meterman)

Small-eyed, small-eared, a mole perched like an ace of spades on one eyelid, a mastoid-depressed void behind one of those ears, pale of complexion, shoulders it seemed worn down by weights almost too ponderous for life, Jimmy Griffith was the essence of obscurity as he leaned on the bar of the Vets Club. All members knew Jimmy by name and by sight, but few had ever heard him say much more than a good morning or a goodnight, or "I'll have my second beer now, Al," or "Brownie," if Brownie Latefox was on duty. This was the two-a-day ritual at the end of walking his route about town, measuring water consumption, reading the meters down in fieldstone cellars or the utility rooms of newer bungalows. Read the meters, jot the numbers, cheat a bit for a friendly face, or go a step further, like disconnecting a meter for six months at a time, not a soul at the water department or in the confines of Town Hall ever the wiser. Nobody knew how happy Jimmy was to have the job, nobody in God's creation. Or why.

Slab Glasko, dues paid up for eternity, overt proof that all of life's complexities merge mostly in personalities difficult to up-grade, did not like Jimmy Griffith for some reason unknown to the other members of the Vets Club. A big, boisterous guy with shoulders of a long-time lobsterman, mouthy, often insolent to visitors or strangers, Slab found Jimmy a suitable target for what always ailed his own person; too much silence about, too little noise, some part of life threatening to skip past him. "Goddam, let's have some music here. Perk the sleepy chickens. Wake up, world! Get off'n that effin' perch, boy! Life is here."

Slab's eyes seemed overactive below his dark brows, the forehead broad as an ax face, his ears, on close examination, a bit broad even for that prominent brow. He bodily ached for noise, for center stage or spotlight's glow, all essentially accountable, and agreeable to him, in one man's life. As he would say whenever queried on motive or outlook, "Life is noisy and you damn well better make some noise while you're on this side of the grass." That philosophy was always an opener for his wartime exploits to be expanded into the conversation, subtle as crutches or an aluminum walker. "I tell you this, when this old boy was in Paris with the Third Armored, everybody in town knew Slab Glasko was around.

Turned that town on its goddamn righteous Frenchie ear, I did. I'll bet a few Glasko genes are still afloat over there." Whatever container he grasped at hand would be emptied, dramatically, acute as punctuation. And then, with such pronouncements in place or echoing, his hugely knotted, salt-forged fist would slam on the bar loud as a keg falling off a trucker's tailgate, the vibrations mobilizing to the end of the countertop.

People often said Jimmy Griffith could tell what kind of activity, dependent on water, took place in a house. Probably could write a book or two, some of them said; who showered often and who didn't, who pooled or who didn't, why some lawns were much greener than others. For forty years he had been on the same job, since he had come out of the final noise in Europe in 1945 a tired Dogface. Meek-looking upon sight, a loner, unmarried it promised forever, Jimmy was often seen in season fishing with a fly line the back waters of the Saugus River on Saturday mornings, waders stretched to his crotch. Other off days or holidays he'd be that bent over figure digging for clams on the tidal marsh flats near the end of Bristow Street or mornings after storms scrounging for beached quahogs on the littered sands where the Atlantic dumped the mosaic of its own debris. Content to be alone Jimmy was, not a talker, and never a mixer. At no time did he ever spout any brand of politics left or right, or deliver any personal exploits of his younger days, but hung gray and stuck in neutral gear and almost out of sight in just about every situation, mostly accepted for what he was, Jimmy the Meterman, a numbers reader, of small account.

Slab would keep up his pageantry. "You were in the friggin' army, Jimmy? That really amazes me. In my army? In my very own army? In Europe against the Heinies, the invincible Heinies? The panzers. Germany's best, along the hedgerows? You a cook or what? You ever get in the combat zone where the real war was, down between those bushes?" The dark green Heineken bottle emptied itself down his throat. A few of the old members, stilled forever, were prompted to turn away, the ones who sought their own special silence with applejack or schnapps or a cutting ale, who left Gold Beach or Omaha Beach or the Anzio beachhead where they had found it, back in Europe, or Kwajalein out on the wide-blue. Brownie, slow to anger, yet with wild gray hair at odds with décor, cheeks like some brought-back Mescalaro warrior, moving resolutely behind the bar, a sense of timing working his frame, said to Jimmy, "Ready for your second, Jim?" He'd have him out of here before Slab

84

could get going, turning for the home stretch; three more beers and Slab'd be on fire for the night.

Jimmy didn't answer. Slab slammed the bar right beside him, thunderous as a sledgehammer. "Ain't talking again tonight, Jimbo? Jeezus, man, you give me a big puzzle. I keep trying to figure what the hell you did in The Big Two. You're like one a them culls crawls off into the corner of the tank watching the world go by. You gotta do some jivin', Jimmy." He turned and smiled at a few Third Armored cohorts idling on stools, real Slab fans that would appreciate his turn of a phrase. Jivin' Jimmy made him laugh out loud. "The world is full a culls, Jimmy. You gotta make distance, make time." He noticed Brownie standing at the end of the bar, staring openly at him, those high cheekbones shining with their particular dark varnish, the eyes dark as muzzles in the brush. Sliding down the bar to his pals at the bar, Slab muttered a loud aside, "Shit quiet again tonight, boys. Shit quiet." He would not look back at Brownie Latefox, once the very top soldier in the entire Big Red One.

Jimmy finished his second beer and slid off the stool. With a deft pat on Brownie's hand, he headed for the door, leaving a whole nightlong conversation packed into the solitary gesture. Brownie said, "See you at the parade, Jimmy." Waving a hand over his sloped shoulders, Jimmy slipped into the late evening that swallowed him up wholly and immediately. The small town of Saugus, accepting night and all that came with it, waited on him in the gathering darkness.

Slab muttered an unintelligible remark making his pals laugh unnaturally loud. Brownie, thinking they'd laugh at a cough, pulled five empties off the bar and wiped down that section of the bar top. Staring at the door Jimmy Griffith had passed through, he saw a few stars twinkling atop the parking lot out on the slow horizon, on the vast plain of night. The unforgotten war had been out there on that plain, small features of it leaping back at him even now, close to half a century later. A faded picture of Jimmy Griffith in army fatigues, somewhat fictional, possibly wry in its presentation, twisted in the back of his head, but he could not place Jimmy in an activity where those worn fatigues were common. The fished-for moment did not materialize, hard as he tried.

Memorial Day burst over the center of town, and the parade units bunched and lined up and headed out on the march, drums and bugles at a blaring cadence, twirlers prancing, pride dancing, and the crowd in exhilarating echo. A cool breeze walked in the air and sought company with hosts of balloons and winged and propeller-fixed toys and noisemakers of every sort and color. Young boys on bicycles, numerous as water bugs on Lily Pond, flitted through the crowd and along the parade route. The air was continuously brittle with trumpets and bugles and the ruffle of drums at a Monday morning's tattoo.

Slab Glasko, ill-fitted in an old Class A army uniform, buttons of his blouse at full strain, stood in the front line of the veterans group, chest out and shoulders back. Martial and galvanic music throbbed in his veins and the thrill of it forced him to stare into eyes along the march, challenging, seeking acceptance, demanding honor. There were non-veterans he knew who would not look up at him, and he found those in the ranks of watchers he was positive would never look him in the eye. The small pain at his hip did not bother him for one second. I was through a helluva lot more than this, he thought, thinking of his whole run through Europe, counting his scores. Long-known banker Ellis Milwood, standing smartly suited and elegant at one intersection, kept his gaze locked down at the pavement. Screw you, pal, Slab muttered, you couldn't know for one minute what it was like. His shoulders, squared to another degree, put him at another level. The crowd must love this, he said to himself, puffing his chest anew. He wished he could scream out the old cadence count alive and beating in his veins, the drumbeat of it in the back of his head. It was the way he nightly dreamed of convoys slashing across Europe, the Third Armored's lance, him out front, parting the Wermacht like Moses at the Red Sea.

Then, in one quick glance through the crowd, he caught Jimmy Griffith at the entrance to the cemetery. Jimmy's eyes looked red, recently-wiped red, teary-eyed red. Slab fixed both eyes on Jimmy Griffith who slowly turned, found Slab's eyes, stared back. Cast in concrete came the stare. This was new for Slab, this move of the quiet man. Those reddened eyes did not waver for one second, and Slab noticed a set of the chin he had not seen before.

There was a small break in the parade's tempo. Slab could feel those eyes of near-mute Jimmy on him, and he swore every man, woman and child on the parade route could see it, could measure it. An icy chill at his neck said this wouldn't do. He walked over to Jimmy, put his arm over his shoulder in a feigned show of comradeship and whispered, "If you got something to say to me, pal, spit it out like a man." That was telling him, cull of culls, flower on the wall. No way he come through

86

Europe.

No sooner had Slab uttered the admonition to Jimmy than he felt Brownie Latefox at his side. Three up and three down for chevrons in his prime, almost immortal in the ranks, Brownie put his hand on Slab's shoulder. "Can I listen in or is this some more private shit going on?" Slab about-faced back to the march unit.

Brownie looked closely at Jimmy. "What's the matter, Jim? You look like hell run over you."

"I was down there for a while earlier," Jimmy said, nodding toward Riverside Cemetery. "I got a couple of special buddies down there." Brownie could feel a leverage in the air. "And there's another one they never found," Jimmy offered, the final comment of his essay.

A few hours later, at the bar, Slab carrying on about how great the day was, how much the whole town paid honor to those who marched in the parade in their old uniforms, Jimmy Griffith started on his fourth beer, precarious and unsure.

"This is our day, baby." Slab waved a Heineken bottle in the air. "You hear the applause and shouting when we went by? Great day in the friggin' morning, wasn't it? Our day, baby, our day, for all the shit we went through. For all the hard times, for all the shit and shinola and rat ass Sergeants and green-ass second Louies we had to listen to and take crap from and pick up after. Today, this is it! This is our day, baby." The Heineken spilled all over his ill-fitting uniform. His Third Armored pals laughed and slapped him on the back.

His fourth beer gone, the glass empty but standing as a totem, Jimmy Griffith spun on his stool. At the end of the bar, four frothing Budweisers in his hands, Brownie Latefox snapped to attention.

As if changing his mind, or his approach to the matter, Jimmy leaned back on the bar, rested his elbows on it, only slightly less obscure than usual, but only for the moment. The small eyes, now bred of trouble, were hard as marbles, the concrete still in his chin. "You know what you are, Polack?" His voice was different, cutting for the first time ever. "You are one big loudmouth. You're all asshole. You have been ever since the first word you ever said in here. Why don't you smarten up and realize this day isn't for us, not for us who came back. It's for the guys who didn't come back. Like a couple of my pals down there in Riverside counting up on forty years or so. Don't go waving the flag on me, pal, or stuffing your friggin' ribbons in my face. It don't work here." He drank off his last swig right from the bottle, placed it on the counter, spun on his heels and walked out before Slab, mouth ajar, could say a word.

When Slab found his voice, telling his pals, "That little peckerhead probably never fired a shot in his life," Brownie was standing at the end of the bar, his arms folded across his chest, nodding assent to some internal thought. The next evening he went to his nephew and asked a favor. Two whole months later, the club quiet for the most part, no words at all exchanged between Jimmy and Slab, Brownie's nephew came into the club and handed him a piece of paper.

"This guy knew Jimmy in Europe, Brownie. He was evacuated and spent almost three years in a hospital. Says Jimmy was up for a medal and big time. Here's his phone number out in New Mexico. He was company clerk until he was hit and shipped home. Says Jimmy was kind of quiet but exploded a couple of times. You ought to talk to him." He handed Brownie a copy of the American Legion magazine. "I started with this. You can see it in there. A couple of guys wrote back who remembered Jimmy being in their outfit. This Alcindo was one of them. He's your best bet."

"This is Brownie Latefox calling, from Massachusetts. My nephew gave me your phone number. I was top-kick of the Big Red One, just for name-dropping. I'm interested in Jimmy Griffith, a pal of mine. I'd like to clear some things up about him."

"Kind of a loner, he was, Sarge. Pleased to meet you, by the way. Never said much, Jimmy, but popped a couple of times. I typed up his citation the platoon Louie had written."

"Citation? Why didn't we ever hear about it?" Brownie was suddenly aware of a string of snafus he had been involved in where paperwork went off the board for one reason or another.

"Jeez, Sarge," Alcindo said, "when I was bailed out of there I thought I was on my last breath. It was a long haul. Still catches me sometimes, but better than a lot of guys had it."

"What was it?" Brownie said, as if nothing Alcindo could say would be unknown to him.

"Mortar, they told me, right beside the orderly room."

"That's a messy lot. The paperwork get processed?"

88

"Don't know that either, Sarge, but I know the old man didn't like Jimmy a whole lot."

"What do you mean?"

"Stuck it to him a few times when Jimmy didn't do a thing to deserve it. Just was quiet all the time, not the old man's type. He liked the bluster, the PR kind of guy. He lives out in San Marcos right now. Saw his name a few times in the Legion mag. Still a gunner of sorts, big time. I never did like him. Not for what he did to Jimmy, that was small peanuts, but the way he generally was, mostly asshole if you know the type. I've met a dozen of him since then. You kind of remember them, not that they're supposed to be memorable." He chuckled. "We hadda have 'em. Made the world go round."

Brownie said, "He probably ditched it. I've seen it done. Let the war lose it. I'd love to have a copy of it, but that's too much to expect. Remember who the Louie was?"

"Never made it back, Sarge. Took a round right off the helmet. But it may not be a total loss."

"What do you mean?"

"Well, long after I got home, a train came into town one day and the stationmaster calls me and there's a duffel bag on it and it's mine. The Army sent it to me. It's been sitting in the back shed for years. I wore a few of the shirts one time, but there's some papers there I've hardly ever looked over. Might have something in there. I know I had an extra copy of the citation. I'll look for you."

Brownie gave him his phone number. "Anything comes up, any kind of a reference, give me a call, okay."

"You got it, Sarge. Say hello to Jimmy for me. Tell him I still remember him, even if he was mostly quiet."

"Mr. George Croughmartin, please." Brownie had dialed the San Marcos phone number." He was alone in the club, the bar not yet opened, the air vaguely stale and cut with a drift of ammonia, shadows sitting in corners like lepers.

"This is he." The voice was strong, level, and authoritative. "Who is calling?"

"We've never met, sir, but I was top soldier in the First Division, Big Red One, Europe, 1944, 1945."

"Well, Sergeant, this is a pleasant surprise, old comrades in arms.

89

What can I do for you?" Brownie detected roundness in the voice, a voice without edges. He'd already constructed a face.

"It's going back a long way, sir, but do you remember a citation or commendation written up for a Private James Griffith in one of your platoons, November 1944?"

"Is this one of those make-up calls, telling us we did not do our jobs as officers? I sort of resent that, Sergeant." Now there was a distinct edge to the voice. Brownie could feel it right through the phone. Immediately he knew he was accurate on the facial structure. It was like television.

"Do you remember, sir? It's kind of important."

"That is a long time ago, Sergeant. Memories fade, lose their luster, go out like the tide but never come back. I really do not recall the situation. This Griffith must have been not quite memorable, as I see it."

"Well, I was hoping you would remember, sir, because I've been in contact with the company clerk, Alcindo Requerto. He was wounded, evacuated, but remembers it fully and is pretty sure he has a copy of the citation come his way in a duffel bag the army shipped home for him long after hostilities were over. Says he probably kept it for a specific reason, but I don't have any knowledge of that reason." Insinuation was a tool in itself; use it as leverage "I expect a call from him shortly. We are going to make amends for a grave oversight, for whatever reason it happened."

"This Griffith, was he a quiet loner, not much of a soldier? A person of small stature. I might remember him at that."

"The citation, sir. It was apparently never processed. "

"The rigors of war, Sergeant, and the inevitable losses in every corridor." Now, thought Brownie, listen to that shit. He's going back on himself.

"One way or another, sir, we're going to get Jimmy Griffith his due. Any recollection of the incident at all?"

"Might have had something to do with him retrieving some wounded personnel. Yes, and going back someplace and getting a couple of radios and the weapons left behind. Those were cataclysmic days, Sergeant, as you well know. Something just fell by the wayside."

I bet, thought Brownie. "You have any personal records could shed some light on this, sir? It's long overdue."

"I will undertake a search, Sergeant, you can be assured. Perhaps this company clerk, this Alcindo, might come up with something. Does he think or does he know he has some reference?" The edge in the voice was like an open book exam, no questions unanswered in it. Don't get caught out in the open, it said. Cover your ass, it said. No bad press, it said. Go with the flow, it said.

Brownie pinned a copy of the faded but original recommendation on the wall of the club, at one end of the bar. Alcindo Requerto had found a copy in the duffel bag in his back shed. Croughmartin had been pushed into remedial action. Jimmy hadn't gotten his medal yet, but it was in the works. Slab didn't say much anymore, pulling into a minor shell, then stopped coming by the club altogether.

Jimmy moved on to three or four beers a night, the club now quiet, solitude and peace there generally for the asking, and one day, in April 1990, the trout working their silver and blue magic in the Saugus River way up behind the Cedar Glen Golf Course, a groundskeeper spotted the body of a man face down in the water. Jimmy Griffith, PFC with eventual Silver Star, the real quiet man, fly fisherman, meterman, had left this life, perhaps long after he might have left it.

Brownie Latefox had one of the members make two oak frames, one for the faded document, and one for the real thing when it came along. The second one hung on the wall empty, for over a year, before the official citation was inserted.

On 27 November 1944 Private James P. Griffith made three trips through a ravine that was under a relentless hail of enemy fire to rescue three seriously wounded comrades, working tirelessly for three hours to save the lives of the three men. Private Griffith also returned with a radio and three weapons the men had been using when wounded. Again the very next day Private Griffith left his covered position to cross terrain open and without cover in the face of heavy enemy fire to administer first aid to a comrade. Determining that the wounded man could not be moved without a litter, and realizing that the company was about to make a withdrawal, he remained with the wounded man, despite the withering enemy fire, for over ten hours until the company objective was captured. The gallantry and intense devotion to his fellow soldiers displayed by Private Griffith exemplify the finest traditions of the American soldier.

The original commendation was signed by 1st Lt. Royce Abnodder, Inf., Company C, 414th Infantry, United States Army (to which Alcindo Requerto had appended KIA 17 December 1944 RIP).

Every time Brownie Latefox turned on the tap to pour a beer he thought about Jimmy Griffith. He could see the small eyes, the mole on one eyelid, could see him twist an empty and hear him say, softly, so as to disturb nobody else, "I'll have the next one, Brownie." He remembered the wounds he wore, and that death was his neighbor.

Slab Glasko never entered his mind.

An Awed Submersion

The moon, maybe the night, perhaps the damned river itself, had begun to suck some of the beauty out of her. He could see it happening, the edges beginning new exposures, showing new lines. She was different, emergent, from or to. Something had moved away from her, a departure subtle at first but now gathering an identity. He thought how strange it sounded, his declaration.

Carmella couldn't stutter if she tried, but the words came out as if she had, "I don't understand why you're like this," while her hands were shaking, drama at full exhibit. Maybe she had practiced for this performance, an actress doing her lines for the director, her becoming something else right there in front of him. They were under stars, on the bridge, and eye to eye but only for short intervals.

They had been arguing on the bridge for more than an hour, where the river begins its snaking, its slow uncoiling, slipping off to sea like it was out of breath all the way down past the First Iron Works in America and the docile marshes and the lobster boat fleet at rest, and the huge General Electric plant hovering downstream like a ghost on the far side, the whole magnificent route lined with growth that fed on saline tastes, upland deposits, whose cast-offs became another man's treasure.

"Oh, not that," Eric said, "not that again. It's just because you can't hear where the river ends up. It disappears and becomes something else. There's more than mystery here." He wondered if she could understand another approach to the matter at hand, doubting it at once.

Meantime, the water flowed beneath them, past too many bends ever to be heard from this point, even at midnight when the air became as thin as the old lace curtains in her mother's parlor.

He was deep in thought, the words threatening to be vocal, but held in place. "Oh, yes," he was thinking, "the one place where our hungers truly met, blossomed in a burst, in your mother's parlor, on the Persian rug. Wild and beautiful. I swear your legs at times like a referee's touchdown signal. You were ignited and lovely that one time, a rose before cruel July kicks the hell out of it.

"You're too slippery on things, Carmella."

It was said. It was out. Then he added, as though a piece of him was talking other than his heart, "Just too damned slippery."

There were parts of her he'd already forgotten, out of reach; a

93

curve of whiteness so sinful it could choke him, a curve near a hip taunting from first appearance behind the sheerest silk and darkness, her Mound of Venus, complete with gesture of wish, of command, like a finger drawing him, a road marker.

One of her breasts, he realized, was more perfect than the other. Just then he could not remember which of those stars lit him up. Once, during a night at the beach, hidden by dunes and sea shrubs and high grass, everything dizzy in proportions, a seed seemingly broke loose from that nipple, which he savored for hours. Did she miss it? he wondered. Did she even know?

That time she waited almost two weeks before she said, "Why didn't you do something at the beach that night?" It was the only way she could say anything like that, sliding at him later, coming at an angle, never saying what was foremost in her mind. It was another piece of her mystery.

One late evening, during a walk beneath occasional streetlights, in the midst of solitude, she suddenly blurted out, "What in God's name," spun on her heels and hurried home, leaving him in silence. She had plenty of similar moments, so many they faded into indifference, lost in the current.

Carmella was not at all like some women he had known, remembered without restraint, so direct they were beautiful, saying, "Do you know what I'd like to do right now, Eric? I'd like to suck that." Or another loveliness saying, after her same bit, "Oh, Eric, you're fuckin' suckin' beautiful," even as the gin vapors rose in the night air and she from her haunches, silk talking a language he thought he'd understand all his life. And her repeating her words, saying them three or four times, making sure she'd be one of the women he'd remember, her words alive forever.

A smile crossed his face, a tremor of a smile, saying it worked either way; he knew her now, and often.

As a result of the rush of memories, the one night of true mystery with Carmella came back in pieces, but it was all attached to her aroma, her taste, with a rush quicker than the river; electric it came, her straddling his mouth in trepidation at first, her eyes locked down on his armor, one hand eventually holding him and stroking him in disbelief, then shifting, moving, meeting, assenting, moving again, and again, dropping slowly in acknowledgment of the deed.

94

At the moment both of them were cresting, he saw the door open just a slit at first from the hallway and her mother, a matching beauty of 40, a widow, eyes deep and dark as sin itself, standing in the midst of her own awe, hands to her face, studying them, her frame twisting subtly into a wholly and sudden emptiness, yet a wanton release, almost a cry he could hear, until her eyes locked onto his staring back at her.

With sudden desperation and loss taking her by the hand, she slowly closed the door on them, with her eyes still locked on his, drawing something from him up off the Persian rug.

But who knew what, for her?

Remembering every detail with a sudden helplessness, right there on the bridge, water trickling over rocks, whispering an evening song in his ears, he admitted he didn't know which one of the women he loved the most, Carmella the daughter or Carla the mother.

There were arguments.

The fading of Carmella's parts was dramatic, the way she came out of spells, the way he came out of day dreams of her, near trances where the flesh stayed master longer than he might let it. Some of the parts, he agreed wholly, were gone. Had they gone behind that door when it closed, gone with her mother? Had her mother owned them from the beginning? Would their ownership be proved?

The here-all? Lie? Lay? Lain?

The words jumped all around him.

Caught he was between the matter and the form, between the harshness of beauty and the spirit of beauty. The look on her mother's face hadn't left him; it came as acceptance, as desire, as a promise of what could be. It didn't end up in a small niche, that feeling, but made a continuous assault on him, kept touching back at him from wherever.

From then on, in every instance of thought, Carla, perhaps in her mother's destiny, seemed more desirable, more mature, more woman who would sacrifice her own passions for those she loved, not those she wanted or needed, or had made an overture to.

The punch of it all came at him again as he looked down at the water flowing under the bridge, going wherever it was led by an accustomed route, shaped, pulled, pushed. And Carmella looked down too, most likely seeing something other than what he saw, another image, and another idea so new it might have frightened her at first.

Eric realized he had brought Carmella to the bridge because of deep curiosity and a need for comfort. It was a place that caught him in general ease. A hundred times he'd been here, fishing, dreaming, and seeking resolutions. It was his place. Here he'd been caught up in the romance of the plants and flowers that had drawn him to many illustrated books about such growth, and the litany began to spill from him as if a torrent had broken loose, like the river in April, the rush from inland: the landscape in a thousand parts coming with it, torn loose by awesome strength, ripped out by brute force, or eased away by the same unknown power of green growth that separated concrete walks, parted asphalt with its green knife. He knew crowfoot, toad-flax, snap dragon. Columbine, dog's tooth violet, arethusa bulbosa, horned sedge, sea pink, Plymouth gentian, oysterleaf, riverbank wild rye, marsh marigold, sweet aster, bloodroot, poke weed, squaw root, papoose root, lizard's tail, wool grass and cord grass for miles and miles. For miles and miles. The water below him, in its run, nurtured such growth, provided cover in the growth and feed for animals of all kinds, and had filled his mind for delicious hours of study and contemplation.

"Here's a list of plants to choose from," he had once said aloud to nobody but himself, not abetting his memory but enjoying a near-movie of filmy images: thyme, rosemary, rock rose, lavandula, rugosa rose, seaside daisy or fleabane (erigeron strigosus), catmint, coastal golden wattle, bougainvillea, valerian (centranthus ruber), vinca minor, cape plumbago. Never once did his tongue trip over a name, even those in Latin or another language applied for classification.

He was lost in his own comfort zone when she said, looking at him and then back at the river's flow, as if an answer had come to her, eyes sunken, cheeks gone dead flat, without an ounce of charge in them, no eye lights or highlights. "You just don't care about me anymore. You wander. Well, I'm pregnant, that's what I've been meaning to tell you, trying to find a way to say it the way you'd want me to."

With that delivered, her hands and arms in cheerleader flings, before he could move, before his mind came back to him from her mother staring into his eyes, or from a litany of flora and fauna, she jumped over the rail and into the river.

Taking her unborn child with her.

He did not hear the splash.

He did not jump after her.

Not immediately.

It was more of her thinly clad dramatics, he thought, because she was an excellent swimmer. The river was not dangerous, though it had sudden twists in its course, hidden obstructions, debris of the ages one might guess. He couldn't remember how many times his fishing lines were hooked onto some hidden clutch while he stood at this very spot, the only solution being to cut the line with a knife, try again, never knowing what clutched at him, grasped at parts of him.

She didn't surface.

The river ran its way, past the arrows of reeds, the cord grass and glasswort, on bank after bank at every turn where flowers fought for a grip, where upland debris and dosage piled atop itself, for good, for now, for the tidal change to creep and seep its way back home.

He looked for her bobbing head, the one he had seen so many times come up in the water of the lake, her hair as if it had been combed back severely on her head, her mouth wide open at last and drawing air. All he saw was the unbroken flow of the stream; no bubbles, no foreign objects in the float, no sharply-combed head of hair. Nothing.

Nothing!

Panic, in its moment, swiftly obliterated her mother's wanton gaze, and swung through him pushed by its own bellows.

Off came his shoes, wallet out of his pocket and dropped on the bridge for a signal to someone coming onto the foot bridge, anyone, or for preservation of contents.

On the bridge were his shoes, his wallet, his last thought in the air as he jumped over the railing, hit the water, found himself deep, screwed himself back to the surface, looked again for a bobbing head, saw none.

He'd been in here before, in these same waters for a youngster fallen from the bridge on a prank, the boy's pals on the bridge all stunned, all screaming their fright. The boy's wild commotion in the water made it easy for him to be found, Eric's hand clutching him by the belt of his pants, drawing him up for air, onto the banking, his pals still screaming, but now in joy, in release.

He remembered how the boy tried to clutch at him in the water, and how he'd held him apart, not harming his own success at rescue. He'd get Carmella the same way. Heard himself telling Carla how it was: I found her in the grasp of lower water, near the bottom, near dangerous roots, debris, the awful stuff the river brings with it to the sea; it was not going

97

to take you away from me.

He actually said that, afraid of being a failure here, at this attempt.

He rose again, arms pumping, his head up, eyes scanning the river ahead of him.

Nothing.

He dove again. Saw nothing.

Rose again, dove again, searching underwater for a commotion set off by Carmella.

Only the water provided motion, slight debris with it in the seaward march.

He did not see the old fender of a car, or the jagged edge of metal strip ripped from place by an accident so far in the past it might have pre-dated his birth.

But he felt the slim edge, sheer, knife-like, as it sliced down along his stomach under his shirt, felt the initial pain, felt its grasp settle directly under his belt buckle, like a lure by a striper that once had come this far upstream for his hook, almost to the foot of the bridge.

How could he tell Carla he had failed? Would she hate him? Would her eyes still hold his eyes like that one time? Or his eyes hold hers?

He tried to rise again. The clutch would not let go, and then he could no longer see ahead of him in the water as it become too cloudy. The last word from him was "Blood" as the red swirl moved with the flow.

He said, "Blood," loudly, open-mouthed. He couldn't find a name he wanted to say.

Downstream, the excellent swimmer, nearly around a bend in the river, rose once more, took a deep breath, made for the cluster of saw grass and reeds on the nearest bank, and saw, in a flash of red and black, a red-winged blackbird rise free from its hidden nest in the high grass, in the reeds standing like spears in a quiver.

Born to Wear the Rags of War

Vatcher Sexton McKee, Sergeant of Infantry, already as cold as he'd ever been in his life, could not hold the pencil securely in his hand. He'd broken the lead point three times and worried about handling the rifle, managing the trigger when the time came, expecting a new wave of Chinese infantry surging uphill in another three hours by his estimation. He stuffed the latest letter home into his parka pocket, to be finished when he could get back to it.

Earlier, the cold wind, not a storm laden with snow, but a nasty body of cold wind in burrowing waves announcing another quick freeze, had swept down the valley on the brink of the Yalu River.

He observed that ice on this slope of the mountain was a living thing, moving in the night, taking over, going into all the secret places it was knowing again, like an explorer making new sign on an old trail. Ice had visited here before, would come again, perhaps in the same sly way, but taking over every nook and cranny the mountain had to offer. And there was no way to hide from it, no escape, no secret route subtlety leaned into, or grasped by sudden moves or sudden ideas. Ice had made the awful though subtle introduction: I know you and now you know me. It was so simple, but had distinctions; there was never an odor to it, as if it bore virginal cleanliness from the onset, no odor, no taste, no identifying proclamation in the throes of it ... just hard ice in every format, every level, adjuncts to life on a winter mountain in Korea.

His toes told him first of ice, and his ears, and the little fingers on both hands, the near unconscious maneuvering of them. Asian ice, supposedly, was no different than the blocks of ice that he and pals had sawed out of Lily Pond in late Decembers back home, watched the blocks go up the noisy ramp into Sawyer's or Fiske's ice house, into and under the spread of sawdust as insulation in the coming summer, thereafter fishing awhile, sliding along on the amorous arrows of late canoe rides, watching daring girls at midnight (some of them most demure classmates), on the island, skinny-dipping, the moon a heady perfume slipping past the eyeballs, contorting, embellishing all the possibilities that existed.

If he wandered into those images, he had to rush out of them. The realization was a loud bang at the back of his head, in the eyeballs like an echo seeking them out. Bang! it went. Alive. Move on. Come back here where you belong, in this mess.

He heard himself say, "Oh, Mom, you wouldn't dream who some of them were; a few of your very favorite girls in their soft calling, their intentional visits to our house, their secret touches of selves that were bodily revelations, invitations, experiments in young seduction. How to bring them back? Initials? No, too open. Second initials? Ah, yes; like a Muriel Stinson now lives as UT, breathes, moves back into the promise of a novel, finds her own page for starters."

"Oh, girl, how splendidly you dive into the night pond, slim, silvery sylph."

But ice would make a comeback in his book; that was a bold, bald statement, more promise than previously held: Ice, he would paraphrase, would do, would suffice, and all he had to do was get the single word of it into a single letter, mask it somehow, tell his mother nothing mounted any more interest in him "at this lazy moment under this piercing sun than a glass of your iced lemonade."

Ah, yes, Robert, ice will suffice. Leave the fire to its own making. The ice, herald it, would run ahead of many images, yet come in its dogged, silent way, like a footpad, a night thief, a Jimmy Valentine on the job, its approach on a lengthening, slimming icicle the same damned way glaciers move along the dreaded, huge white edges of a continent to find a sea all their own.

"Oh, Mom," he said into the cold air fighting for his teeth, "one of your ice-cold lemonades!"

He spun about at the thought, shaking himself alert, looked down into the bunker of logs, sandbags, rocks, ice clinging fast as quick-dry cement on this home-away-from-home, this *uichi*, b. 1951, Bong Ha Lee, architect, ROK, RIP, went home on leave once with a basket full of yen in his backpack, came back, caught a high hard one he never saw, never dreamed of, taking most of it with him on that last step. Master tinkerer; sewed tent canvas, salvaged Jeep U-bolts for horseshoes in one reserve area, made watch crystals out of clear C-ration spoons, played the guitar like an Ozark strummer. BHL/ROK/KIA/RIP, half a line of memory held in place.

Tom Durocko was still sleeping just inside the bunker. He could see the Chicago Kid's simple, private body motions of slow breathing, as though napping on a beach in a better place, or a select place on the lake shore, though Lake Michigan had its own winter horrors. He'd not be dreaming, but McKee envisioned him making do in the Coliseum or any arena where hand-to-hand combat held sway, where true guts were required one more time each time. The kid would be wide awake in two seconds when he had to be, ready to go at anything coming his way. A born tiger, he was, made for this stuff, McKee agreed, and nodded at his own internal image, seeing the Chicago petty thief standing before the judge who simply said, "Jail for three years or join the army just three doors down the street, and where you can be useful; you owe us, son, you owe us heavy."

It was the first wake-up the kid ever had tossed in his lap, for him to handle or fumble, carry the ball or drop his life short of any goal line.

The judge had slammed the gavel down on the dais, trying to scare the hell out of Durocko, who did not flinch, who smiled back at him, and the two of them, each of them out of their own Loop's Hells, had to smile at each other in appreciation. One day he'd write Durocko and the judge into a book; all he had to do was cover him in one of the letters home; bring the code, find a name for him, leave the essence for his typewriter to find again: TD scored on a Korean hill, field judge's arms raised. All the sly, coded inclusions would snap at him, shake him when the time came to yank these tidbits out of the lost column, bring them into the ranks, find order for them, for him. It would be a cinch; all he had to do was get there, get home, and find the spark again. Piece of cake!

Downhill, behind him, all the way down the slope, snow littered the trail the way old snow plows used to leave it, and comrades' bodies in their slow movements stood upright like trees. He strained to see any comforting activity, support of any kind at the lower levels, the bubble of help moving up from vast supply depots the winter kept pounding at, the narrow mountain roads piled up to consistently slow advances, every turn on a rising road an adventure, the six-by drivers he swore as good as Indianapolis drivers. He'd seen one go, on a treacherous turn, starting its slide as though it was moving slowly and cautiously into a parking space, felt the brakes without grip, the ice smoother than butter, frictionless, take that whole god-damned six-by right over the edge, the driver frantically trying to get away from the cluttered cab, a guitar in the way, his boot probably caught between a pedal and the guitar, his last look saying he really didn't like music that much, the last wave of his hand coming off as an orchestrated goodbye.

A few replacements, raw as onions, hesitant, not in any way eager to mix it up with a veritable horde of the enemy, were moving uphill like an ant hill being emptied during normal work hours. McKee, swapping places with the replacements, knew their terror, their lost place in life a moving treadmill sending them uphill, silence moving into the heart of death. None of them spoke, he assumed, stunned into silence. They'd obviously seen the stacked bodies piled stiff as logs between the stakes down the line, a place they might come to even before the day was over, feeling stretched forever on a no-account hill. Even their inner voices surfaced behind his eyeballs, gaining ground where they didn't belong. He had trouble finding quick pity; there wasn't much left to deal with. Not here, nowhere in the whole world, home so far away it might not count any more.

Where they were now, in this slow ascension, he'd already gone through, been there. He knew them now, this minute, this image coming again: this new shot at memory: John Maciag was all bone, knees, elbows and jaw, Hated his rifle, proficient at killing, wanting home so badly it burned his soul. We leaned up that mountain near Yangu, frightened. War's hurricane tore our ranks, trees of us lifted by roots. I came running down three days later. Like cordwood the bodies were stacked between two stakes, all Korean but that jaw of John Maciag I saw, a log of birch amongst the scrub. The Sergeant said move on. I said, Maybe never. I'm going to sit and think about John Maciag's forever, whose fuel he is, what the flames of him will light.

The images, the ideas, the possibilities running free ... a single Chinese soldier, from a valley of buried gods, standing in place and refusing to move, a puffed, quilted warrior maybe not yet fifteen years old, a wily and warm veteran of other hills, this hill; they'd been on top here twice before, leaving their marks ... the deepest bunkers, sundry lost artifacts carried by warriors for perhaps three thousand years, how many millennia, strange names left on log surfaces as undecipherable as freight car graffiti speeding past a midnight crossing or past a break in midnight trees. Time bears enemies and allies. Memories. His codes. The heady stand-ins he was using.

He jumped again. Images did that, setting the way, breaking ground, finding their way via ink onto a blank page and another page, a long paragraph without the first punctuation mark coming into place for 350 words, or such. Life moving on in a breathless paragraph, chest caught up just before a period came to life, a STOP sign. Rest.

The trees that once made their way on this side were gone, every one of them, the mountain shaved down from the crown to the base, the last of them dropped for bunkers slid into the earth, where the troops slept through solemnity hard to imagine any more, the touch of all solitude embracing them one at a time or taking on a whole squad at one instant, like a malaise moving hand to hand.

For a split second, it seemed, time did not matter, having a place where it could hang out by itself, neutral, on the other side of a mountain like this one, dreamy, silent, rice-borne, a sort of Valhalla where old friends, or dead comrades made a habit of shaking hands again, letting him know they'd be there at the finish, once it arrived. That was the big doubt, not if they'd hang in with him, but if the end would ever come for them. If there was anything he could not understand, it was his imagination, up and at him, boisterous, jumpy now and then, and mostly now, leaping at lost images, old faces, buried ideas. His father had once said, so solemn it might have been left over from a lost vesper, "Time comes for every idea; make sure you're ready for it if you can."

His father's whispered asides were inevitable and commanding, him gone blind, hastening around on two crutches and one leg, leaving echoes for the long run. On the job long after he should have left it, socks bloody every day after work, a false smile on his face.

McKee had written, "Dear Folks, Upon this hill the sun shining bright and hospitable is a good sign for us ..." the lie in place as usual, the weather up front in the first line of the letter like a window shade snapped up in the morning sunlight, best of starts for the folks, but the letter, like all of them he had written for them at home, always coming off sweet as syrup, a new blossom his mother could nearly smell, the gentle touch of falsity hiding his place in the combat zone. The fiend Death, to the unwary letter writer, could too often slip into the written message.

So every letter for them went off loaded with key words that he'd decode later, positive of all the keys built into them (the dotted letters, the Os filled in or circular portions of other letters of the alphabet, the Ts dotted or double-crossed, location names misspelled so they'd never check on them (La Plaza Solay, La Coste Solte each coming back in his later interpretation as Seoul, where he was yanked to surfacing as Yang-du), the military unit numbers a jumble of math equations impossible to breakdown this side of the Enigma's Ultra machine he'd heard about. His mind jumped at the possibilities of his encryption being broken, but that

103

would hardly be achieved within the family. It was a fancy he was pursuing and shook if off just as a shiver came back to life at the nape of his neck … and down inside his parka. Aversion is as good as diversion; no place to run to, but getting there. There were times it was plain and outright juicy to hang his hat on impossibilities.

He admitted that strange thoughts pursued him doggedly, for there were times he didn't know who he was, not really who he was, or why he was here. It made him think of Oppenheimer's The Great Impersonation where the main character was lost in the pages so many times he, in his reading, kept putting the wrong face on him, the wrong place in life, the roles so twisted even the character would have trouble straightening it out. In the midst of momentary silence, his admiration at such ability stung him with a singular force, like a bullet might hit home.

Nor did he know what he looked like any more. The last time he'd seen himself in a mirror, the question still lurking about him, had been almost a month earlier, on the side of this same mountain … only halfway up. What he remembered were the same lines about his face his father had, and before he was 40 years old, all of life throwing its concrete blocks on his back, making him tote them too early in his days. The lines scored his eye sockets and ran crevices of a sort from the orbs down past his mouth, and he recalled how people looked at him, trying to guess his age. His father had that problem, not knowing if he was 40 or 70 from one day to the next.

Doug Henderson, dependable corporal, Georgia-born and created, looked up one day at the foot of the hill when he was still embattled with Oppenheimer's book, before the first try at ascending this hill that became a mountain, and said, "Vatch, if you ever find out who the real guy is, do you promise to tell me. I can hardly wait." The hearty laugh followed. They'd knocked the book around a few times when he'd shown Henderson a few pages, letting him stew in as much doubt as he had, never giving him too much of what bothered him, letting him get as deep as possible … just where he was.

"It sounds like the damned amateur hour Major Bowes ran, one man plays several parts and best part wins."

That made him shift his thought immediately to home and a day in school, one of the transfers endangering him daily in this mountainous place. The translation to another self became swiftly evident to him, so swiftly he looked about, woke himself up, and went off again, telling him

104

it happened too often, but so far all the changes had come off as harmless: he wasn't dead, he hadn't been wounded, nor had he accidentally shot a comrade in the back, his attention brought back from its wandering and wondering to allow him to function as a Sergeant of Infantry.

Oh, some of the wanderings he went through, zipping into him like barbed wire messages from his past, the recall of events so sharp they frightened him to think that he was someplace else and this part of Korea was nothing but a dream. When he remembered looking at Lee Bong Ha with his backpack filled with payday yen to take home, he thought that to be a part of the dream too. Bong Ha was a magician with tools, with inventiveness, with his dreams. Were his dreams so similar? Did he too shift around in his mind? Was he building some kind of a collection bound for the unknown?

Oh, he had wandered again, his mind shooting ideas and images on wild tangents, in crazy unmatched pairs, but coming at one time from one mind.

Yet a laugh gurgled in his throat as he thought about the formula for the Solvay process, the test answer so elusive in his high school chemistry course. Of course it came back now, clear as ever, when he had no need of it at, and never would have need for it, but the memory stung him blatantly for its uselessness, $2 NaCl + CaCO_3 \rightarrow Na_2CO_3 + CaCl_2$. The formula would be engrained for eternity.

And so came a view of the home reception of his letters after simple and quick readings and grimaces of ignorance on their part, but, as requested, put into a box in the back hall or in the attic, or in a closet, to be held for him ... for in the collection of letters would sit the heart of his novel to be beat into a life, to crawl away from his letters one letter at a time on the typewriter, crawl on its hands and knees from that clutch of letters, to come together on that machine, to breathe on its own merits, to make real what might now be a dream.

If his grandfather was still back there, the Yeats reader, the tobacco smell coming along with Yeats, he'd be sleeping with his letters, at his bosom, as his pillow for thought, his stretch of night, a coverlet for a child in a poem he'd forgotten right from the old man's lips like they were Yeats' lips. And he heard the old man say again and again, "Hear the music, Boy. Hear the music in the words." Then he'd qualify it all by saying, "The words with handles. Get them, Boy. The words with

105

handles; they'll do the deed for you."

His grandfather's rhythms lived; they were now his. He reached once more, the fingers moving, one on each hand, grasping a word with handles. Owning it, taking it down inside, twisting it, turning it, making it work an old way, a new way, his way. Oh, fucking halleluiah!

There were times in the midst of a battle zone that he imagined the smash of his fingers down on the trusty old Smith-Corona, locked away in the backroom closet, kept the blood circulating in his hands, in his fingers, making the final demand up along his biceps, the shoulders feeling it ... imagined but so useful. Sometimes he'd remember a word or two, now and then its root looming into a sentence asking for completion, for housing in a paragraph, in a chapter, the full message of a word making its way down the long haul. "They'll do the deed for you."

He dreamed sounds, expressions, the musical tattoos coming on wings, a word, hard as stone yet moving, sliding like a tailback, Tommy Harmon, Bruce Smith, Nile Kinnick in command, penetrating the line, finding open air, taking flight.

Over the edge of the ridge, atop another blast of frigid air so heavy it slammed him aside the head with the punch of a fist, the enemy bugle calls came uphill again and promised they'd be coming back, waves of Chinese infantry as thick as the cold had come in its own crunch, onward, deliberately massed, fearsome waves of humanity with nothing to gain in the whole world of possibilities but another useless hilltop.

Durocko was locked and loaded. "Hey, Sarge, ain't we been here before?"

"Up 'n' at 'em. They're coming back," he yelled. "Flex your fingers. Make sure they work. Fit the trigger. Get ready."

His look searched along the line of his squad, measuring his men, hoping for the best of them to step out again, as they had in the previous thrust. The new lieutenant's body was in the bunker with a damned good chance of getting buried there if a shell hit it, or a flung grenade. The platoon leader's dog tags were in one of his pockets where his fingers touched them, perhaps the last sign of him here on this earth. Who was waiting on him, what was waiting? He hadn't gotten to know the man in the few short weeks he'd been here, only that he could stick his head up at the wrong time, see death coming straight at him. They had all seen the curious, the unwary, the doubters of quick death.

Of course, it would be like that with some men. He tried to

remember what he looked like, the new lieutenant, but nothing came except his stare directly at his own death. It was all uneven, no balance to it, this art of dying. The awareness had been the lieutenant's from the first minute of combat. The others of the unit, the hep ones, the alert ones, knew how the lieutenant's mind worked and had consigned him so quickly it might now have been forgotten.

Hell, now it did not count. Other considerations loomed.

His letters counted. Every damned letter in every damned letter. Every word. Every paragraph. Every suspicion. Every fear. They had been transcribed from so many angles he hoped he could find the level to finish them off the way they came at him when he had first thought about the book, that idea shaking him awake the first night he had slept in a bunker on a hill in North Korea, words beating at him, the tempo taken and accepted, the rhyme and reason and all the phonetics telling him where he was on the journey ... though at the start, "You are on your way."

He went back to the book without pages.

He came back from an odd paragraph. An awed paragraph, the kind that get so good they kill you when you lose them. And lost they are; perhaps to come back in a slow moment of life, his head on a soft pillow, time on his hands, death behaving itself.

Perhaps they'd go MIA. It happens.

A bugle sounded. He thought of a bugler, a trumpeter. He said the name "Al Hirt" not knowing if he could see the right spelling, but he could hear a song, the muted parts as well, the notes like letters in a paragraph, on the page ... and he was tone deaf to begin with.

It was enlightening. It was book.

He yelled, he thought as loud as the bugles, a sense of bravado riding him, finding the words, the words surfacing for the composer on simple demand, words to be used.

"Hell's coming up here for another look. Do the devil down, boys. Do the devil down."

He eyed the movement downhill, at the edge of piled-up snow. "Do the devil down." He kept saying it.

One more flash came into the back of his head before multiple bugle calls came anew, and odd drum beatings: the current letter for home, for the file he was building back there, was #153, and like the last 20 letters written, not yet in the hands of the mail service, but wedged into a deep pocket of his parka, bound as tightly as a secret. There had been little opportunity to send the letters on their way, and the business at hand, the war itself, throttled further chances of sending them on.

The beginning of his book was there in the letters, and the middle of it, and the end of it after the hills came into it, the high hills, the falls down, the climbs back, the names of characters, the constant name of his hero, Mack Tribbley, the 31st Infantry Regiment as an entity, heaven and hell and all else deadly.

Snow was a character, and the cold. Devils about.

Those thoughts rushed him back to the living fact: they came, rushing uphill. He was glad they were not Gurkhas he'd read about, but they were almost as good. The war was happening for them again. Battle, on the edge of consciousness, came renewed. Ground support from the rear roared overhead, dropped in square parameters, hit in the midst of the enemy, and then crawled along the edge of the hill, his hill, bumpy, banging, like the Dodgems at Revere Beach, hell on wheels for kids now conscripted for death and dying; only adults may serve in the combat zone … like hell.

Overhead the artillery observer in a Piper Cub wagged the wings of his plane, and the onslaught from the rear continued, slamming like an old-time break-in of a bank vault, Chicago style, no Jimmy Valentine in this war, on this hill.

The Piper Cub signal was irreverent. Down the line a captain of infantry fired his M-1, emptied it, at the plane loading up death for an erroneous target. Friendly fire, my ass, he'd say.

Came separation, noise, screaming, his ears pounded by blasts, concussion, and a sense of reeling, on a dance floor, on a skating surface, in a roller coaster like the Cyclone at Revere Beach with dives the way he had seen some Mustangs bite the dusty clouds and wing home in a scream. The headline gone over the hill. The tattoo of escape.

He woke up shaking, the noise a horrible roar inside his ears, banging on his eyes, rolling across his scalp.

"Remember this," he thought he was screaming. "Remember this. Put it in the numbers, in the names. Save it all. This is it."

He tried to stretch a hand, to search.

It could only be a chopper riding the turbulent air and as he tried to move, shift his weight, he felt the binds holding him in place. The fall out of the stretcher cradle might be hundreds of feet, straight down, back to

108

the beginning. Back to the start of memory. He could not hear the roar of guns or cannons, or the bugle calls rising to chase him. Al Hirt's sounds no longer downhill. Just before he had been shipped to Korea, he had heard him on the radio with Horace Heidt's Orchestra and marked him, loving the sound of a contemporary musician probably only a few years older than he was. There was acceptance and grace in being tone deaf. He tried for a trade-off.

The binds prevented him for searching his parka for the packet of letters. The pocket felt empty against his side. Loss and separation and calamity, in unison, hit him broadside. In a momentary flash old words came from nowhere: They had been strangers beside each other, caught in the crush of tracered night and starred flanks, accidents of men drinking beer cooled in the bloody waters where brothers roam forever, warriors come to that place by fantastic voyages, carried by generations of the persecuted or the adventurous, carried in sperm body, dropped in the spawning, fruiting womb of America, and born to wear the rags of war.

The blackness ascended with the chopper's lift. Air rushed someplace, going past, going fast, then faster.

He woke up far in the rear of the battle lines, far to the rear; warm, arms bare, burnt steak aroma in the air, a place under him that was off the ground, minutes of absolute silence making him think of a kind of death. He saw a nurse first, younger than buds, her lips pouty and soft as she looked his way, the mound of her being pressing against her white uniform, a signal of survival saying its name, him wondering if he was still whole. It was impossible for him to reach, to check. He kept trying, kept failing.

The nurse spoke to him, a piano voice speaking, the keys appropriate, delicious; "You're near the coast, in a hospital ship marked with three red Xes bigger than life. At the pier behind us Japan sits with welcome arms in front of a new cortege of injured warriors. Your comrades are still coming aboard. There are a lot of them." She became real, with tears. "It's like a fucking parade."

Her face was in her hands, her tears shut up.

Her breasts said he was still alive in some parts.

She was crying, but she was movie beautiful, like Debra Paget in the last film seen. Where was that? Camp Stoneman? On the other side? At the real beginning, at the embarkation point knowing absolutely nothing of the life to come as they boarded the ship, no weapons in their

109

hands?

The thought of empty hands brought back the panic. He could tell that the packet of letters was missing. "I had a bunch of letters, a bundle of them. Where are they?" His voice was loaded with undecipherable emotion.

The nurse knew nothing of the letters, or the orderlies or the aides, or the tough-looking ward administrator, a blonde with dark eyes that seemed to be brooding, big lips, no breasts visible, arms that might lift kegs, her whole person sadder than Christmas Past.

She said, "There was no packet of letters with you, or on your person anyplace, or in your gear, what little there was, when you came aboard. Other matters were more important to us."

It was almost apologetic when the administrator added, "There were others with you, from your squad. They've all moved on," and she added the saddest commentary, "one way or another."

They had ganged up on him, the two of them.

He didn't ask them to qualify the manner of separation.

Just one letter he had sent home he remembered coming came back to him verbatim: Save all my letters and put them in a safe deposit vault in the bank. Keep them for me. They are important.

If only his grandfather ...

In the hospital stateside, no visitors, he was morose. The letters hounded him, but there was salvation, he hoped. He didn't dare write and ask about them. There would come a letter of disaster, of no concern, of little care, so like the past being the past. The roots had no importance. Today counted, this morning. That was all. The thought shot him down again.

When he got home, and after the mini-celebration, he went looking around during the night through the house ...in the cellar, the attic, as many closets he could get into, the back hall leading to his room where there was no heat, where few would enter on cold weather or in the heat of summer, secret hiding places in the structure of the house he thought no one else had ever found.

He found no letters. Not a single one. No map developed by text. No coded city. No hill number shrouded by equation. No misspelling leaving footprints of his travels. Nothing. No fossil. No clue. His mind shorn.

Finally, his live-in cousin said, "I'm afraid of something here.

110

Somebody thought they were just diversions for your mom so she wouldn't get upset like she did about big brother Jack in WW II. They were such innocent letters, a lot of jumble and hieroglyphics in them, things we couldn't read or make heads or tails of, and we thought sure you had lost part of your mind and we wanted to protect your mother. But they were thrown out by accident, I think, in a box that was in the hallway when we cleaned up the spare room for you, knowing you were coming home. I think one of the kids threw it out. I'm not sure."

It was as severe as a wound, like shrapnel in its rampage, the unseen touch of it, ethereal but conclusive. What corpsman could heal this, what nurse? What ward companion looking for his own way home, saying what he felt but never what he might know? ... "We're not through with this yet. Parts will hang on; they have a grip you'll find again."

He walked out, left home. Twenty years later they had not seen him, all that time in New York City trying to recreate every word, every passage, finding some, but not all, finally finding one complete letter in his mind and blowing it apart so that it fell in place for him. Like an elocutionist emptying the last word said but leading to the one waiting in line, parts came together, linked, lead onward, up one hill and down the other side. Parts came back again, without prejudice, in another millennium. He knew the weight of an M-1 rifle on a web strap hanging on his shoulder, the awed knowledge of a ponderous steel helmet atop his head, press of a tight lace on one boot, wrap of a leather watch band on his wrist, and who stood beside him who stand no more. At length he knew all those who were born to wear the rags of war, the children of men, the men as children.

Once his mother said, on her dying bed, "I think he was angry with us for throwing out all those letters. He thought he was fooling me all the time, but I knew him better than he did himself, that's why he left. I never told anybody, but that's why he left. His life, since he found himself over there, was wrapped up in the book he was going to write. He used to talk about it in his sleep before he left, like he was dictating to a stenographer or one of us if we could have sat still long enough, but none of us could."

He died on a bench with a book on his chest in New York's Central Park. The wallet ID said his name was the same as the author's name, Mack Tribbley, the book was Born to Wear the Rags of War, and stuck in between pages was a review from the New York Times.

A patrolman who was a reader and a veteran from Pacific campaigns of warm sands and hot jungles found him and the cradled book and his curiosity was aroused, the ID proving to be a phony at first look and an old one to boot. No person with that name appeared in subsequent searches of records, but the name of Vatcher Sexton McKee, lost, missing for more than 20 years, was bold on the dog tag hung on his neck on a length of silver chain, along with an Infantryman's Combat Badge, its blue background faded, formed into a bracelet with a small chain on his left wrist, a special grasp on brotherhood, where in the locked room of his mind it finally broke free and he was able to say in the one voice of them all, in its place in the book found across his chest: The day had gone over hill, but that still, blue light remained, cut with a gray edge, catching corners rice paddies lean out of. In the serious blue brilliance of battle they'd become comrades becoming friends, just Walko and Williamson and Tribbley sitting in the night drinking beer cooled by Imjin River waters in August of '51 in Korea. Three men drably clad, but clad in the rags of war. Stars hung pensive neon. Mountain-cool silences were being earned, hungers absolved, a ponderous god talked to. Above silences, the ponderous god's weighty as clouds, elusive as soot on wind, yields promises. They used church keys to tap cans, lapped up silence rich as missing salt, fused their backbones to good earth in a ritual old as labor itself, these men clad in the rags of war. Such an August night gives itself away, tells tales, slays the rose in reeling carnage, murders sleep, sucks moisture out of Mother Earth, fires hardpan, sometimes does not die itself just before dawn, makes strangers in one's selves, those who wear the rags of war. They had been strangers beside each other, caught in the crush of tracered night and starred flanks, accidents of men drinking beer cooled in the bloody waters where brothers roam forever, warriors come to that place by fantastic voyages, carried by generations of the persecuted or the adventurous, carried in sperm body, dropped in the spawning, fruiting womb of America, and born to wear the rags of war. Walko, reincarnate of the Central European, come of land lovers and those who scatter grain seed, bones like logs, wrists strong as axle trees, fair and blue-eyed, prankster, ventriloquist who talked off mountainside, rumormonger for fun, heart of the hunter, hide of the herd, apt killer, born to wear the rags of war. Williamson, faceless in the night, black set on black, only teeth like high piano keys, eyes that captured stars, fine nose got from Rome through rape or slave bed unknown generations back, was cornerback tough, graceful as ballet dancer (Walko's opposite), hands that touched his rifle the way a woman's touched, or a doll, or one's fitful child caught in fever clutch, came sperm-tossed across the cold Atlantic, some elder Virginia-bound in chains, the Congo Kid come home, the Congo Kid, alas, alas, born to wear the rags of war. Tribbley, reluctant at trigger-pull, dreamer, told deep lies with dramatic ease, entertainer who wore shining inward a sum of ghosts forever from the cairns had fled; heard myths and the promises in earth and words of songs he knew he never knew, carried scars vaguely known as his own, shared his self with saint and sinner, proved pregnable to body force, but born to wear the rags of war ------Walko: We lost the farm. Someone stole it. My father loved the fields, sweating. He watched grass grow by starlight, the moon slice at new leaves. The mill's where he went for work, in the crucible, drawing on the green vapor, right in the heat of it, the miserable heat. My mother said he started dying the first day. It wasn't the heat or green vapor did it, just going off to the mill, grassless, tight in. The system took him. He wanted to help. It took him, killed him a little each day, just smothered him. I kill easy. Memory does it. I was born for this, to wear these rags. The system gives, then takes away. I'll never go piecemeal like my father. These rags are my last home. ------Williamson: Know why I'm here' I'm from North Ca'lina, sixteen and big and wear size fifteen shoes and my town drafted me 'stead of a white boy. Chaplain says he git me home. Shit! Be dead before then. Used to hunt home, had to eat what was fun runnin' down. Brother shot my sister and a white boy in the woods. Caught them skinnin' it up against a tree, run home and kissed Momma goodbye, give me his gun. Ten years, no word. Momma cries about both them all night. Can't remember my brother's face. Even my sister's. Can feel his gun, though, right here in my hands, long and smooth and all honey touch. Squirrel's left eye never too far away for that good old gun. Them white men back home know how good I am, and send me here, put these rags on me. Two wrongs! Send me too young and don't send my gun with me. I'm goin' to fix it all up, gettin' home too. They don't think I'm coming back, them white men. They be nervous when I get back, me and that good old gun my brother give me, and my rags of war. ------Tribbley: Stories are my food. I live and lust on them. Spirits abound in the family, indelible eidolons; the O'Tribbleraugh carved a myth. I wear their scars in my soul, know the music that ran over them in lifetimes,

113

songs' words, and strangers that are not strangers: Muse Devon abides with me, moves in the blood and bag of my heart, whispers tonight: Corimin is in my root cell, oh bright beauty of all that has come upon me, chariot of cheer, carriage of Cork where the graves are, where my visit found the root of the root cell---Johnny Tribbley at ten running ahead of the famine that took brothers and sisters, lay father down; sick in the hold of ghostly ship I have seen from high rock on Cork's coast, in the hold heard the myths and music he would spell all his life, remembering hunger and being alone and brothers and sisters and father gone and mother praying for him as he knelt beside her bed that hard morning when Ireland went away to the stern. I know that terror of hers last touching his face. Pendalcon's grace comes on us all at the end. Johnny Tribbley came alone at ten and made his way across Columbia, got my mother who got me and told me when I was twelve that one day Columbia would need my hand and I must give. And tonight I say, 'Columbia, I am here with my hands and with my rags of war.' I came home alone. And they are my brothers. Walko is my brother. Williamson is my brother. Muse Devon is my brother. Corimin is my brother. Pendalcon is my brother. God is my brother. I am a brother to all who are dead. We all wear the rags of war.

The Eagle's Son, Camouflaged Hero

Police Lieutenant Roy Cryder of the Chicago Police Department screamed at one of his subordinates, Sgt. Leo Blaney. "What the hell do you mean all you found was a goddamned bird feather? You telling me a goddamned bird flew in here and spoiled a crime scene. Are you telling me that, Leo?"

The two policemen were standing at the head of an alley, a dark alley.

Already red in the face, puffed with anger, the ticket to his seat at the Hawks game in danger of being given away, he continued his tirade. "The damned place is practically roofed in, the whole alley, like all them alleys down here in the Market District. How the hell could a bird fly in there and drop a feather? Let me see it."

He held out his hand for "the alleged feather found at the scene of the crime."

"I didn't bring it out. It's a crime scene, Lieutenant. 'Don't move anything,' you said a thousand times."

"How did this damned bird kill this guy, Leo? He carry a .38 Special or a .357 Magnum? Tell me." Face-off was only half an hour away. He hadn't missed a game yet, the season already three weeks old. He couldn't wait to see Patrick Kane on the ice once more.

"All right," he said. "Leave it. Rope it off again, the whole alley. I'll be back after the game, or on the morning if there's no overtime. They kept me up twice last week. Fill me in by phone if there are any developments. Real stuff, mind you."

A week later, Cryder's phone rang in his office. Sgt. Leo Blaney said, "Roy, we had a call. About a homicide. Down on Navy Pier. 'Member that guy, Red Lobster, who just got out two weeks ago? Well, we found him as dead as he'll ever be."

"He deserved it. What else? I feel like you're keeping something from me."

"We found another one of them feathers. It was just lying there, like it's a sign, or a clue, like someone's telling us something."

"Oh, crap. Tell me we have a vigilante after the bad guys."

"That's what it looks like, Roy."

115

On the fourth of July in 1981, a Sioux maiden named Pure of Eye gave birth to a son, which was the result of a rape by an unknown man near the Rosebud Reservation in South Dakota. An older Sioux woman, Gray Ledge Lady, assisted at the birth, and noted at the moment the boy was born, as did the mother, an eagle floating across the Dakota sky, his wingspread an awesome sight.

When the boy was old enough to understand what she was about to tell him, his mother told him how he came to be, and about his name, which from his birth had always been Eagle's Son.

In her Lakota tongue she said, "*Ciwablieeshniyatekioihakewanil*," and said it in English so there'd be no misunderstanding: "The eagle is your father forever. *Ciwablieeshniyatekioihakewanil*."

"He is your father, from that very first day," she explained. "And he'll always be your only father, watching over the world, watching to protect young women and others from attacks upon their person, just as I was attacked by that vilest of men. That is your destiny. The next day, after your birth, as I sat at the edge of a great field of grass, I saw the same eagle set upon a coyote attacking a lamb on the prairie. When old Gray Ledge Lady went out there to check on the lamb, she found an eagle feather on the ground, a proud feather. The poor little lamb with some deep cuts was still alive. She brought back the lamb, but left the feather in place, as if to warn the coyote or his kind, that he was watching ... and protecting all lambs. When she was very young, the old ones told her stories about the eagle, about *wabli*."

Pure of Eye watched her son as he accepted what she had told him. Somehow, as certain gifts are bestowed upon people in this life, she realized he was probably feeling the first urge of his destiny come upwards from his soul, perhaps grasping a small piece of his mind and holding on ... forever. For days she had waited for an eagle to show itself for him.

It was not her pure eye that saw an eagle at that moment, but the eye of her son, and he raced off to the edge of a large field when he saw the eagle swoop low in a threatening dive, only to veer off and swoop away.

But a feather fell to the ground.

He left the feather where he found it.

Pure of Eye knew he understood.

Eagle's Son became a celebrated athlete in high school, an

excellent specimen of grace and strength, skilled in a variety of sports, but found no lasting interest in them after high school. He joined the military and served in two branches, excelling as a Navy Seal, asking for his discharge and volunteering for an advanced reconnoitering army unit. Again, he excelled. Some Afghanis called him "The Ghost of the Mountains."

No matter where he was after that day, in Somalia, in Afghanistan, every day since he came stateside, he heard Pure Eye say, in her melodious but foretelling voice full of the centuries, "*Ciwablieeshniyatekioihakewanil.Ciwablieeshniyatekioihakewanil.*"

At 30 years of age, Eagle's Son became a civilian again, and chose Chicago to live and work. Soon he realized he could see as much in a crowd of people as he saw in the mountains and valleys of a strange land, a land that fought back at him as did its people in the high places. His talents and abilities were in place: The whisper of a breath on a leaf could be heard by his tuned ear. The movement of an insect on a log can be marked by his discerning eye. "Pounce" is part of his talents, as much as it is in scorpions or tarantulas, or the eager young fox leaping for a mouse hidden under snow. So he was attuned to separation, selection, identification, closure and pounce.

More than two months had passed after the Market District incident, where the feather was found on site beside Red Lobster, when word came to the police of an attack on a young woman near Garfield Park. She reported that an unknown man rescued her by severely beating her assailant who was tearing off her clothes.

"I managed to get out one scream, just one scream," she said, "and he was there, that stranger. He moved so fast I still don't know what he looked like, but I'll tell you, he hurt that bad guy as bad as he'll ever be hurt. I heard bones break. Bones. Not one bone, but bones, and he made him cry too, that rotten pig!"

She paused and said, "He said something else, though, like in a foreign language, but nothing I could understand." She had, of course, heard Eagle's Son say a new version of, "*Ciwablieeshniyatekioihakewanil,*" which came as "*Ciwablieeshatewayekioihakewanil.*" "The eagle is my father forever."

But she couldn't repeat it, though the shadow of those odd inflections sat in her ear like the echo of a bell at Sunday Mass.

For more than an hour of testimony, she carried the same story,

117

and Cryder admitted to his staff, "I can't figure this thing out. Is this guy, this semi-hero of sorts, stalking some loser until the loser loses it and tries out his specialty, perverted or whatever? And then, like a lamb dropping a ball of fleece, he leaves a feather. C'mon, guys! Get with it!"

In Cryder's squad was the youngest member, just brought up from significant work as a patrolman, a young man who showed certain skills at deduction, but odd habits for a criminal investigator: his name was Billy Cutlass and he spent many off-duty hours at the library. Some of his section mates called him "The Bookworm."

Cutlass had some definite ideas about the feather findings and went looking for additional leads.

In the library.

And he wasn't the one who leaked the word to the newspapers, but he went looking for birds of North America and photos of feathers. He found the right book.

In the library.

Eagle's Son, standing at a downtown corner, where he had moved with grace through crowds of people, had been watching the antics of an otherwise indistinguishable 40-year old man who had kept a corner vigil for over an hour this evening, watching girls leaving work at the quitting hour. Streams of secretaries and older women, probably executives in their elegant dresses and fancy briefcases, moved onto buses, taxis, into husbands' or boyfriends' personal vehicles. Some of them walked straight off to nearby apartments.

The parade was endless, but he had seen the same man do the same thing the evening before, the man having left his vigil only for coffee on a few occasions and a light quick-food lunch another time. He was as constant as a security guard but, as Eagle's Son suspected, had fallen to the other side of the fence.

From the third floor office of a friend, he had been watching the passing scene for over a week, and had taken pictures of the area on each day at the exact same time. He spotted his suspect in repeated photos through the use of overlays. His military training had come full circle, back to an old pro at a new assignment.

One moment in the office he had uttered the old stand-by,

"*Ciwablieeshniyatekioihakewanil,*" and almost in the same breath added, "Thank you, Captain Water-Bear," his illustrious leader in Afghanistan, a true Sioux, who had guided him in the art of observation during his tour in their advance scouting unit.

Down at the street level this day of action, Eagle's Son, expert in current observations of people, their body language, their talking without saying an audible word, their sudden movements of alarm or recognition, saw the girl at the same time the suspect did. She was glorious in a slinky red dress, her high heels stretching her elegant frame and long and shapely legs. She was a knockout in any league, on any busy square or corner of any city ... or any dark alley to which she might be forcibly introduced.

Eagle's Son was dressed in a nondescript black windbreaker (with three eagle feathers in an inner pocket, which is against the law, as we all know) and a weathered baseball cap that a mucker like Trot Nixon wore in his Red Sox days. He had seen him in newsreels of White Sox-Red Sox games in old Comiskey Park and the new U.S. Cellular Field. He had admired the hustle of the man, "down and dirty" he had said of him, like some Afghanis he had known. And he knew that his own hustle was now needed, for the suspect, without a doubt, was on the trail of the woman in the long legs and the classic red dress many women, and some men, often dream about.

He kept pace with the suspect who kept pace with the woman, and then watched him hurry his pace, to get right behind the woman. When she was abreast of a dark alley, the suspect's right arm slipped around her waist and his left hand covered her mouth.

In a whisper the pair had disappeared down the alley.

Nobody seemed to notice, or took any action if they had seen the capture.

When Eagle's Son soft-footed into the alley, he smelled the steep, heavy odor of chloroform.

The pictures came to him like quick still photos; his own mother in such a plight, the strange hands upon her.

He came upon the man upon the woman, at abusing her.

He clubbed the assailant with the blow of a fist on the back of the head. Punched him again. Grabbed his arm, and remembering Pure Eyes telling him how her clothes were ripped off, broke the man's right arm in one single two-handed snap across his raised knee.

119

While the man writhed in pain, and began to scream, Eagle's Son hit him again, a chop to the back of the neck, dropped him over the edge of an open dumpster, gathered up the woman after re-assembling some of her clothing, and carried her from the alley.

But not before he reached into an inner pocket of his jacket and dropped a single eagle's feather on the ground beside the dumpster. The new thought sounded; *"Ciwablieeshatewayekioihakewanil."* "The eagle is my father forever."

He sat her, conscious but dizzy, her eyes unclear, in the entryway of an apartment building. Walking across the street, he yelled to a woman in a first floor window, "Call the police. There's a woman over there, across the street, who's been attacked by a man. He was going to abuse her."

Billy Cutlass, off duty and heading home, heard the call on his police radio. He was the first one on the scene, heard the woman say she had been dragged down the alley and did not know how she had gotten to the entryway of the apartment building. "But I think someone carried me here. I still can't walk. Can you smell the chloroform? He drugged me."

When the police cruiser showed up, Cutlass walked into the alley.

He found the feather in the beam of his flashlight.

It was an eagle feather.

The newspaper were at it again, even before Cryder got to his office in the morning, read the night reports, called Cutlass into his office.

"Where do we stand on this stuff, Billy?

"I have some ideas, Roy, but you might not want to believe them. They're a little off our course."

"Smarten me up, will you. You kids come from another world. I can't wait to retire, re-marry my first wife, go back to the farm, raise some wool and wheat and get comfortable for the long haul."

Cutlass laughed, as if bidden, and said, "Let's take it one step at a time."

"I'm all for that, Kid." He smiled his appreciation, lit up a cigar, and put one foot on the desk.

"One, I think we have a vigilante. Two, I think he's some kind of an Indian, because the feathers we've been finding are eagle feathers. Three, Indians have a great respect and reverence for eagles. Four, this vigilante is telling us it's him without giving us his name. Five, I hope we

120

don't find out who he is because we'd have the biggest problem with PR on our hands than ever."

"I'll forget the last part you said. How do you know it's an eagle feather?"

"I looked in a book I took out of the library. It's in my desk right now."

"Go get it. And then tell me if you know anything else."

"I'm checking that out too, Roy."

"Where?"

In unison they said, "In the library."

"Like what?" Cryder was hooked.

"Indian stories, culture, beliefs, relationships with the universe, the land under their feet, and all the animals on that land and in the air over that land. And that includes you and me and the lady in the red dress and a few victims, wounded or dead, like that Red Lobster creep from a few weeks ago, who I'll bet was teased his whole life about his name and took it all out on the women he attacked."

He almost spat on the floor.

The newspapers, of course, ran wild and red, headlines half a page tall, often with photos or drawings of eagle feathers as if they were the lead-in paragraph to each article: The Eagle has Landed! Again!" "Read about feathers of this bird whoever he is!" "Who flocks with him is in deep trouble," came right from the heart of a tabloid front office.

Somewhere now in a major city of the country, on a darkened corner or a daylight-safe public park but which becomes horrific in promise on some nights, is a hero in night-time camouflage, his keen eye observing movements and intentions that others do not see, are not aware of, and may never hear of ... until that ghost of the city streets is apprehended by police, who would/might/could turn their backs on the final collar as they hear him say, "*Ciwablieeshatewayekioihakewanil.*"

Send Galabicus

The midget Galabicus had one problem at spelunking; his crawling and narrow aperture insertions always caused a huge erection, for a man his size a vivid and sometimes embarrassing erection. He never knew if it was caused by excitement or abrasion, but it came about every time a desperate or dangerous situation occurred and he was situated in the bowels of Earth.

As for me, I'm afraid of caves and all such mucked-up underworld. I have been since near being buried in a hillside bunker in a war zone; darkness scared the hell out of me. And just imagine... this thing with Galabicus was always a bit notorious for a little guy, people always grabbing the early edge to push down on somebody. His plight here up front, of course, is confessed as fictional, but I am privy to some real inside information that throws such a stand entirely on its ear. To boot, my old pal Tremont Consul nursed a weighty sense for justice, and thus for the midget Galabicus, a small man who had reached heroic proportions on a number of dangerous escapades, and other events, with that previously-spoken, oddly relevant phenomenon.

Galabicus, as I've said, was a midget of the first order, and was perceived by many people as a mere afterthought. Some men said he was the little devil from darkness, with a wee bit of concern in the wink of their eyes, in the tilt of their head, and a kind of mock disdain setting on their lips. It appeared initially he didn't count much in the matters of men. Or of ladies for that matter: Small feet, runt thing, the ladies might have said behind cupped hands in the ladies room late in the night, or at the edge of picnics where tales were swapped... the tittering, the giggles, the gross assumptions of reality. He was child-small, but not badly distorted in his framework.

Some ladies knew it all, as they've said in one degree or another. Some of them, it developed, called him names other than Galabicus. One fashionable cave lover said he was the perfect trade-off. She had carried on, saying, as if it was an announcement to one and all, "Whatever the guys call him, he's definitely not the runt of the litter." There was not a trace of redness on her face.

But this day of which I am speaking, as it proved, would turn inevitably, and completely, on Galabicus's size, his courage and his true manhood, even though he was cheated of many things at the outset of life.

Considering just the sound, the first rock that came down, nearly atop the group of cave explorers, was the real kick-off for the day. Tremont Consul, cave veteran, wiry but thin as a shingle, leading the group, had the worst feeling ever in all his visits to the innards of German Vettum's Cave, smack in the middle of Chawtenauga's Valley of Holes. Now, at that site for about the hundredth time, he was making deep inroads with a new gang of spelunkers, raw amateurs through their ranks, mere potatoes in another ordinary stew. But they paid their way for the exercise.

The first minor slide ahead of them, Tremont noted, was followed by a silence eerily disturbing him. "Oh," he said lightly, breathing the word in, becoming aware of a sparse tingling at his feet, a barefoot tingling as though he, bootless, had made entry here. The noisy gabbers in the group were instantly mute, some with their mouths agape, caught in the middle of address or redress. Tremont, noting their stiffness, dreaded the possibilities emanating with the tingle at his feet. And the rock, without doubt, was a runaway, the kind that carries omens or leaves such notice in its wake. He'd been caught in Earth-shifts before, where the core of the planet was disturbed by deep and multiple penetrations; as if asleep, the whole planet had been rudely awakened.

The ensuing silence was part of the warning.

In a first thought of emergency measures, he wondered why he had not roused wee Galabicus earlier in morning. Instantly he recalled, in a series of quick vignettes, the little man pursuing Marta Vergensa through a night of possible true bliss for him and, as much as it could, setting a benchmark for all the little men of the world... little mark but big score.

Running one hand down his long frame, Tremont checked the presence of the cellular phone holstered at his belt, the way a sheriff assures he's armed for uncertainty, for any desperado's sudden appearance.

Tremont and the amateur group had entered German Vettum's Cave at the stroke of dawn, just as the sun came up with a slam over a mid-point saddle of Mount Hebron, the way it does at Stonehenge, and mysteriously marked the face of the cave. Tremont, as always, was stabbed by the significance of sunrise at the burst of day, and its quick punctuation. Daylight, as a tool, was important to him and his entourage as it carried a known attention about them on the outside while they were in darkness.

And far behind them, back at the Spelunker's Grand Lodge, the last of them, the last of the true professional spelunkers in the whole area, wee Galabicus, the erogenic midget, was still sleeping in the small garret room, probably dreaming again of hustling the bustling, dark-eyed Marta Vergensa, for sure twice his size and then some.

Often, in deep hours of self-content, Galabicus thought it grand that he might someday be grabbed for ransom, and tortured to the very end of his manhood! Oh, Nirvana! There had been times, he realized, that the embarrassment got the best of Tremont the boss man, a stickler of sorts when it came to his touring charges, especially the women, the gigglers, the touchers, the curious groundhogs of spelunking. Dark caves, it appeared, moved them into odder dreams quicker than a subtle pass of hand or eye. Tremont and Galabicus had seen it time and again... foreign territory, new touches, the expansion of dreams, the dark underworld filled with all its possibilities. Sex under cover of another sort.

For a long time Tremont had thought personal abrasion was a specialty just for women. Cave women, he'd come to believe, carried a long history of manipulation, of conquest. Times there were he was aware of a Cro-Magnon smile lurking in a shadow, behind a stone blind, an essence almost bubbling from darkness, a saber-toothed tiger smiling at prey. The genes carried the smile, and the next step. And then along had come wee Galabicus, nee Giant, in his own riotous way righting all the wrongs found in spelunking.

But Tremont this morning, his mind now at movement in all directions, came back to that disturbing rock... hearing the silence again, knocking him fully upright with thought and imagination. It was a runaway, the big and singular rock that had come loose from forever, the harbinger's lot.

A message from Mother, he professed.

And the soles of his feet, without doubt, talked to him again.

Immediately he recalled a stone he toed once in cold Maine, Maine as cold as it could be, with the ocean running away from him at Hermit Island, tossing itself down the sandy way, leaving him alone with the universe and the ocean touching at his feet, at his bare toes. That day, the reverberations, the echoes, the last cries from the world's circled wagon train, came at him. He swore he could feel the temperature of Hermit

124

Island's sea water. Hell, he thought, Maine was always cold, except in the haymows of barns, near witness of the Golden Fleece, at moisture's interception, when all Earth was younger by thirty or more years.

Yet, in a remote confine of German Vettum's Cave, the one most recently opened up to torches and eyesight and still the least explored cave in all of the Chawtenauga's Valley of Holes, a small shift of earthly proportions had first come to Tremont as an earache. Then it went real, pushing air down odd shafts, along tunnels, coming long serpentine ways, and a full minute later crossing his face, its sound flagging like a semaphore.

"Oh shit," he said, feeling the cool edge of air, knowing the shift of air was pushed by turmoil of all Earth itself.

Sexy, high-chested, ebullient Paula Abreau, rolling right and left by touches in life, had consistently filed right behind Tremont in the cave journey, bumping against him anytime she could, at times being answered back by his lingering hand. She felt the quick sheet of air breathe at her eyes, at her lashes, and then heard Tremont's small curse.

Ever raw and hungry with her black hair and dark smoky eyes, Paula pulled back her dangling hand. She had loved the cover of near darkness; now, she knew, it might grab her. Yet it all could not be over for her love life; there were hands and mouths and tongues she had not known. Even here, in the dark deposit of this cave, there had been, up till the last moment or so, fulfillments she had only dreamed about. Tremont was on the top of that list. She had remembered, early this morning, the command he exercised in instructing the tour on what the day would be like. She liked his mouth, how he formed words, used subtle inflection rather than a distinct change of voice or tone. He wore his blond hair in a boyish mop, making him a tease of the first order with the brilliant lagoon blue eyes of innocence. When he stood at the head of the group the day before, briefing them on the morrow's escapade, laying out the law for them, she could taste him. He wielded significant messages that positively came only to her, and were therefore meant only for her. She had taken the message to bed with her. Under cover. Under cover. All hers. And now there came her sister, Earth, wrapped around them both, the grip perhaps tighter than any encounter.

She heard a distant grating, the soft muffle of another sound. And the earth shook anew, like a flag raised, or a trumpet sounded on some high concourse. She heard Tremont again say, "Oh, shit." He was, she knew, smarter than she would ever be. It made her stop thinking about sex, darkness no longer being the carrier of lone, sweet correspondence.

Tremont said, the tone now more menacing than his words, "Nobody move. Stay close together. We might have a problem developing here." Damn right, they did. He'd never been wrong about the deep touches of Mother Earth, how she'd announce all her decisions with a subtle piece of advice, of warning. He remembered a whole tunnel being suddenly obliterated in France many years earlier, when he was studying the Pre-Adamites, and how Mother Earth had spoken to him, as if directly, as if she had said, "So, Big Man, you had to see all this crap for yourself!"

Tremont Consul squared his shoulders. In utter darkness trust made its own demands. He'd mouthed Mother Earth in his normal voice, the way he inflected humor in any other than humorous situation; his hand being steady as a rock, the usual rock of significance, not the kind old Mother nudged into prominence or sudden being. If something came here, he decided, it was Mother Earth announcing to him that she was unhappy with some long-standing arrangement of her dark parts.

It was said in all sections of the valley that he had courage, ingenuity, perseverance. He could be relied upon to keep his cool in front of the others in the face of trouble. He hoped there'd be no fools in their midst. Once, down in Kentucky, on the calmest of mornings in the deepest of caves, another spelunker had thoughtlessly dropped a small boulder over a precipitous edge, to satisfy her woman's curiosity… and started an internal landslide that had shaken everybody in the tour to the bottoms of their souls. A lesson had been learned and Tremont hoped there'd be no such learning this day.

Earlier, in the approach to the entrance, he had spoken to the small group. "It's been quiet here in German Vettum's Cave, probably since the finish of the last Ice Age, which certainly made its way through the region and did, in fact, give us German Vettum's Cave. German came here over a hundred years ago, finding the opening behind a huge piece of ledge that had been sheared off the cliff by an awesome power. I doubt that anything has ever happened since he came here, but we must always be on our toes. I've made this same tour more than a hundred times, and I find something new and interesting each time. But Mother Nature's always at our elbows and at our feet. So keep your cool all the time." He paused

126

and then added, "Don't ever treat this as a Sunday walk in the park. It sure isn't that."

Tremont, after the slide, then held his breath, wary yet, and stood still, the light in his hand aiming into the bowels of the cave and he watched the steady ray of light as it played on a far surface of stone; behind him, Paula Abreau breathed a little more evenly and inhaled a scent of the man standing so near; ten other spelunkers stood in a suspenseful ignorance of the sudden void about them.

Then, as if in one breath without another warning of any sort, Mother Earth collapsed a tunnel, dropped a hundred tons of stone, broke down a wall, filled a wide cave end with stone and dust, sent that near abrasive dust careening for escape in the air rushing past the dozen of them.

Someone cried. Someone screamed. The echoes rang short notes, the way a wall cuts them almost in half. Tumultuous Earth moved abruptly, spasmodically, but with an awesome energy. Paula, suddenly thrown into the air, had come down with a thud on her back. A presence was in her face. It was not Tremont. It was not a man. It had no manly odor. No sense of being. It was, she finally acknowledged, pure stone. It menaced her. Tremont's fears had come alive. She could hear the awful echo of his words from a moment earlier. The hand that had been so close to danger then was now endangered and a pressure was pushing down on it. She tried to move one finger and could not.

Huge boulders and slabs and slices of rock menaced all of them, and at them came the mouth-filling sense of ferric dust as if an old colliery had been opened anew. Tremont felt the pain in his ankles first, and knew he could not move, but was glad he was alive. With one hand he touched his chin, felt his face, and breathed against that hand. At least he could function in some manner. Paula Abreau, whom he had sensed so close to him a second earlier, with a whole night coming compromised in that sensation, had been tossed onto a slab of granite that had settled atop other slabs close to him. Her moans called at him. Other cries came from behind her, back the way of the tunnel. Escaping air, almost filled with iron dust it seemed, rushed past them toward an obvious escape, compressed by the fall of stone ahead of them.

Tremont valued that knowledge, that sufficient air was available to them, yet feeling a magnet would steal much of its content. "Be still," he said, with as much confidence as he could arrange. "If you can, tend to someone near you. Don't scream. Ask for help. Tell each other what has happened to you. My ankles are caught by stone. I can't get loose. Use your flash to look behind you, to see if the way back is open. I can feel the air escaping. There must be a way back that's open."

A voice replied. "The way is blocked. A pile of rock's in the way. It's up over my head.

I can't move very far either, but I can breathe."

"Anybody else near you?" Tremont wondered if somebody had been crushed. All Mother Earth had moved.

"Harry's down in front of me. I know his arm's broken. I can see it twisted awful. He's not conscious. I can't see anybody else."

"Who are you?" Tremont said.

"Morton Chalice, here," the voice said. "Morton Chalice. I was the last in line. I damn well didn't want to come in here but my wife wanted me to. Said it would make me more interesting. So much for frigging interest."

Another voice said, "Grady here, Morton. You get out of here and you can talk her ear off for the next forty years. It'll serve her right." His voice paused, a dry crackle in it. "What's that damn taste in the air? I swear it's gonna suffocate me, like it's stealing my pile of air. Goddamn, Tremont. What is it?"

Tremont, without an instant answer, liked Grady immediately. Then five others spoke up, picked up by Grady's sense of humor.

Once more, but in a more subtle manner, Mother Earth spoke. It was like a rustle in a nearby thicket, an animal in the brush. Tremont understood the subtleties of the old lady and trained the beam of his light backwards. The stream of dust rushing for an opening came to an abrupt halt and he knew that the latest noise had signaled the cutting off that escape of air and the dust that flew with it. A sense of panic rose as he contemplated how long a dozen people could last breathing air in a closed space. Some of the old campfire stories, out beyond the caves, tried to reassert themselves. He shut them off even as the taste of iron came heavy in his mouth.

He reached for his cell phone in its holster. By a miracle it was still in place, though the holster was torn. If he had but one call left because of possible damage or that single message getting through, it had to be short and specific. The beam of his light went back the way he thought they had come. It found only rock face and boulders, and the pale face of Paula

Abreau smiling her last hope at him. Time, though it had crawled around them all weekend, might now be sprinting away from them.

He called up the emergency frequency on the memory face, thinking of the shortest and most informative message he could send, and simply said, "Send Galabicus... with air."

Three times he said the same message and the face of his phone went blank.

The hours passed. Minor repairs were made by some on others. Some of the party did not respond. Grady Parcell kept up his sense of humor, often going back to discuss Morton Chalice's wife. Paula Abreau had not moved except to stare at the beam of light when it came off Tremont's torch. Trying to be positive, she found it extremely difficult to bring up a smile for Tremont's torch. Only Fate and Destiny could touch her now. She thought of slowly being squeezed to death by the flat slab of rock hanging above her. After a while she kept her eyes closed. Back to her came a moment in her fifteenth year in the rear seat of Lefty Weller's Ford when she unhooked her bra for a clumsy Bobby Caithness. It was the only time she ever had to do that. It found a smile for her someplace.

Tremont calculated the taste of iron in his mouth. It had lessened, he assumed, as the dust had settled. But at the same moment he realized the air was staler than it had been. Once he believed he could taste an essence of Paula Abreau in its passage. He began to take smaller breaths, and instructed the others to do the same. "Don't squirm around. Keep still. Don't breathe too heavy. Someone will respond to my call. All we can do is wait. So save all the air we can. Don't breathe too heavy. Don't moan or cry. Be as still as you can." His pause announced a small touch of hope. "Keep listening. Someone will come."

Galabicus, dreaming, still locked in Marta's arms, nearly having the breath and life squeezed out of him, heard the pounding up the stairs. The door flew open. Mansard the deskman yelled at him, his voice bouncing off the walls. "Cave in, Galabicus! Cave in! They say Tremont called for you. And he called for air. What's that mean?"

Galabicus rolled off his tiny bed. Like a fireman at call his little legs dipped into rolled pants and into his boots. Mansard thought he looked like an elf called in an emergency by Santa Claus. He almost smiled, and thought better of it. Tremont might punch his head off, he favored the little man so much. "Some of the team's downstairs right

129

now. They said to hurry." Galabicus was on his way out the door, a short-handled thumping going down the stairs.

All the equipment had been carried into German Vettum's cave as far as the blockage, a mass of boulders and rock slabs in a huge jumbled mess. Galabicus fixed his compass, accepted the air line, and began to seek his way through the maze of stone. He went slow and easy, dragging the air line through small ways, assuring its entry and passage between large obstacles. He knew it would be most difficult to go back, as he found no place where he could turn around. He thought more than once of being squeezed by Marta. It made him smile as he worked. Life will always go on no matter what it presents to us, he said to himself. He had known that forever. Even as a child he had known it. Knew it made him tick, now and then felt the abrasions coming back at him in life's continuity. It's endless, he accounted, and continued to slip and slide and grind his way through the mess Mother Earth had loosened from her grip.

Marta came back to him often, and then was just whisked away by some other measure. Once he recalled being part of a midget wrestling team in a late-night diner in black New Hampshire, trying to get the attention of the man behind the counter, to order five black coffees for his teammates. A robust, noisy customer at the bar finally said to the counterman, "Hey, Wally, I think Shorty here wants some coffee." In three seconds the noisy customer was off his seat and was flat on the floor as the team sat on him. They got their coffee and left big mouth on the floor. And did not pay for the coffee. Between two enormous stones, Galabicus laughed again. He had laughed a thousand times thinking about that night.

Tremont, too, came just as often and just as quickly into his thoughts as he scrambled, wiggled, and crawled through the smallest spaces. Nobody around here near German Vettum's Cave can do what I am doing. Tremont knows that. He counts on me. Tonight I will tell Marta all that I will have accomplished. He wriggled some more and the erection came back. He was in no way disturbed, not even with the mission being at hand. Life will always go on no matter what it presents to us.

Paula heard the sound, a stone moving, a rock losing its grip. It yanked at her attention. She held her breath, though she wanted to scream out at Tremont and the others. She didn't know what to say: Someone's coming, or watch it! It's going to start again. Her mouth stayed wide open in indecision. The rock near her moved again. It slid on another rock a mere inch. Then it moved again. It was being manipulated, controlled. She heard breathing. She heard someone breathing. Perhaps the hissing of air. Joy leaped up in her as she felt the presence again of the slab hanging flat above her. She finally whispered, "Who's there? Who is that? Is that you, Lisa? I hope it's you, Lisa. I haven't heard a sound from you. Are you all right?"

"Galabicus here," came the answer. "Who are you? Where is Tremont? Is he okay?"

Paula could not see him, though the beam of his torch came directly at her. "I'm okay, but kind of locked up here. Tremont is ahead of me and he says he's caught by his ankle.

He can't move to get to any of us."

"Can you breathe okay?" Galabicus said.

"Yes, right now I can, all of a sudden, though it's been getting really stale lately. Thick. Rancid. Almost rotten." She paused, felt exhilarated, added, "Boy, am I glad to see you, though I can't see you." Immediately she was grabbed by her choice of words. Boy seemed to echo along all the stone faces.

"Boy glad he's here. Tarzan come later." They both laughed, the humor bustling, hope realigned in the spheres. His hand touched her leg. The touch was delicate but manly. She leaped with joy and memory.

"Ho, Tremont," Galabicus yelled, "your old pal here, making passage with the air line. I'm dragging it with me. I can't turn around yet to push it forward. You okay? The team's behind me. It may be a few hours, it may be a few days before they get here. The line leads them this way. It's tight but they'll open it up. They've sent for our pals at Kitty Mount. The Crawlers will be here in a matter of hours, the other little guys."

Galabicus said to prostrate Paula Abreau, "I have to get this line through to the others. I'll have to pass over you if I can find the room."

The lady tittered in the darkness. "I'd be delighted," she said, even as the stories came resurrected about the little man. All hope sprang eternal once again, and she was aware the world around her was still larger than she was, larger than her constriction.

Tremont, listening, nodded in darkness, the taste of iron still in his mouth, knowing that Galabicus had one more story in his heroic arsenal.

131

He trained his light on Galabicus as the little man crawled over Paula Abreau, who had been so close to him such a short time ago. He saw the radiant smiles on both their faces.

The Long Look Home

The sun warm, the air pleasant, but me like a beggar lost in thoughts, I stepped up to the back door of the old farmhouse on Route 182 in Franklin, Maine. Home at last from the army was topping off my day. Coming home from military service, I'll swear forever, is better than birthdays, weddings, or vacations.

Or should be.

The homemade back door had faded to pink from the deepest red imaginable, and checked lines were visible stripes running down the frame, like veneers ever show slightest diversions. And doors, as you know, homemade or not, glossy paint or not, front or back, always deliver some kind of message. Houses have the power to say hello if you're listening.

A cloud's shadow passed over the land, swooping across the back stoop with premonition speed, much like the shadow of a large bird in flight across the face of the sun. Just as quickly, the farm reclaimed its properties, and the barn, regardless of its condition, caught my eye; I knew varied birds' retreats once and always, the ridge pole talking silently about age, the sagging sides near final implosion or burst. At one corner, faint as mist, even fainter, as though slipped from long secrecy, old whispers escaped captivity, hushed but audible, known again.

I felt my soul shifting in place, searching the properties of the farm, seeking perhaps nothing more than the warmth of a welcome, the drift of a word nearly inaudible, a soft halleluiah sifting out of a forgotten place heavy in shade. From nowhere and in no hurry, a large shadow tagged the barn with ease, and in a slow passage tagged one corner of the house where two window boxes once laden with pansies and impatiens sat empty as the broken down truck in the rear of the yard. Again, as an adolescent youngster needing to break out of myself, I was reading the land and all the objects on it, taking measurements, finding revelations.

At first the emptiness of the house was bigger than day, filling it, spilling over. I thought I might be swallowed right off the stoop, stolen by absence. Sentry duty had been this way, looking for anything breathing, verbal, shared, getting sucked into a singular interest; trust residing only with your own senses, though one at a time; smelling fear, touching danger, hearing refuge breathing someplace local but out of sight.

A sound snapped from inside. Different. Calling for attention. But

133

something was wrong from the usual.

I had never lived any place else. The house, my home for 23 years, was downhill from the Little League Field, across the road from acres of blueberry patches and standing wood that could warm one family with 20 years of firewood. Sometimes there had been pigs as big as all-out commotion in the pens, now and then a cow, a pony, and corn and tomatoes growing right up to the back steps, in fall replaced by stacked cords of split wood in military columns.

I reached for the doorknob, rolled it easily in my hand, and pushed the door open and waited to be pounced upon by kitchen smells I carried in my mind like rich baggage ... the piccalilli promising such livid accompaniment at the table in the corner, an open jar of strawberry preserve flooding the air with dark toast right off the top of the stove, or the yearn that went scratching for recall of a beef stew so thick with potatoes, onions and carrots it needed no crackers, no bread to sop.

Every cotton-picking mouthful grown right on the farm.

Then, at another quick thought, it might be my mother turning at a task to smile at me, staying bent to her work in a sweat-stained pale blue dress, early-gray hair hanging across her face and trying to hide the smile but unable to do so. She'd never say hello, just "smile me warm into the kitchen," and go back to her task. Her fingers had touched everything in the house; fabric, furniture, materials, hearts, dreams and toils.

Somebody had to work hereabouts, she might have said, though she rarely condemned the devil himself.

Turmoil, reality, came loose with my foot just inside the back door, as though I had carried it all away with me on deployment travels and brought it back without a single change.

The red and white checkered oil cloth still dressed the kitchen table, the curtains on the high windows, now a pale blue when they had been a pale green, still sat with their off-colored humor against the folksy wallpaper so long hung no one knew who put it up; the clock, which no one looked at, said 8:23 of a forgotten day as it had for years on end. But the dial face of a kitten was so pleasant to start the day that nobody would chuck the clock even though it carried no hope of ever working again. Mother said it was her best happy face, to contend day with, or nights too full of old haunts.

For close to two years I had dreamed about this arrival... but this wasn't home any more.

Such rapid revelations dig deeper than you think. But don't ask me, I'll tell you: On the boat coming back to the states, things started to shake loose in earnest. The sea, that chameleon Atlantic, withering calm some days, like an ogre on other days promising a bad night, the anchor chain loose for endless hours on a section of hull that happened to sit right near the head of my bunk, on that sea my mail caught up to me.

In the last letter I received in my enlistment, my sister wrote that they had sold the farm. My father had taken the easy way out. The family got a free house, way over in Vermont, from grandmother who died, then my folks sold the farm for a few bucks to Eben Gregson because I was not around to do most of the work, my brothers not old enough yet, father being at the bottle too much of the time. Once the seed was in the ground, the wood cut for the winter, he'd fall to the wayside, suffer afternoon naps, dream, find places he had forgotten. He thought life owed him a big debt, that now he could rest, shoot the breeze with like cronies, wile away the remaining best hours and days of production. My mother would not say boo to him, afraid of the night later on when the whiskey would come roaring up out of him in some horrific manner. Of every black and blue remnant on her arms, her legs, she'd say it was from a bump in the night, one of the animals, a log off the top of the woodpile when she wasn't looking ... but tell me, whose mother never looks, doesn't worry about her kids in every single action, dares not be wary for herself and thus them?

Of course, damned few.

It had all fallen on me, gone two years in the army, back a mere day, and it all fell on me, as though my departure had yet to exact its payment, being dunned for the two years I was away.

I was furious about the sale.

Instead of going to the house where they now lived in Vermont, and most of the way up the state, past the end of lake Champlain, so New Yorkers were next-door neighbors, I went back to Maine, all the way back home. I sidestepped the family confrontation. I was tired of fighting. Tired of waiting in line. Tired of failures. Tired of some of my recent memories.

Oh, there'd rush me some days, those memories, often the hard core of them pouring forth, hanging around until they got tired on their own.

We had come down Route 182 in the pick-up with father and us

135

six kids looking for cheap vegetables from road stands, the best buy for the family, spending as little as possible, him saving what he could for a few drinks. Blue Hill leaned over our shoulders, Cherry Hill too. The shopping list was long, mother's meals planned as if she was cooking for a regiment and toward a schedule while fighting for supplies. That year, for some reason, we had gone through much of what little was left of the preserves … the peas, the corn off the cob, beets darker than blood, tomatoes stewed and bottled under cap, rhubarb swimming like eels in the special way she did them, and the bins getting empty of onions, potatoes, yams, squash. Gone were the berries we spent whole days drawing up in buckets and tins to mother's table, red and blue and green.

When father said, "That's enough in the order," to a woman at a roadside stand, putting the balance of money back into his pocket, I knew it was for the drinking later on. His calculations were exact. But I knew he was cheating. If I told mother, she'd rail at him, and in the morning there'd be a new bruise, a new testimony that she had gone too far for he had gone too far.

The more he was exposed, the more she'd rail, the more he'd respond in his way, until she'd rail no more.

But we had the good days in between. There'd be a warmth in the kitchen when seed was put down, or a day spent splitting wood and stacking it against the barn first and then against the house, and the piles would leap along the yard like frogs from the pond, and in one day it would be over. He'd be measuring, calculating heat and energy and, most vivid of all, the dryness in his throat that demanded payment. He would dun himself right down to Barclay's Tavern and would not pick up an ax or a maul until the next summer.

Once I caught mother as she looked out the window, after looking at the calendar under the clock that never moved, under her kitchen kitten, as though she was seeing when the cold days would ensue before summer was on us. For father had just planted his maul into the middle of a chopping block with a magnificent swing that nearly split the old block, the thwack of it resonating on the air; It was his statement swing; he was done for the year.

She knew that swing, most likely had seen it the last year and the year before and who knows how far back … six of us, near two years apart, had been born here in the upstairs bedroom, looking out on the yard, the fields of blueberries across the road, looking uphill where the bear had come one year, black as the old flivver in the yard, and father killed him at least ten times over with his rifle, thinking of us picking the berries sooner or later.

There were moments.

I had come back to these memories because they were not done yet, they could not be wrapped up until mother allowed it, wanted it, sat in her kitchen and smiled out the window, warming us all back in ... and father in the bunch; the tender times were memorable too.

The attention-grabber in the hallway came back again as I stood with one foot inside the kitchen. Eben Gregson, open-mouthed, stared at me from the hallway, a raggedy-Andy as far back as ever. Even with my father's time off for drinking and his notorious and sudden cessations of work, he'd get more done that Gregson ever dared. The man worked on sympathy, cajolery, a sense of timing that prevented his energies being displaced, a heady control of inertia.

"My God, Paulie, is that you?" The surprise was authentic; the news was late. "Your folks don't live here anymore." The half-apology broke free, like he was in the confessional; "I bought the place from them." The other news was stale, too; "They've gone to Vermont, to your grandmother's old house." More authentic surprise; "Didn't they tell you? Haven't you heard? My God, Paulie, I would have sent word."

Gregson's word didn't own an ounce of integrity.

"How much did you pay for it?" I said, jumping right in, demanding an answer, which might not carry much with it. Much as I had studied my father, I knew the neighbors as well. Gregson was the one a few years back paid me a whole dollar for shoveling his whole driveway, paying me like it was a late Christmas gift. "I want you to spend this wisely, son, not frivolously; you worked hard for it. Real hard."

Oh, he was a piece, I'll tell you any time I get the chance.

"That's my business and your pa's," he said in answer, probably, I was thinking, he might have recalled the dollar present. Still, he hung his head the way front-row kids did in school when they blew an answer in a class quiz. Oh, I had seen that move a dozen times, hang-dog coming up an excuse, assuming forgiveness from the transgressed.

This man was not going to get loose from me; I'd seen his fade-aways. "It's my business too," I said. "I worked here as hard as he did, since I was a kid, but longer in the evenings than he did. How much?" I started counting on my fingers, the way a fast teller can snap-count a pile

137

of dollar bills.

"Four thousand dollars." Goggle-eyed he went, facing me, facing the truth, chances being that he could have gotten 12 to 15 thousand from someone else if he'd been less thirsty, more knowledgeable.

I came apart at the seams, and was afraid I'd grab him. "You stole it at that price. You stole it from a man who wanted steady nights by the booze. A cripple he was and you sat back and waited for him to fold in on himself."

"That's his concern. Not mine."

"It's yours and mine now. I'll buy it back. How much?"

"Hell, Paulie, I can't pick up and move again. Marla would have my ear forever, knowing I ain't so special with all this." His hands spread the indifference 'bout the farm, measuring what little he too would get of land that needed working. That was a moment of truth with Gregson, no play-acting now.

"You do it for a quick thousand dollar gain?" I had to be careful. I had the money, but not enough to squander on pride, or gentle bargaining.

"I don't know, Paulie. There's a piece of work to get done."

"The Douglas place is for sale. It's half a mile down the road. A simple move. A day's work and I'll help. I heard Les is hurting. You can steal the place. It's better for you. Smaller, not so much to do. And you'd do Les a great favor, like you did for my father. I saw Les's son Earl down at the store, and Les is going to move in with him, now that his wife split on him."

"It's a deal," he said, his eyes lit up like dreams were alive in them. He could be out of here in the morning, everything catching up to him in three days, the whole package. A thousand dollars richer. A year's saving in a few days, with a few signatures.

Mother would accept the return home, but father would likely want some restrictions laid bare, rules of the land, but his voice would not count now.

Once more, an older day grabbed me:

Father was at the woodpile, and the pile of logs yet to be split was daunting. From across the road, in the trees, I could read his body language, the drop of one shoulder clear as a diagnosis, his malady afoot in him, a cavernous ache, that other emptiness. It was a signal, the way he looked about, at the house searching for mother, and with a monumental decision proceeded to smash in a mighty swing the six pounds of the maul

138

just past the edge of the chopping block; the handle shattered, the maul head bouncing on the gravel, the year of wood splitting coming to rest almost right there at his feet as smooth as a sacrifice bunt.

I was caught up in a mixture; I'd been too many strange places, known too many discomforts, making myself over again for those people I can barely remember now.

They'd better come home. I was home to stay. If he wanted to drink at night, let him, but I wouldn't pay for it. I'd just let him be, some things are just cut out for people on their way through here.

Hell, I had a platoon commander was drunk every night and died a hero, on top of me soaking up all the shrapnel like it was made to order.

I painted the name back on the mailbox.

139

I Flat-out Didn't Like the Way She Looked at My Flowers

What I do best is water my flowers. I do it daily, making sure I can get back from elsewhere in time to do so before the day is gone with the moon. I am faithful to that compulsion, and when this chick comes along, made nice in a certain way, yet points out dismal little failures in the front garden or the narrow plot beside the driveway to an occasional walking companion, it pisses me off no end. I've heard her through an open window say things like, "Wouldn't you think someone would know better than to plant the short ones in the back." Or, "Don't you agree that his color scheme is a bit off base? Needs a little more imagination?" Or, like one totally elliptical occasion when she said, "Who does he thinks likes so much orange?"

No green thumb do I really have but I like the way my flowers pop yellow and orange and rainbow parts somewhere during the summer, sort of a last retreat from the cataclysmic world that blossoms about us, strange as it might seem, like Iraq never letting go on the television and my Korea not that far back. Many of my flowers promise to hang on in their special way until October rolls around, now and then someone pointing out a clutch of colors breaking the day apart; you only have so many chances you know, pleasing the customers, getting a dime's worth for your nickel. The mums are spectacular I think, like ice cream cones or spun candy, as are a half dozen annuals, pink and gorgeous, I spent a few bucks on and which manage to light the place up like searchlights were on. Two rose bushes, mighty red Americans on trellises and against two front windows, are for real, until July heat knocks the hell out of them. Short but sweet. So what else is new with a short breath rose bush?

With all my business at the flowers, I don't even know who this chick is, the complainer.

Nicely is, I've always said, is nicely done. I've been on my knees weeding a time or two when she passed, with that punctuation walk of hers as she moved by. I bet I heard huh or a short harump a few times as she expressed almost silent judgment on something not quite at its best color or shape for her taste. Tough shit, lady. Lump it or leave it. Take another route for your perambulations. I won't miss you.

She's persistent, I tell you, in her twice-a-day. I've seen her a couple of dozen times, make the corner at the head of the street and start down my way. It's been a solid three months or more that she's been making that turn and coming my way on a double-daily basis mostly. Her way takes her right past my stubby little lawn and my old colonial house a stone's throw from the First Iron Works of America. The whole area feels like a piece of history coming to a slow crawl, or a halt. History downhill, if you'll have it. Yet Harry Trotter takes a long gander at her every trip just about, standing like a shadow beside his garage until she goes past and then steps out to follow her with his eyes. You'd swear he could be rubbing himself. Until, of course, he sees me looking at him looking at her. Well, he's a hunk of history too, yet pretty agile for an older buck when he jumps back out of sight. I bet his wife makes him jump like that too. He's the type. So's she.

So this near-silent, discordant, unsatisfied walker, with a bod and a half to say the least for her, doesn't change her flight pattern and keeps going by my place in her generally most pleasant T-shirts until it finally hits me that she really isn't displeased with my flowers, but has a yen for getting to meet the green thumb revolutionist who happens to be in the single life, widower going on ten years and with no serious bites as yet to change that stance.

First glance at her marked her as being in her mid or early forties, damn good shape, leggy in a healthy and provocative way, blonde hair in tight but neat curls that sure does things for the imagination every six or seven seconds on the clock, the way guys are. A closer look, from the open door one day as she pranced by, made her more like the late forties or early fifties that a half decent life must have granted her. I think it was an upper arm thing, the giveaway, trying to break the cellulite free or let it get out of hand. But, from all points, a damn good looking woman with decent mileage left in the chassis. Probably could damn well outrun me, me being in my sixties, not much on exercising but kneeling and stretching and tending the garden; only now and then, and only by reference, seeing an occasional woman for a short stretch or a short run.

Could be she's done some investigating, like clicking a search button on my name in the computer. But, for all of that, I'm as patient with women as I am with flowers, and so for this perambulating knocker of things floral I plant a small, innocent row of late seeds (right alongside the front walk and perpendicular to the house and the sidewalk, which I have never done before) and begin to water them with my usual care. When she knocks them, if and when she does, and I'm betting she does,

141

I'll pull her aside and tell her they were hers in the beginning. Touché, lady, and up yours.

The water works, faithful as Old Faithful itself, and one morning, as I get down close for real inspection (nose-to-the-ground kind of thing where you can smell the rank, sea-borne, salty drawing power of Mother Earth herself in all her frigging glory), there's this mild trickle of green starting to follow the line of seeds I had planted. They're like a butch haircut at first, or a new flat-top, whatever you want to call it, or again like a stitch line in a Celtics' jersey. They're new, they're young, they're eager and I'll have to weed with extreme care, I tell myself and promise myself.

A few days later, perhaps a week of not really counting, the sun every day busting out of its pants on the nearby hill, the dew swept up in the first rays coming on the powerful slant, she bites. Down the street I see her coming, the floral perambulator, the flower and garden knocker with legs swearing they carry promise itself, and Harry slipping out his side door to loiter carefully at the garage purposely at an accidental errand. He'd probably been watching for her through a window on the other side of his house that's flush on the corner of the street she comes from in her turn. This is her second trip today and I'm betting Harry's wife is bullshit. Earlier I was in the back yard and only caught a glimpse of her sashaying by with her walking pal. Again, she was pointing back over her shoulder, at punctuation's gesture. I suppose we can all guess at some thrust of her comments, what called for her wagging finger, what denouncement: new shoots, I'd bet, the green line of new stitches at the edges of my walk, the newness of a strange little plot in front of the old colonial. Change for the unchanged.

This time she stops. If invitations are never printed, one must guess.

"Why something new for an old house like this?" she says, nodding her head, taking everything in, hands on her hips the way a teacher might stand. I notice that her breasts are taut against the whitest T-shirt and I swear there are no other restraints on the dark orbs I see pushing out prominently. Another tone about her seems to say, "Why's an old geezer like you doing something new?" Or, "Are you still able to make such decisions that come around occasionally?" The way she stands demands notice. She goddamn knows what she's carrying. There's a thrust to her crotch that grabs my eye most immediately, not that I am fully satisfied

142

with flowers no matter how pretty or sweet smelling they've become. Like the man says, "There's no substitute for lemonade in the right glass." I forgot who said that, but he knew whereof.

Mystery abounds in a sudden growth.

Green eyes catch my eyes. She nods. Shadows of crow's feet talk happiness and excitement in a quiet, graphical music. A minor and subtle sensual displacement takes place. I'm not sure what it is, where it begins, how it gets where it does, but she nods again and movement happens. It gets there. Something shifts in place. A neuron change.

The laboratory of a woman at endless work. She knows. She knows everything.

This opportunity, after months of walking by, has come down to the nub. She broadcasts, airs herself out, reveals, lets go, knowing the one chance hoped for has come around. This casual passerby has cut the edge of patience, has opened a new door. I can feel it swinging wide. I can see beyond. I can measure experiences that are displayed just the way my flowers are. Class and patience have done it, on both sides of two people at odds with destiny, and time and the awareness of the passage of time. It all leaps around us; the roses are gone. The last one, hanging on, bewildered like the last leaf on the maple in the backyard caught in a late November Northeaster, is an insignia of all that passes through life. That last rose does not want to let go. It has hung on through perils of August heat, deadly rains, and my ineptness at times. It clutches the lean stem that is connected to the ground root and is still sucking moisture right up out of Mother Earth's lap. It wants more time. It demands more time. And the peonies, so glorious, so ebullient for three long months of beautiful tapestry against the front of the house, are closing their white and pink blossoms into little brown fists full of brown passage. Their story is the same. This summer, this life, is going too quickly.

She sits on my front steps, her hand stretched out to touch the granite horse holder that stands three feet high with an iron tether ring through its column, a mark from pre-Revolutionary times when this house was built in 1742. It gives off a sense of age, of use.

The house is old but it's still standing, though the roses and the peonies are gone to their brown withering. On the top granite step, abutting the solid panel door with an antique brass knocker, a pair of rolled-iron boot scrapers is separated by the width of the slab step. The scrapers have performed 260 years of menial service, though Hal the mailman wonders at their utility.

Sitting on the steps her knees flash a sense of mystery and inner paleness, the best kept secret kept yet. Her lips are moist. Her eyes are as green as a leaf in the earliest spring day. I feel the bud coming out of its long grip.

I say, "All beginnings have mystery in them. You have mystery about you. I am well aware that this is a beginning, and while some manifestations come quickly to me, and to you, others will take slightly less than forever, much to endless satisfaction."

She says, still pale as a petal elsewhere, "My name is Justine."

She blossoms.

144

Contemplation of a Drawing

Josiah Gibbons, another of Grady Walker's cousins, a Yale student working on his PhD in history and art, had won a closet on the third floor with his pick out of the hat, a small closet at the head of the second staircase on the back side of the old house. Grady knew an angry Josiah in a few hours would be wailing away with the tools he brought with him. His body language, for most of the night after the hat was passed, proved sickening. Once, he declared he was "visibly upset," but in other words, loud enough for all to hear him. Grady knew Uncle Cheesy would turn over in the grave if he heard the mild curse. Nobody had ever heard the old man spill the simplest curse.

Harvey Cheesy Cheswick, PhD, LLD, had been beyond them all, just as he was now, cavorting with other gods.

Grady stood in the middle of the room he had picked in Uncle Cheesy's lottery. It was not high noon yet. Debris lay at his feet and across the floor; large chunks of gray plaster and molding of various sorts. What he was doing cut through him swift as a needle. Lazy sheets of plaster dust shifted in bars of sunlight streaming through two windows, their motions so hypnotic a trance could have taken him in tow.

In one hand he held a pry bar; in the other, a fireman's ax. Sweat rolled off his brow, stained his shirt at the underarms, and a streak worked down his back. Two more hours belonged to him. With his pick out of the hat at the drawing of room numbers, (the lott'ry as his cousin from Maine called it), praying for a room of good size, not like Josiah's closet, he had gotten this upstairs bedroom. Second floor, next to the last door on the left. No furniture in the room.

With the furniture removed, the room looked larger. A good-sized closet sat against an inner wall. The two windows looked out on trees. The same molding and cornice work borne in all other rooms loomed lone as guardians. Grady feared the room was closing in on him even with the debris at his feet, with the dark maroon and purple runner still on the hallway floor, after climbing the stairs. It made him think of Dorothy trying to get home again, back to Kansas, to Toto, to Auntie Em. Cheesy had run the film for them many times.

Last night, when the drawing started, Josiah walked to the printed layout of the house tacked on the study wall. With large letters he had written his name in the closet space, the ends of his name spilling into the

145

adjoining rooms. The act couldn't have said anger any plainer. With a crazy head of hair, he was tall and gawky and too jittery for a long-time student. Since his arrival two nights earlier, Grady driving him from New Haven, he wearing a blue Eli sweater. He continually squeezed a rubber ball in his hand, swapping hands every few minutes, his level of pushing iron, getting hands and arms ready for the tools and next day's task.

Josiah's assigned number, 20 for the closet, was listed on the schedule as Tuesday 2:00 PM-8:00 PM. The Drawing had begun, Josiah taking the first pick out of the hat, one of Cheesy's winter caps, ear flaps in a knot. He never wore the hat but Grady remembered it hanging on one bedpost for over a year. Fun was attached to it.

Grady's number turned out to be 17, a bedroom he had never slept in, though he found a faint recollection that his parents slept in the room during one vacation. His schedule, on the study wall, said, Tuesday 8:00 AM-2 PM. In the square of the house plan he had written his name, lone, level and as neat, he thought, as round the decay of that colossal wreck, boundless and bare, the lone and level sands stretch far away. Cheesy's voice also came back from that elsewhere he had gone to, saying the poem for the hundredth time maybe. His likes were limitless, from Dorothy and Toto to Ozymandias.

Despite the size of each room, the 6-hour limitation was uniform. Josiah made the biggest stink about the rule. "Just think about it," he had muttered to one group in a corner of the study, "you get the dining room or one of the main bedrooms and you don't have any more time than anybody else." Staring some of them in the eye, it looked like he was practicing for the courtroom rather than a life with the arts.

Another cousin, from Maine, said, "Josie, don't you really mean that you've got an advantage with such a small room, or you're being penalized for being unable to swing your ax like Paul Bunyan, being too restricted?" The snicker was evident.

"Don't call me Josie! You know damn well I hate that name, Conrad! And I'm not complaining." He said Conrad like it was Cornnn...raaad, a real dig at his Maine cousin, boondocks deep in his trapping and hunting, backwoods written all over him.

"Could have beat me with a stick that time, Josie," Conrad answered, and walked off to see another cousin. On one hand, at his side, a middle finger prominently displayed what everybody knew he was thinking.

146

Josiah and Conrad and Grady were some of the thirty-two relatives of Harvey Cheswick, PhD, LLD, etc., etc., etc., so gathered for the occasion. Harvey had died a year earlier, having spent ninety-seven years of near grace on this planet. For fifty of those years he had been the curator of The Lampford Museum of Art, in Cambridge, Massachusetts, a most celebrated and respected museum. In addition, he had garnered an enormous collection of his own, which some connoisseurs declared to be one of the most valuable private collections in the world.

Now old Cheesy, as many had called him, was dead, and all his collection had been accounted for, delivered to named inheritors around the country, all notable museums. Not one individual made the gift list. Neither of his two sisters, both elderly and in nursing homes. Not his ex-wife, ten years abroad on the Continent, as she would say. Not his only son Harvey Jr., somewhat of a gadfly, a spendthrift of the first class, nor his daughter Juliette who was now married for the fourth time. This one was as promising as the others, as whispered by some of those involved. Both children had fallen far from the tree. One item of the collection, Cheesy's favorite and his most valued one, a Rembrandt, had not been accounted for. Not before, supposedly, and not now. But, in the will of Harvey Cheswick, however, there had been the promise that this piece of art will become the property of the one who finds it...all in proper order, time, and as directed by his will, in an exercise either he or his lawyer had dubbed The Drawing, now underway.

All nuances allied in The Drawing, both the blunt and smooth edges of humor and irony of the farthest reach, said each one had been picked by old Cheesy's sense of humor and justice for those involved. The prize, itself a mystery unto itself, was also said to be merely a pen and ink sketch by Rembrandt. But it had never been seen. Though listed in the description and insurance documents of his collection, with date of its creation, no one had seen it, including the family. All that helped bolster Cheesy's reputation in his mission for the arts. His assessed value of the sketch was six million dollars. The insurance company accepted the valuation. Anybody would knock down a few walls for that much money.

As a youngster Grady, a grand nephew of Cheesy, had spent several summer vacations at Uncle Cheesy's house on the hill, sitting upstream on the Concord River in Concord, Massachusetts. Young relatives who came for tidy, fun vacations under Cheesy's wing, and at his expense, called the house The Playpen. Older relatives called it Mount

147

Ararat, Cheesy being god-like in his own way. Children gathered to him like a mystical grandfather, a figure from an old fairy tale, a saint from a fainter volume. Adventure itself hung about the house on the hill, and hidden dramas. Old auto tires hung from great long ropes in the elm trees on the backside of the hill, some ropes hanging sixty feet from high limbs. Downhill three Maine-built canoes graced his own slip onto the river, and beneath the rambling house lurked a dark cellar full of strange ghostly shapes, formations, and secret things only the young talked about late at night under warm, secure covers. The haven kept secrets of its own.

Grady, still in the middle of the room, studied the ceiling, eyed his watch, measured his useless plunges at walls, his wild swings and ripping of plaster. Nothing hidden had revealed itself. He stood motionless at this point, recalling the early days of noise, gaiety, and the mystery of seeing a new painting suddenly hanging on a wall. Nobody ever saw Cheesy hang a painting, as if each one was hung during the night or when not a soul was about, a ghost figure working in the house. Was there a message there? A schedule for utter joy? No one ever heard a nail driven to hang a picture on, or the twist of a screw through plaster searching for a lath. And Grady, still shaking his head, visualized Cheesy sitting back and enjoying the whole shooting match. The laughter came from the far horizon, from elsewhere; distant, secretive, but audible. For all the physical mayhem in the house promised by searching for The Drawing, a ton of humor waited to be revealed.

Grady thought he loved Cheesy more than he did at the beginning of this personal wreckage, if that was possible.

The Playpen, three levels of it, sprawled across the top of a low hill on the westerly side of Concord, the river meandering below like a stream of brown molasses. Each room in the house was accessed by a deep maroon and purple runner that seemed to go everywhere in the house. Grady thought the maroon and purple runner must have been played out from one roll to cover the hallways in the house and climbed, still unbroken, both flights of stairs; the grand staircase up from the front reception area and the darker one at the backside of the house. One vacation, on his own, he had tried to find the beginning, or the end, of the runner. He still didn't know where it was, or if it was.

"What else have you heard, Grady?" Josiah was all curiosity on the ride to Concord, interested in how Uncle Cheesy unseen managed to hang a painting, or where they came from, or in what manner. Were they

148

delivered? Did someone else hang them? Was there a secret room in the cellar or in the end of the attic where one door carried a big padlock? Josiah's glasses, thin and rimless, sat professor-like on the bridge of his thin, Anglican nose. His head, ever at an angle, inquisitive, tilted towards answers.

Grady replied to a question about the hat as if it was old hat. "Cheesy's lawyer, Harmon Askins, said it plain and simple as far as I know. A hat will be passed. We'll each draw a lot, a number I guess, corresponding to a room in the house. He said any room with four sides to it will have a number. Thirty two rooms are in the house, including closets. There are 32 relatives. I counted them, in my sleep. Some I haven't seen in years. I wonder if Cheesy has. The Sketch, as I call it, and Askins does too, is hidden in the house according to Cheesy, so you'd be damn foolish to rip wildly at walls. But the contents of the room you draw in the lottery is all yours, if anything's hidden there."

Pausing for added effect, staring at an 18-wheeler sliding by them, Grady said, "Askins thinks Cheesy wanted to tear down the house. Maybe that's our part in the whole thing. Get a leg up on tearing the house down. Hell, it needs a ton of repair work. Ever notice how bad the front staircase creaks like it's ready to let go? I think the runner might hold the house together, keep it in one piece. And think of this ... maybe The Sketch is not even there. He's done funnier, stranger things, old Cheesy. 'Member when he took the screw out the bedroom doorknobs one vacation? We slept out in the screen house, all of us. Had to cook our breakfast on the Coleman stove and his cast iron grill half an inch thick. God, I can taste that set-up now, breakfast so damn delicious that morning. And he was in his glory, showing us how to get it done. One of the best vacations I ever had here. So Askins thinks Cheesy doesn't want to share the house with anybody. The Sketch is enough to leave to us. But he's left so much else."

"How do you interpret the rules of the game," Josiah blurted out in his haughtiest fashion, "like not going past the laths in your assigned room? How the hell can you do that, or not do that? Damn, you could be in the next room in a matter of seconds, working on somebody else's wall." His energy was almost visible in his seat. Grady noted that Josiah had not brought up any of the salient points he'd advanced in to the conversation. It was evident that Josiah had forgotten a lot of what Cheesy had set aside for all of them starting way back.

The rules of the game had been posted a month earlier, and all advised by mail. Each letter had contained the return address of Harmon Askins, Concord Village. In between times, a thief tried to break into the house. A hired security man with a shotgun had driven him off, a dark-clothed person. Twice it happened, and then no more, as if twice forewarned was sufficient.

Josiah kept on. "And the room upstairs with the lock that's been there since the day we first saw the place? Maybe I'll draw that room. I've thought about what's behind that door for most of my life. Haven't you?" Josiah dreamed of hitting the big one. Grady wondered what his study habits were like.

Grady's father, Gardner Walker, a youth counselor, full of blond curls and a ready smile, had signed his name to number 28, an attic bedroom. When he walked back from the plot marker, his wife Constance said good luck and hugged him, and they both nodded at Harmon Askins whom they had known for thirty years, and then yelled across the room to Grady. "Good luck, son," they said, a duet in perfect sync. The delivery irked Josiah, the corners of his lips saying so.

All the thirty-two relatives of Cheesy Cheswick were gathered in the large study on the first floor. Many places on the walls revealed where paintings had hung for extended periods during Cheesy's life.

A contest began trying to remember what painting had been hanging on what spot for those years. Jug Handl, barkeep and owner of a small 6-unit motel in Maine, loud as a cheerleader but warm at the same time, swore he knew two of two paintings. Jug was a big guy, busting at his jeans, and more comfortable sitting than standing. "No more'n two that I can say. Beside the fireplace. On the left was the shepherd boy with this stick he carried, twelve or thirteen I'd of guessed, and a dog at his heels. Like a twin, the one on the other side was also a young 'un, with a dog too, a terrier puppy, but that boy was a swimmer. Like he'd just come out of the sea, all shiny like. I remember the rocks and the seaweed and wondered how they were painted so damned real. Like they were from different places or lives and meant something to Cheesy."

"I think you're wrong, Jug," said Bill Cheswick, a tall lonely looking man who hadn't spoken much since he'd arrived. "Having two boys on either side of the fireplace means balance." The words moved a thought across his face.

He smiled, nodded, looked away at some point in the distance, and

150

said, "Jug, I figure the on'y one missing is your ole kid partner, Rafe Tucker, out there in Klamath Falls. I 'member how you guys got along one summer. Never been here since his eighth or ninth birthday from what I hear, that Rafe, but never could afford to come anymore anyways. Rafe's one of them good ole boys."

Another thin man spoke from the corner. "What's Rafe up to these days, Jug? You hear from him at all."

"Rafe's a mechanic now," Jug said. "Says he has a little two-bay shop keeps him ahead of the game. But couldn't get up enough dough and time off to come out here for this big gamble, if it ever pays off." He took in a small breath of air for such a big guy.

They all thought Jug was about to make another observation, but Harmon Askins looked at the schedule, well underway, and then at his watch. He double checked it with the clock on the mantel, and said, "Gary Plagent, you got your tools, son? You're up in ten minutes." He looked around the room, sadness sitting in his face, loss of one kind or another, one observer could have determined.

There was a hush across the room, like a freeze game at recess. Everybody stopped talking, stopped moving. Some looked at each other and smiled, and a few nodded at relatives closer than others. A few of them had been out and back, and were hanging around for a surprise, a party, whatever was planned. Cheesy could've handled it all with his bank account.

Jug Handl burped loudly and a soft titter moved through the room and faded away as if it hadn't even happened. All could tell that Askins liked the sudden silence, for he smiled at each group around the room, like they were separate flower beds in one garden. He nodded his warm acceptance of all of them, liking most of them, as Cheesy had. Over his glasses, rims dark as Hades because of thick eyebrows, he looked again at Gary Plagent, fifteen years old to the day.

"I got them right outside the door here, Mr. Askins. Long as I can bring up what I brought with me, I'm all set. I got the bathroom upstairs. Can I take a bath when I get done? I got a date tonight. Got to be done before then." He let go a know-it-all smile.

The room filled with nervous laughter." Leave it up to a kid," one relative said.

Harmon Askins was like a teacher, with instructions for a test. "Long as you only got hand tools, Gary. It's alright by me whatever you got. You get those tools ready because Harry Tilford is now about due from his assignment from the main bedroom." Again he looked at the clock, and then at the schedule. "We have to be out of here in two days. That's part of the rules."

The sadness sat in place, as if Askins owned it all.

Everybody in the study looked at the clock over the mantel and then at the main hall door. Sounds of boot trudging and tool dragging bounced down the stairs. A small curse came along as company, with a faint, "Excuse me," and a softened, "Oh, damn."

Harry Tilford, in coveralls over lumberjack shirt whitened by plaster dust, and a pair of Novie boots riding up to his knees, pushed the door wider and dropped his tools on the floor, swapping places with Gary Plagent as the youngster rushed out of the room and off to his quick destiny, six hours' worth.

Harry was a teacher from high in the Laurentians and his voice was in perfect pitch with his appearance. "I'll take that drink now, Harmon Askins. Goddamn room is in smithereens, nothing to show for it, and my throat's parched as The Dry Tortugas or whatever the hell old Cheesy used to say about some place without water." As an aside he said, "D'ju ever make that trip with him?" Then he continued his litany of wreckage: "Floor's still there, but the walls are down and the ceiling and not a damn red penny for all of that. Thought I'd find at least some kind of builder's or carpenter's amulet or charm or talisman, but not a philter or a scarab in the whole passel. Not a damn antinganting for the whole six hours. Not even a simple two dollar gold piece from back when this place was built." He took a deep breath, his chin rising and lifting a long chin and a lean face, and said, "I haven't worked so hard since I shoveled manure as a kid in the mushroom house for Fred Penney, and that I will tell you, with excuses to the ladies, was an awful lot of shit."

"Nothing to show for it at all, Harry?" Jug Handl, dreading the work required toward possible fortune, kept his seat. Looking at Tilford, covered in dust, he appeared tired. "No secret holes? No hidden caches? No little rooms or cubby holes none of us ever didn't see? Not one?"

The Cheswick clan, as must be told, was somewhat short of women, for there were only five of them in the room, five of them on the invited list. One of them, MaryAnn Coulter, 35, asked Harry Tilford if he really expected to find anything. "Don't you think it's all a joke, Harry? No adjoining rooms being ransacked at the same time. Separation

152

counting for something that I can't figure out for the life of me. I don't know why I came."

She had told a few people that the blue coverall suit she was wearing was one her mother wore as a sweeper during her World War II days at the General Electric Plant in Lynn, Massachusetts. She had kept it her hope chest for all those years, along with her father's Purple Heart still in its box. The suit fit her like a laundry bag unused for years, wrinkles in place, pressed by old memories.

"The joke's on me for the time being." Harry laughed and repeated his search for the drink. "I'll have a double scotch on the rocks, Askins, and ask Jug to pour it for me. He and I are going to have one hell of a time before we get back home, that's for damn sure."

'M'I right there, Jug?" He pointed at Jug Handl spread on the chair like dough rising.

"Amen," Jug added, shifting weight, getting ready to prepare the drink.

The scene in the study, in bright pieces like a new checkerboard, kept coming back to Grady as he stood in the middle of his assigned room. The ceiling looked too daunting for him, but he shrugged his shoulders, forced the pry bar into a slash in the ceiling he'd made with the ax edge. He yanked down on the pry bar. Like a cloudburst, the whole ceiling rained down on him in innumerable pieces, like a short cannonade, and every ceiling lath was exposed.

No treasure was found, and he was ahead of schedule. "What the hell," he said, and then picked up his pry bar, searched for the ax, and found it after some effort under a pile of plaster. He had two hours left, but gave up the ghost on the spot and walked out of the room. He started to laugh. He laughed the length of the hall and stared out a window at the end of the hall. Multiple banging sounds came from other parts of the house. A wall near him shook. A man cursed. Out the window, on the side of the hill, he could see a tire on a long rope swinging slightly in the breeze. Downhill, on the river, the same breeze moved simple ripples as if an old man was walking there, god-like, across the surface.

"Old man," he said loudly, "you are frigging beautiful!" Exhilaration lifted him, at first with a sigh and then with a rush of wings, part of him leaping away, part accepting the escape. He'd have trouble giving any account of this exchange. Out of all of them, only Cheesy wouldn't need an explanation.

153

Of course, later on, someone had to go get Josiah upstairs, for he had stripped the closet in twenty or so minutes and was well into the room on the backside of the closet. He was screaming foul play all the way down the stairs. Someone told Grady he had gone out to wait in the car, waiting for Grady to drive him back to New Haven and away from this god-awful foolishness.

The study was crowded as Harmon Askins rang a bell in the hallway outside the study. It was Wednesday, 6 PM. He had been looking closely at the mantel clock for a good ten minutes. And he, as much as anybody else, looked tired, some of them saying Harmon had not slept in the time they had been there in Cheesy's house, this trip. "Nor me either," was a repeated echo.

When Askins stood up, people moved, shifting about, some also stood, stretching legs, whole bodies, twisting shoulders, screwing necks loose from long-locked positions. There came a small but collected series of relief noises; yawns, sincere little giggles of release, short half-hearted curses, pleasurable grunts at one level or another, twinned tittering of two women who had not seen each other in a dog's age. Faces revealed as many studies as there were people in the room. Individual ailments were exposed for the moment, the stiff knees, the arthritic joints, and the eagerness to be away for some of them, but afraid to leave before the show was over. "All the relative stuff," one wag was heard to say as he stared down at the river.

The clanging of Askins' bell ran up the stairs and echoed in a distant place, as if it had run out of breath. The rest of the relatives were coming down the stairs and scuffling along the hall. A curse was heard here and there, but also high tones of laughter, people letting go serious consideration for why they had taken part in the exercise.

The Sketch, of course, did not appear. A bunch of them had not expected anything. They again had been taken in by the old man.

Jug Handl offered a bit of summary. "Cheesy wanted us all to get a last chance in the house, the last visit. Lots of us came here for a long time, for years. We had fun. Some of us grew up here when we took the time to look around. Of course, we had to go on our ways too. But we came together for one slam-bang affair. I enjoyed it. I'm glad you all came. I wish Rafe had made it. He's a good ole boy, like Bill said."

MaryAnn Coulter, still in the laundry bag coverall suit, said, "Mr. Askins, is there anything else we should hear before we leave. I must

154

admit, I'm tired after all this." She showed a blister on one hand, in the groove near her thumb where Cheesy used to charm her, bouncing one finger on her open-hand fingertips. She said what Cheesy had chimed when he did the trick, "Johnny. Johnny. Johnny. Johnny. Oops, Johnny. Johnny. Oops Johnny," as he'd go back over her fingertips. She had not thought of it in more than 30 years. It showed on her face.

"Well," Askins said, "whoever found The Sketch could have the house. He provided for that. Somehow, Cheesy knew that person would be worthy of it, I'd hazard a guess. But if not, then no one was to get the house ahead of anybody else, and it would be well on its way to being razed. Which is now quite evident. I'll call the wreckers in the morning." After a quiet moment he added, "It will be demolished definitely. Tomorrow comes to Mount Ararat."

The sadness came again.

"There's a bit," Grady thought, "sounding like someone out of the Bible." It put a little fear and a little more respect deeper into place. Looking at Jug still astride his chair, with the loneliest look on his face, Grady wondered how close he and Rafe might have been in another time, at another age. It made him feel as sad as Jug looked.

This was his last visit here, where life had been filled with fun, explorations, drama, and a great deal of love. He was in no hurry to get away, in no hurry to get Josiah away from all this god-awful foolishness. The ride, at least to New Haven, would be borne in a solicitous fashion.

Wanting to be alone, savoring a recess in a life that would never come again, he said his goodbyes, slapped Jug Handl on the back and wished that he and Rafe would get together some time down the road. His parents had left early, other duties calling, so he said a loud goodbye and walked outside.

Behind the house a tire moved on one of the long ropes, a slight breeze teasing it into motion. Grady felt the wind in his face the way it rushed at him as a youngster, one of his parents or Cheesy pushing him on the tire. He heard the poem Cheesy loved. Imagined life going on in some boundless plain, yet always in sight. It unnerved him in a strange way. His mind leaped in a hundred measures, a hundred appreciations. Jug's last look came at him, saying how much he had missed in life, not just a boyhood pal. Rafe, he hoped, was happy in his own little world of mechanics. He was thinking of Rafe happily working at a motor job, slipping new rings into an old engine, bringing the engine back for

155

another forty thousand miles of the road. It pleased him as he passed the garage sitting on the side of the hill. As though a magneto drew him, he went in the side door.

Cheesy's old frame making table was still there. And all his tools. The fine little saws and edge trimmers. The tiny plane that was as good as sandpaper on the scrolled edges. The magical miter box with the magical saw, Cheesy saying that each cut of a frame had to be made from the backside. Oh, the pieces were falling into place. Knowledge leaped at him. Disclosures came.

The pile of basic woods Cheesy used to make his own frames lay heaped against one wall. The colors and grains were diffuse. Grady played with a few red oak pieces feeling solid and life-like in his hands. Mahogany reflected a dark cocoa, smooth as a new candy bar. A delicate but beautiful piece of walnut strutted its stuff, the grain speaking its mind. Fifteen or twenty pieces of wood were of serious grains and colors, like a collection unto themselves. It was game time again.

With a sudden twist of one wide mahogany board, a piece of common pine fell onto the floor. The Sketch, it said in ballpoint script, has been given to a museum in Italy, where it belongs. I wanted all of you, who shared the good times here, to be in at the end, for there is no more sharing but with yourselves. The message was in Cheesy's hand and signed in his distinctive flourish.

Askins was not surprised when Grady walked into the study with the piece of pine. He was alone. The others had gone.

"Josiah said he couldn't wait for you, Grady. He got a ride from one of the others, all the way to New Haven. Said he didn't think you'd mind. Good folks don't mind the waiting or the showing up."

"That's okay," Grady said, smelling plaster dust, old wood shaking loose, a strange odor that had no name, Time falling all around his ears, Uncle Cheesy's house taking one last breath the way memories are announced.

One hundred yards down the road Grady did not see the small spark, the ignition, the sudden flare amid the clutter and wreckage as Askins, now lost without his Cheesy, whom he loved more than all the others put together, sat alone at last, oblivious of that now climbing around him, gaining a full grip.

Guaranteed, there'd be no more sharing here; both of them were freer than ever.

156

One Prisoner Too Many

The sound came once more. He stiffened. It was closer. His whole body knew it was closer. It was not just in the hearing. It approached. It made inroads. It said so many things. The metal toe. The kick. The slash. Ping Too smiling through his teeth. Oh, would Ping have a thirst for amontillado! Oh, were he himself the finest of stone masons, setting Ping Too up for the full sentence; to make an end of my labour, to force the last stone into place; to set the best of mortar, forever.

Caught between the professor and the captain!

Again.

In the darkness, in the cell, he had himself convinced to use all his body parts, to get them all into the game. It was the only way to pass time, evade terrors abounding, to keep a thin shred of sanity if nothing else.

Thumb and finger. Thumb and finger. He had them poised, ready to clutch, grasp, snare the crawling vermin dared be caught. If the smallest of the lot trod the ground between those pincers, he'd have an addition to his meal. Perhaps the entrée, though small as it promised. In the pit of darkness, this room with no aperture, no stars allowed, no moon, no haze off the unseen horizon, silence baiting him as always, he could not see thumb and finger. But they were there a perilous distance apart. Then for hours, in the absolute darkness, they were but a whisper apart, a hair's breadth, and at times his whole arm trembled from the concentration. Sometimes, the length of that side of his body, down to his toes, knew that tremble as arcing electricity, knew the burn it could threaten.

Now, there was another thing…. the toes. Time after time he had tried to master the manipulation, to squeeze a big toe against its neighbor when he felt the vermin at that extremity. Way back in his memory, from an old news film maybe, he could picture a man making baskets; weaving, for god's sake, baskets out of strips of dried grass, with his toes! Toes like fingers! Toes using a double-edged razor blade to strip the grass into long, slender pieces! A lifetime at it, most likely, and that a likely mental reservation of his own. "I'm due a few," he said aloud in the circumscription of the imposed cell.

Would toes be at a greater advantage or vermin catching, them so unsuspecting? Ha! thinking like that! What an attribute for them! Or

157

then, there was that other man he remembered without arms, who typed with his toes, he too in an old film of sorts. Oh, he could see the carriage return sling backwards harsh as a bolt in a rifle, could hear the bell click on an old L. C. Smith/Corona, a metal monster with music in its own right, the dumb, inert, potential of great novels, short stories cutting to the quick, poems that could melt him in their abject simplicity. All from that black giant of quick mechanics. He could hear it again and again that musical bell, that energy sign. Oh, the short sentences of the typist, Hemingway stuff, stripped down, adjectives cast alive into the stream, the return bell ringing and ringing. Most likely an A Flat, he'd try to convince himself, though tone deaf. The bull charged. The people ran. Pamplona exploded. A Flat, without a doubt.

Then the itch, invariably, would begin at a point on his back he could not reach, and it was arriving again by the clock, perfectly timed in its entrance. At the small of the back, as if in between the cruddy vest remnants he wore, forced on him by the prison captain, and the worn and thin blanket he tried to sleep on, infested no doubt with creatures warmer than he'd ever be again. Bare, the air talking on his skin, his arms, at least the one not shivering, felt the chill, knew it to the bone, trying to be company with the itch.

But he knew he was evading the truth. The hip pain was the real odd lot, and so persistent in nature, hanging on like a bed of leeches, making him accept the challenge, keeping it busy, trying to suffocate it, kill it with its own pain. Coming beyond his skin it grew, harsh scale and rind, a covering thicker than ever meant to be. In places black lesions had taken root, like century-old stitches left for the ages. And the emaciated scalp he could withstand, its scalp crud crawling beneath scabbed striations, and too the conglomerate sores festering about like a geography on the planet of his body, the small rivers of dry fluid marking all the territories, the apathy of sores, abrasions, abscesses. For hours on end he'd stay in that one position, cemented in place, calling on reserves by the ton, demanding the recall of the core of hip pain, daring it to take him under. At times he'd curse, the words, all at abomination, coming through his throat swift as evil itself. St. John of the Cross's pain had nothing on him, as if the saint's chain itself, heavy and cumbersome at the waist, hanging awry with each and every link, took its iron into his soul, branding, torturing, being conscious grains of ache with each breath.

Only the Shroud of Turin could have enveloped so much, dared so much; nor had he yet thought of a crucifix. But the chain was real, the linkage. Again he cursed.

A shiver, a body's full shiver every once in a while, the entire course of him, was the most pleasure he might have for hours. It would attest to his total consciousness, his whole being, as much a passage fully memorized and fully realized from his old reading days taking hold of him, finding his soul: It must be understood that neither by word nor deed had I given Fortunato cause to doubt my good will. I continued, as was my wont, to smile in his face, and he did not perceive that my smile now was at the thought of his immolation.

Oh, dear Christ in heaven, he had catapulted now through E.A. Poe to the captain; jailer extraordinary, stick wielder, percussionist, with the long yellow teeth, the sneer and contempt embedded in his face, hatred in-born for America and the mothers of prisoners and the Grand Canyon and a Saturday full of football. The captain, Ping Too, long and fanged and yellow-toothed, with the metal toe on his shoe, just the right one, meant for backs, shoulders, elbows, bone, sinew, body, the very reach and portal of the soul. He did not know if it were Poe or the quickened sound beyond, a noise in the night, like the swagger stick striking on another back, across bare flesh. He and Fortunato, he and the captain, the captain and Fortunato. Where did it end or begin? He could hear his old professor, John Norton, reading the passage, coughing his cigarettes into the paragraph, posing his hand between belt and self, sitting on the edge of his desk, nodding at the words, his voice alive, the tower bell ringing at the end of class, May smothering him with trees and the promise of evening.

His voice repeated itself: Caught between the professor and the captain!

It was at him again. The then and the now. Still, he clasped that finger and that thumb, those entities in the darkness, poised, relentless, waiting. Hunger, he realized, would accompany him all the days of his life. Oh, such weariness it could sustain. A being in itself. It would never change. No matter how many times Ping Too kicked him, no matter how many times the stick flashed in the air and he could feel its slash before it hit his skin, the void in his body would reassert itself, the ever-calling vacuum, wanting, needing, crying for food, more food, decent food, one solitary piece of rye bread soft enough for his teeth where he held off the pain. It would do no good to get pain there, in his teeth. If he let it in it would be with him forever. He'd suck it out of his teeth before he'd let it come at him, gnawing its way home, coming like an insidious disease, taking over, controlling, as conscious as breathing. Suck the teeth dry of pain, that was the trick. Call on perseverance repeatedly. Make it stand-to. A man made demands on his body, on his complete self, the ego and the muscle, the sinew and the thought, the search and the grip. The echo came in the back of his head, even if it had to be that way until the last day. What he feared most was the lack of measurement, the inability of allowing or creating reference points, two points around time, and time at the center of two points as distant as stars. There was that hunger for the sight of stars in this room without aperture. That hunger was there like an organ of skin, enveloping.

It was déjà vu, it was a turntable event. The sound came once more. He stiffened. Again. It was closer. Again. His whole body knew it was closer. It was not just in the hearing. It approached. Again. It made inroads. Again. It said so. The metal toe. Again. The kick. Again. The slash. Again. Ping Too smiling through his teeth. All over again. Oh, would Ping have a thirst for amontillado! Oh, were he himself the finest of stone masons, setting Ping Too up for the full sentence; to make an end of my labour, to force the last stone into place; to set the best of mortar, forever.

"Yo!" he said into the darkness, quickly alert, his voice making an attempt at strength, soldierly, once again in the ranks. His mind leaped another leap. The finger and the thumb! No matter what joy comes, keep the finger and the thumb deployed. Be vigilant. Be ready. Anew came the full shiver. A shot of joy few minds would ever understand came over him. Alive and alert was he, down to his contriving toes. Oh, one grasp. One grasp! Oh, but for Christ, one grasp.

Then, as if timed by some legitimate god, a god of the deserts, a god of the deep unknown, a moan came out of the darkness, serious, cutting, soul-filled. It arched through his body. The rotted vest, the filthy piece of cotton beneath him, felt cold as stone, as hard, and as brittle if he moved an inch the wrong way, crumble and shatter its promise. Once more he was penetrated and violated in the darkness. Ache was in his soul, he was positive of that. It had a presence he thought immeasurable, untouchable. But here it was, at him, in him, with him, paining him as no pain had ever come to him.

Even yesterday, when Ping Too had kicked him so many times that

160

he lost count, where the metal plate in his shoe was now felt anew, was not as bad as hearing that moan, knowing Ping Too at new carnage and employ, speaking indirectly to someone's mother. It nearly cost him his concentration. The finger flickered, tremulous, came back to place and the organ of his skin searched its wide expanse for the presence of vermin nearing that vise. Courage came anew, and vigilance, determination. There would ever be the thought of mortar setting in place, a cry lifting itself to the limits of the universe, a metal toe plate rusting back to its beginning.

He thought his eyes had closed for a moment, that sleep had come in the place of Ping Too, that the moans and other sounds faded into the stiff darkness, lifted off to a distant place, yet to be remembered with vivid clarity.

Sleep had come. He woke, this prisoner, stood up roughly with ache anew, stiffly and absentmindedly slipped the rotted vest off his torso, and removed the remnant pants torn at the crotch, torn the length of one leg, letting the frayed string belt fall away. He dropped them and the worn cotton blanket into a tattered cardboard box at his feet, kicked the box under the cot. In dawn's first precious light he looked at his brother's picture, the major's leaf on his collar, the distance in his eyes, his brother seven years a prisoner of war, dead of an abrupt stroke on the rescue plane, never to come home.

He touched the picture frame, cool in the first sparkle of light, spoke the words again, as he had every morning for more than a year, and stepped into the shower, the words echoing, beseeching, apologetic in the bedroom behind him: I know, Charlie! I know! I know!

Once by the Short Hairs

There was a one-way look on her face. Hardness curved her lips, moved out from her eyes in spider web lines on skin that once had been softer. At will her eyes appeared to recess into a center of cold calculation. Only once did she soften her face when another car passed hers and a child waved out the rear window. For that fraction of a second an earlier beauty was visible, coming out of her past like the resurrection of an old photograph, conquering the hard lines she knew were there and were not hard to find. At thirty-two, life had made its early claim.

I'll show them bastards, she said under her breath.

She drove the old station wagon as if possessed, her hands gripping the wheel hard, not allowing the vehicle to veer the slightest bit. It was a faded blue '86 Ford.

The rear view mirror flipped over easily as she hit it with her fingers. The eyes looking back at her were harder than she wanted them to be. She relaxed her jaw, tried to let some of the build-up slip out of her body. Down at herself she looked. The blue dress was perfect. The bra was torn in half right at the cleft. It had taken a strong yank to part the material. Her breasts were half way out of their cups.

I'll show them bastards, she said again to herself.

Relaxation drew at her; she wanted to look sexy, to feel loose. Jerry had spent years telling her to loosen up, to lay back and let it happen. It had been so difficult. She began to think about Jerry, how deliberate and slow he had been, how tenderly he had come to her. "Just wait, honey, when the juices start, you're on your way." But it had taken so long.

The thought of the truck tipping over made her flinch. Always she had believed his last word had been her name. That's the way he had been. After him nobody had ever touched her. Nobody ever would. Jerry was the only classy guy she had ever met. He had told her once about the set-up. For a long time she had forgotten it, but times get tough.

"I'll really show them bastards," she muttered, as the big truck rolled up beside her car.

The big semi rolled past her and the striker sitting in the rider's seat waved down at her and winked. She winked back, aware of the dress riding up on her thighs, her breasts flooding out.

Blue's perfect, she thought. It was always my best color.

162

When she braked for the light at the top of the hill the semi was right beside her. The striker looked and saw her looking back up at him, the wide dark eyes now warmer, the mouth softer in a smile of red lips and even white teeth, the bundles of her tits spilling out of their beautiful bib, hair so black and shiny it would spread midnight across a pillow.

At the green light she moved off. The striker yelled, "Have fun, beautiful!" His wave was casual, but he was nodding.

"You're goddamn right I will," she threw back at him over her shoulder. It made her feel good and the softness moved on her flesh, through her breasts, down the flat stomach, into her thighs. The lazy engine fought her foot on the accelerator, begrudged the force and then reacted. The wagon leaped out past the truck.

A great section of I-95 ribboned out in front of her in a long downhill run. Cars, trucks and vans spread out in a serpentine string. Directional signs hung overhead. Restaurants, gas stations, diners and fast-buck operations were as thick as litter on each side of the road. The abrupt introduction of a reservoir on the right hand side offered the only break in the commercial landscape. So distasteful was it, it made her wince. She realized today she was in a wincing mood.

Out in front of her she suddenly recognized the gas station. Into a small recess she pulled off the road. Traffic continued to flash by. Through a small pair of binoculars she studied the station, counted ten cars and wrote all the registration numbers on a pad. She watched and waited. Another Ford wagon pulled in, was gassed up and drove off. A van did the same. Twenty-three vehicles pulled into the pumps and were serviced. At the twenty-fourth vehicle she sat straight up in the seat. It was a brand new Cadillac. Two blonde girls about thirteen got out of the car and walked around the side of the station. Turning the key in the ignition, she jammed on the accelerator. This was the break she needed. The wagon bucked once, twice, and leaped in response. She pulled into the station and parked beside the Cadillac.

A young attendant, about twenty-one she guessed, raised a finger at her and nodded. The two blonde girls came out from beside the station. They looked like twins, precious twins. Her jaw tightened when she saw the activity inside the station. Five or six men had quickly gathered in the lube room. Her face hardened, her breath came in short, quick gasps. Her hands gripped the steering wheel.

Through her teeth she muttered, "You dirty rotten bastards." The

163

girls got into the Caddie, which moved slowly away from the pumps. A heavy-set man was at the wheel. She took a deep breath and let every muscle in her body relax. It was now!

Her left shoulder dropped over as the young attendant came to stand beside the wagon.

"Help you, Ma'am? Fill 'er up?" Her left breast was almost out of the blue dress. Looking up she saw the bulging eyes of the young man staring down at her. Imperceptibly parting her legs she twisted around and looked coolly at him. "Look, honey," she said in her sexiest voice, slightly opening her legs more, "I've got to use the ladies' room to do a quick repair job. I may be a few minutes, okay?"

The attendant, his eyes still bulging, said, "Yes Ma'am! Yessiree!" His two hands were grasped tightly on the bronze gas pump.

"I've got to be honest with you." She decided to turn it on more. "I've got this terribly important date with a big banker who's married and my damn bra just broke! I hope you don't mind if I go in the ladies' room and fix it up. You just fill it up and check what you have to check and just move it over there out of the way like a real sweetheart and I'll be out as soon's I get ole mother's boobs back in place. Okay, hon." She threw him a look he would never forget.

Transfixed, mouth agape, he stood beside the wagon. Swinging the door open until it almost hit him, she jokingly but warmly said, "If you don't move I might just damage the most important part of you." As an afterthought she clucked her tongue at him.

The young attendant almost swallowed his tongue as she slid long, luscious legs out into full view, the dress flowing well behind her, the patch of white telling her that her panties were showing at the crotch. The kid's eyes, she thought, were like turtle's eyes in the National Geographic.

The adrenaline was really pumping, and she turned the body motor on to full as she crossed the concrete pad of the station. She felt like a lioness in the midst of the pride, her thighs vibrating as heels hit concrete, her buttocks bumping their still-sharp saucers against the blue sheath of her dress, her breasts high and proud and nearly out of the dress.

I'll show these bastards, she said again to herself.

In the ladies' room she put her pocketbook down on top of the commode. In front of her the mirror was clean but she did not look into it. Her fingers ran through her hair. Casually, but with a sensuous

164

movement, she opened the two buttons on the blue dress above the belt that pulled in at her waist. Her full breasts flooded out, the utter creaminess that Jerry had loved, evident, overflowing. The bra, ripped at the cleft, hung uselessly from the shoulders. With a teasing shrug the dress was pulled off her shoulders and then came the bra. The exposed breasts were magnificent, high and perky, creamy white, and each bore a near-orange aureole around deeper nipples. No kids and just Jerry all these years. Her lips parted slightly, moist, shiny, caressed by the small signaling tip of her tongue. A powerful awareness made itself known.

From the pocketbook came a spool of thread with a needle, slanted into it, already threaded. The ease of it all moved through her body. Standing straight, head cocked at a small angle, she began to sew. One hand, seemingly with a mind of its own, momentarily caressed one nipple that slowly extended. That slow hand moved again across the grain of the nipple. Slowly, teasingly, she began to massage it. Her eyes closed down on themselves. The bra fell to the floor with the needle and thread still in it. Then two hands were moving on two breasts and her head began a rhythmic swing. Her hips joined the rhythm, the inner music working, a unity taking place. She could feel her panties getting wet as she rubbed and massaged and kneaded the dark-stained orbs. Her mouth opened wider and her tongue slid over her lips, wetting them all over, making them glisten under the overhead light.

Again she thought, I'll show them bastards. I'll really show them.

Her whole body was in tune. She was loose. The juices were there! Again she thought of Jerry and slipped one hand down inside her dress, touched the hair at her crotch, moved further to feel the juices welling there, spilling all that goodness. She stretched her hand, a finger searching, the belt pressing on her forearm. Oh, Christ Jerry, she thought, the times we missed. The times we missed. She mouthed his name. Her tongue followed around on her lips silent as punctuation, tasting the memories.

Suddenly her whole body shook. To all of it she gave extra energy, gave it what wasn't really there to give, hung her mouth open, climaxed without feeling it.

"You bastards got it coming," she muttered.

Her hand came quickly out of her crotch, out of her dress. Her eyes opened clearly, sharply, as she pulled a piece of paper from the pocketbook. Quickly she unfolded it and held it up in front of the mirror.

Jeezus, she thought, I'd love to be on the other side right now.

On the paper, in large letters, she had boldly printed FUCK YOU GUYS!!

Her arms swung immediately back into the dress and it came over her shoulders. She buttoned one button with a deft, rapid motion and grabbed the handle of the door.

All of them she caught spilling out of an inner room of the station, the young attendant, two others in the same blue work uniform, others in civies. Over their shoulders and through the phony mirror she could see the inside of the ladies' room clearly, the overhead light as bright as day.

They were dumbfounded, embarrassed, and ashamed. They stared at her as she took up her final, resolute stance, legs firmly apart, the blue dress fully buttoned, the old hard look back on her face. The transformation was incredible. Formidable she looked in her stance.

"Okay, you dirty bastards," she said, "this is a stick-up."

They stared at her, their mouths opened.

"I want every dime in the till. Every goddamn dime you got in your pockets!" And then she added the first of her threats; "I'll blow the whistle on you guys so goddamn fast your fucking heads will spin."

Not one of the men moved, though their poise was shattered, their eyes hangdog.

"If you don't snap it up, I'm going to tell the guy who drove that Caddie in here a little while ago. Those two kids were his twin daughters in that fucking room. Thirteen years old they are! He's in the rackets. I've got the registration number of every damn car parked out there." Over her shoulder she pointed to the concrete pad and the station yard. "Do you know what that son of a bitch will do when I tell him about you guys. He'll bust the balls of each one of you. He'll probably do it himself."

It was sinking in and she saw it. Hands feebly reached into pockets. Wallets came into view. She opened her pocketbook. "Ole mother's got the collection basket right here, boys. Just drop it in. No holding back, not a friggin' dime." The cash register rang. The No Sale sign popped up. I have them all by the short hairs, she said to herself.

One of the men looked more pitiful than the rest. He irritated her and it showed in her voice. "What kind of work do you do, buster?" she said to him.

He answered trance-like. "I'm a salesman."

"What do you sell? Any samples?"

166

He was near apologetic with his answer. "Chain saws and stuff like that." He shrugged his shoulders.

"Well, buster, you go over to your car and put all your wares in the blue Ford wagon. Now hop to it like a nice boy or all hell is going to break loose around this fucking place!" The threat was close to physical.

The man did not look into her eyes. "You've got all the money, isn't that enough?"

"Look, pal, when your boss and your little wifey hears about this your ass will be dead. I mean it! Thirteen year old kids, for Christ's sake!"

The salesman moved out to his car.

She addressed the others. "You guys, if you are carrying samples or anything, I want them all put in my wagon, pronto. Now move it!"

The men in civies moved out of the station.

Just inside the lube room door she watched the parade of gear being moved to her wagon. Christ, but her pants were still wet. Jerry would have been proud of her. She had carried it off.

The rear of the wagon was soon full of an assortment of gear and boxes and bags. As she walked away from the lube room she pumped her ass one more time for good measure. Let them bring that home with them.

One of the men in civies, a gray plaid suit, nodded and smiled as she drove off with a last wave and smile. Nobody but the docile salesman had said a word. The young attendant finally said, ''I don't fucking believe it!"

They were all standing there ten minutes later, thinking about how she looked in the ladies' room, but talking about the heist, when an oil burner service van pulled into the station. A young man leaped out of the driver's seat and approached the group of men.

He was visibly excited.

"You guys won't believe what I just saw down at the lights where the Fellsway comes in. There's this blue Ford station wagon parked across from me at a red light, heading southbound and a broad's behind the wheel. All of a sudden she screams like she's dying and she jumps out of the wagon. Honest so help me, there's a fucking snake around her neck. I mean a real fucking snake! It scared the hell out of me and I'm way across the road. I don't like snakes no way so I just screwed. Can you imagine that? A real fucking snake! Must have been six feet long, I

167

swear."

The man in the gray plaid suit walked slowly to his car. A wide smile spread across his face as he opened the door. A legend, in gold leaf lettering on the door, said, BURTON'S WILD ANIMAL FARM.

He climbed into the car and drove off.

The Young Man Who Said He'd Never Eat Chocolate Again

Today it all came back. Once again, on another brilliant dawning, the Western Yetness still calling me, I woke with a toothache. A stupendous one! In half an hour, despite quick brushing, the stimulator poked here and there, gargling, all proving useless, the ache remained in force. It was, without a doubt, the chocolate again, or the mere thought of chocolate. I knew I was weak to most any candy, and to chocolate in particular, right from the beginning.

Believe me, me being Paul Legatione himself, that I am so much more than all of this around me. And I remember, vividly at times, how it all started; my father walking away from us when I was six or seven and my mother, Delores, wanting as much time as she could get with her many subsequent men friends, seeing to it that I was judiciously bought off with candy and books. The Big Swap I could have called it. Those friends arrived in their turns, some staying for long spells, and some for random short visits. She must have spread the good word far and wide, though, for she had lots of friends calling on her. And the candy arrived with them, toted as part of their baggage, and the books.

So frequently did they come that I grew up with them... the friends, the candy, the books. But tastes soon developed along with my character needs. As much as I could I declined the friendship of the men, often drawing back into a feigned facade, learning artistic ways of evasion, but I ate the candy meanwhile and read the books. Both, I swear, avariciously, relishing the sweet taste in my mouth, the sweet turn of a phrase giving me music, experiences moving in the back of my head. Of course, from that onslaught, my teeth went bad, but I read the books cover to cover, every word of every book, not that I was selective in the beginning, being reduced to strangers' tastes. I could read a book while worrying a tooth or rooting at that sore member with my tongue, so that I'd get by the aspect of pain, molars my anathema, my digging spots. Slowly, though, I developed my own taste and preference in reading and made suggestions, dropped hints, left notes about the house boldly marked with book titles, or authors' names that eventually began to crawl out of the narrowing selectivity in my mind. Joining the ranks, I guess you could say. By taking advantage of things, the library grew assiduously, and I learned a whole lot, absorbing all I read or reflected upon, every

169

word, every sentence, every illustration. My mother, on such days, was the happiest mother around. And you can say what you want about that happy phrase.

I suspected one time, like I had probably known all along, that she was sleeping with The Creole, a rather smooth but talkative man later speculation said must have come from James Lee Burke's bayou country down at the end of the Mississippi. He seemed like a nice enough guy, with the subtle dominance an occasional man can master, slow and steady, most always in first gear, moving ahead, no woman's piece or part deterring him. Even mother's speech changed for that dalliance, evincing a flair for a soft, slow Louisiana drawl she employed for either pleasure or annoyance... I was never sure which. It was always pointed at me, me the subject and object in what I imagined as an admission of guilt, a clearing of the air. An atonement, perhaps, she had intellectually arranged. It made me think of Huckleberry Finn and how the old boy, Mark Twain himself, prefaced the whole vernacular flow of his novel with that perfect aside right up front. He just set the record straight for his readers, his critics, all that history coming down the line right at him and his marvelous creation, Huck and Jim on the river, a spell of time and its particular sounds.

Of course, before The Creole suffered his entertainment, she welcomed The Corsican, and The Hammer-Thrower and The Glutton and The Sword-Swallower. From the earliest I had reduced her many friends to short descriptors, each of them following one another like trail hounds after my father walked away that day. Obversely I'd bet to a man they called me The Candy Kid. Sometimes I thought about that dictate, how the word must have spread, about Delores and her kid with the good sweet tooth, and it made me sour to my stomach.

I grew, though, while she entertained and my teeth went bad so many times I lost count. Visits to the dentist were horror shows I will remember into the pine box. But I had some innate abilities springing to light in spite of my mother and those dalliances, if I may call them that in polite terms. She bloomed with a man around, or men, did Delores. On other days, the slack days, such a difference came, a laundry sack of a woman... she'd become morose, depressed, near lifeless. There'd be no lipstick pressed upon her mouth, no care to dress, supper a poor substitute for the goodly fare; eggs for supper, fried eggs, quick eggs, or a bowl of dry packaged cereal, an old meal resurfaced, a rushed sandwich without pickle or condiment, her fast-food dictates at hand.

Then came, for me, the red letter day if I may say so, when The Corsican, big as he was, massive at the shoulders, gently cupped her buttock one morning with his outsized hand. Early angled sun dropped bars through the narrow windows of the house. Those bars fell in slanting bands of joyous light across two walls of the kitchen and made the silverware glitter like coins in a till. A dark blue oil cloth on the table condoned a swift mirror of brightness. The room was a warm happy room at that exact moment. The Corsican and mother were just inside the kitchen door, caught up in bands of sunlight set about them like matting in a picture. In a memorial pose were the two of them. Then she leaned her head on his shoulder when he had cupped her rear in what appeared to me to be the ultimate signal of giving all one might have, right there or in the immediate future. The ultimate of promises. I saw it framed. I wondered what her eyes looked like then, what they might have said, for I swear I heard the song in her begin; the near mute tra-la-la making appropriate commentary, the notes that move behind a smile.

The Corsican was a big man with a huge smile and marshaled a look in his eye that could dwarf anyone less than noble or courageous. Hair as black as a night skyline showed his eyes and his teeth to great advantage, making him softer, and gentler I'd bet, to mother. Also, there was directness to his actions, which she loved in strong men; they knew their wants, they spoke their piece, they took their booty. Thus, this cupping day, starting at breakfast, was hers in celebration. The bloom was hers, and the candy was mine. I never fully knew what that dalliance really was, until some years later I met the daughter of a Buick Roadmaster owner, and encountered my first dalliance in the front seat of the Roadmaster hardtop before the engine of that magnificent machine was humming again, though her humming, and mine, went complete.

If you want to know about me, how I was made and how I have come along the way, I'll let you in on just about all of it. Where I learned it I don't know, but it was in my mind and in the touch of my hands, primal, from the git-go. A gift clearly bestowed upon me. I understood things, contraptions, working parts, and their reasons for being, their methods of operation, what part did what job in the collected mission. Theory came easy, complex reads were simple tasks. Connections of all sorts found instant access in my thinking... schematics, plans, routines, processes. I saw it all and most immediately, a counterpart ingrained and

171

open.

Talent came, scads of it, like a flood or a bursting. Was all of it a trade-off? Was I driven there? Did I seek it out and dare not refuse it? Was I being recompensed for the role given me in life, and my mother's? I'll never know for sure, but today, in drop-dead certainty, I can hone a car to perfection (from tappet size to exhaust ratios and you can throw in all the kinds of theory you might advance), or a piano, or a guitar, sometimes so keenly at it that drivers or players exult at the zenith of their capacities. And with my ear I can make a harmonica nearly dance by itself, never mind an old piano awash in the universe, its old keys bouncing like a junk car's shock absorbers. I do horns, computers, VCRs, washing machines, dryers, you name it. I am a player and a doer. I am special and I damn well know it and they do too, mother and her friends. Hadn't that Ferrari and that old Strad peaked at my finger touch, humming alongside the universe itself, all that mellow music at the ear, all in tune with each other? I had it! I had it, every belly-pumping inch of it! Oh, what glorious humming I could accomplish! God, I'd often say, all of us should be so endowed.

But, despite all the ready goodness, all the acceptance and praise, all the tumult of ass-kissing accolades, I kept saying I would not, damned if I would, eat chocolate again. I couldn't afford it, so I kept saying it like prayers: Not a bite, bet on it! Not a Sky Bar chunk or a Tootsie Roll or the heavily-wrapped two dollar goodie she always brings home for me and a potential occasion. I'll not close my teeth again on a Heath Bar or a Hershey or an Almond Joy. Bet on it! Bet on it! Bet on it! Include Snickers and Milky Way and Three Musketeers in the whole toothy arsenal of hits. I'll read the books but I'll swear off the candy stuff.

I said it all the time and I relented all the time. I caved in.

And so I learned about trade-offs.

They caught us in Dockery's Greenhouse, the 3 A.M. moon in the first quarter, the alarm ringing, us stupidly afoot and agape. I was eight years old. All of us kids had seen the chocolate bunny in the window; it had ridden its tongs and grips deep inside. I knew what the grace of chocolate was, that cocoa distinction, that dark softness on the palate, the lingering mouthful of richness, and I enticed them with the sweet promises. And, as vowed, I picked the lock on the back door of Dockery's Greenhouse. It was a snap! And we hefted the chocolate bunny the night

172

just before Easter was to come along, and suddenly there was Dockery himself and the cop on the beat standing in the doorway. There was an uproar, of course, but we were kids and got away with it. I could taste that chocolate bunny even as my mother whipped my butt. But she liked men and I liked chocolate. They came together. I never knew if perhaps Dockery or the patrolman had formed a union with her.

I had my own reputation, I guess you could say. Not just precocious, but handy to the Nth degree. It did not take long to make that point, and to exact fair payment. When I was twelve I was doing a motor job on old Essering's convertible engine with poured Babbitt bearings Essering didn't even know existed. I blued them and scraped them and fine-combed those bearings and tuned all those parts and I made that car hum with a music it had not known in ten years. Out on the pike he swore it raced off at 80 miles an hour and he could hear the sacred humming in the seat of the pants. And he made my mother hum in his own turn, the old Dodge their transport. They rode off in that chariot for days on top of days and came back late. For weeks she was singing in the kitchen in the morning, and late at night. I remember the night I told myself I was a mechanic and she was a lover. There was one trade-off for you! Kid stuff that kids are made of.

And before you know it, there's a Buick Roadmaster being pushed into our garage at the side of the house. One of mother's friends, The Carpenter, had squared the garage away for my use, put up shelving, a skylight, a bench fit for Edison himself. The Roadmaster daughter's name was Amie; I think she came with the car. At least she was with it, it seemed, from Day One, sitting in the front seat, primping, exhaling, being smelled and inhaled above grease and oil flavors, and only fifteen years old in her burst of beauty. Once I caught her fondling herself, her eyes smoked with slow, dark combustion. Soon she was fondling me. I was hanging the exhaust system under that old Buick Roadmaster while lying on my back, part of me under the car, part not. She straddled me, as if she could not have altered those actions in this lifetime. She showed me she wore nothing under her skirt. "I never wear underwear," she said. It was an affirmation of destiny, the role in life, making one's own claim on things to be.

"Never. Never," she repeated, half the world in her eyes. I was to remember that statement, that vision, every time I saw her again, and lots of others for that matter. That day we advanced upward to the fabric of

173

the front seat, me straddled again, her knees against the back of the front seat. I suddenly knew I was different too. Another trade made.

I guess I essentially began to measure things then. My gravitation to all of this. How important Don Quixote had become and Huckleberry Finn and A Tree Grows in Brooklyn, and a man named John LeCarre and the hilarious first part of Freaky Deaky by Elmore Leonard and Robicheaux's fistey friend Clete painted up by James Lee Burke. I guess I began to know my mother better too, the way I began to learn more about books and stories and the people that put them all together.

When The Handshaker came in his turn, he brought nothing but himself. He asked for candy once in a while instead of bringing it, smiling at choice sweetness, thanking me cordially, but never overboard with his gratitude. The huge surprise was that he began to borrow books from me, read them quickly, asked my opinion on a number of books or authors, engaged in liquid conversations with me about where ideas might spring from, knew about Huck and Jim on the river, Mr. Timothy, Francie and Johnny Nolan down in old Brooklyn where the tree was growing. Interest walked with him on every corner.

And my most avaricious mother, my one-road, one-grained, one-mind, one-appetite mother must have sat up one day, suddenly like a light switch had been thrown in her darkness, and saw all that was about her. The Handshaker consistently made points. More than once he ushered a newcomer from the front door, his voice authoritative, at times imperial. Nights full of April lilacs and daffodils he kept to his room in the back of the house, and if they had meetings they occurred when I was not about. One day, after a pretty bad toothache had ground itself from existence, he convinced me and her that I should have many of my upper teeth extracted. That it would be best for me, even at sixteen. He kept saying it was not a sin, that new intelligence about teeth and implants and such things were steadily improving, that my health should be protected from the invasion of poisons my poor teeth kept inviting.

The transition among us was not noisy, but it was in motion.
"You'll smell better too," he added one day later when we were sitting on the porch, both of us relaxing from a book, mother in the kitchen preparing a fish meal he had proposed. "That's a gift in itself." I had not entertained the thought of bad breath. The Roadmaster daughter had never said a word about that. Nor another car girl after the

Roadmaster was driven away.

That's the night he told us about losing a son, how life ached for the longest time, and that a certain comfort had come upon him at our house he thought was no longer attainable. We were sitting on the porch again, one light burning above us, the lilacs with long hands touching us, the fireflies dancing at a distance, continuity expressing itself. I saw the effect on her, the way a curtain comes down on stage, makes separation, allows alterations. I remembered The Corsican's huge hand on mother's buttock, the sunlight on the walls, her yielding and signal gesture. Now silence was a gesture of its own. I heard her silence. I heard her acceptance. I heard eventual change inserting itself in our lives.

I bid the chocolate adieu.

As the philosopher says, The sweet taste lasts longer than the first bite.

The Catch of the Day

Three of us were tight as a fist, and Eddie's call came at 4:00 in the morning. His whisper, not wanting to wake his wife, said "Great storm at sea last night. Want to check the beach?" I knew he had called Ray already. Eddie knew false dawn practically every day of his adult life, his internal clock telling him not to miss anything the dawn brought along behind it.

An awakening grace on my end also told me it was Saturday.

That's all it took in the darkness beside my wife, turning, stretching, eyes blinking, rolling over, going back to sleep. She knew it was Saturday too.

Once before, after a storm out on the Atlantic, we had found a dozen quahogs at Nahant Beach, picked them off the sands with an assortment of sea clams on the mile of curving beach along the causeway linking islanded and insular Nahant to the City of Lynn. For years we swam at Nahant Beach, celebrated with evening cookouts, and watched the girls on long summer days.

In silence, in darkness until I reached the kitchen, I left a note for my wife: "Storm at sea last night. Will be at Nahant looking for quahogs to stuff and bake. Eddie called. Ray and I are going."

The morning was special. A summer nip climbed in the air, saying, as ever, that Saturdays are full of expectations – all you have to do is keep your eyes on the faintest line of the horizon where sky and sea make their ocular mix.

We did not bring baskets or bags (that would call for too much organization), but hurried to view the scene, not to be left out of the treasure yield the storm and Father Atlantic might have tossed onto the beach. On the way, in Ray's car, an old green Studebaker that smoked and made strange noises, we talked about grinding them up for baked stuffed quahogs for munching during TV hockey games, or for freezing them, after being ground up, to use in Thanksgiving turkey stuffing. Some would be earmarked for adding to the menu of a corn and lobster clambake classic in one yard or another, and large copper pots loaded with seaweed sitting atop several joined camp stoves.

In our five mile ride to Nahant there was little traffic, the sun just burping over the horizon, all of Europe halfway through its day.

We hit the beach, and were stunned; in front of us was the mother lode from Father Atlantic. As far as we could see, along the strand stretching away from us in a long curve, the beach was littered with quahogs and sea clams, all sizes, tossed like stars, fragments of an inordinate explosion. In joy and surprise we screamed at each other for not bringing baskets or plastic bags to carry off the loot. Hunger tantrums made way on us. The forgotten taste of baked stuffed quahogs came back in a hurry. Tabasco sauce, a glass of wine or a glass of beer, a kiss from the wild Atlantic. Wives would bustle, demanding condiments as varied as kitchen wallpaper, tastes born of hunger, experience, aromas brought back from mothers off on the long forever ride.

Scrambling for anything to carry them in the trunk of the car, we found an old pair of wading boots and two old work jackets. We rushed up and down the beach, filling all the limbs of those boots and the jackets, lugging them to the car. We filled the trunk and then the back seat. It was exhausting work, running back and fro, waiting for the hungry crowd to come over the horizon, to get their share.

We thought the morning was as complete as it ever could be, the three of us, Pine River fisherman, trout fisherman, who were mesmerized by sea food … lobster, clams, shrimp, the catch of the day stuffed and baked, broiled in the back yard over an open fire and matched with August treasures taken from our own gardens.

But, in another wake-up call, along the paved walk of the strand, on an old-fashioned skinny-tire bicycle might be next seen in the Antique Roadshow, going slow, studying the beach, came an elderly gent. He wore a shirt and tie, on a Saturday, and a blazer. His shoes shined like a car bumper just out of the car wash. Clean, creased, neat as rows of peas in the garden, he appeared as if he was ready to perform a ceremony, judge a criminal case, present the future to any audience looking over its shoulder. He was thin and wiry, but not squirrely. Something told me this straight-standing man was on the same hunt that we were, but likely it was more of a mission, a command he had accepted. The neatness came from by long habit.

We asked him if this was his regular morning constitutional, from insular Nahant, to pedal the causeway out and back, to keep fit what was an 80 year old body, at least.

"Not really," he said with a soft smile. "My wife Mirabel, she's sitting at home waiting for me, we've been married almost 60 years, sent me out to see if I could find a couple of quahogs she could stuff and bake

177

tonight. She knows her weather patterns, the tide climbing and leaving the rocks of Nahant, what happens out at sea that she can read sitting back here in a house she's lived in for more than 60 years; I'm not sure how many years. I know if I'm successful on my search, she'd pull out like magic out of her hat a nice bottle of wine from some place in the house, and we'd have ourselves a grand evening. Rich salt air, a little wine, music from a favorite old opera, and baked stuffed quahogs. The lip-smacking was in order. "It can't get any better than that." He smiled the soft smile again. He was not out to beat anybody.

The old man, we believed, at that moment between the tides and forever after, had found Nirvana and Utopia.

Ray, quick to spread his wealth, opened the trunk of the car. Quahogs, like huge coins, spilled onto the pavement. We filled the little basket sitting across the handlebars of the old gent's bike. A dozen quahogs, loaded with promise, sat like the riches of the Orient.

The air was special. Saturday was special.

Eddie said, "Do you want us to follow you home and make a special delivery, a big delivery."

"Oh, dear, no," the old gent said. "That would only spoil it."

To a man we knew what he meant.

We never saw him again.

We never saw the beach littered like that again.

We never made that trip again, time having its way, and mortality.

But I think about it often, and all the players on that special Saturday.

The Piano Man

Elsie heard the music coming from the garage, guitar music, the chords, the melody, and pretty decent at that. She nodded at her assessment, agreed. The summer air carried them clearly across the short walkway to the house, up onto the porch, coming home. Alec, after all the fuss, really had an ear for music he didn't know he had. Now she'd get her piano. By God, by whatever means, she'd get her piano. There had been discussions, or arguments, but only about fitting a piano in the living room ... what corner? Why? Why not? The children should be hearing piano music every day of their young lives; that's when it counts. She really believed what she was thinking, though work needed to be done, action started.

The chord came again; she'd know it forever, she told herself. She shivered as she thought Alec and her had merged more than one talent.

It was illumination time from both ends of their marriage. From the doorway she called out to her husband who had recently bought a used guitar, but a good one. "Alec, bring that instrument into the house. Play it in here. No need to play in the garage. You are not consigned to the garage. You're not a leper at music. You're not tone deaf. You're not a stranger to a good tune, a decent chord. In fact, you sound pretty damned good ... for a beginner." From her and from the garage, loud and long laughter followed her commendation.

For the rest of the day, even during naps for the two children after they enjoyed their father as a different person, Alec strummed the guitar. Chords, "really decent chords," as Elsie called them, carried into all corners, lifted up the stairs, and went out-bound to the porch and beyond. Ought to grab listeners with that stuff, she thought.

A neighbor's head lifted and cocked to one side as he listened and smiled. In the know he was concerning his young neighbors, and thought, Now Elsie will get her piano. Another chord, vaguely familiar from the deep past, caught him up in quick enjoyment; and an image tried to form itself but lost out, though the chord remained familiar. It would come to him during the day, happening that way, like an unbreakable habit coming unannounced. He went back to trimming the shrubs, the long hedge between their properties, between him and the young couple barely out on their long voyage. Mary-jo's face came back quicker than the lost chord, and then that mysterious chord returned.

He smoothly clipped away at the hedge, and began to whistle.

Doing much of the research on purchasing a piano (she had earlier collected some data), Elsie kept searching, knowing it would have to be a used piano; they could not afford a new one, a good one. Her friend Jess said she'd help by looking in the want ads. An hour later, Jess called back and said, "I've got a phone number for you. An elderly woman in Newton wants to sell her piano. Says it's not been played in a couple of years. Says she's 'preparing the ground work,' so you can guess what that's about. I'd call today if I were you. It's not a long drive. Lean on her about the kids needing a piano in the house, besides your wanting to play it so bad your back teeth hurt." Her sincere laugh followed.

Elsie waited until the children had been fed, showered, storied, tucked into bed. Alec, coaching the golf team, had the team under the lights at a friendly driving range, a donation from a former teammate on their high school defensive line, fast pals, jokers, whistling between plays, driving their opponents to certain distraction, an earlier form of trash talk with a beat, a tune. They loved jazz, country, light classics, but had no great talent at any of them.

Elsie knew he'd be home late. When silence settled its invisible mantle about the house, she dialed the Newton number."

The "Hello" brought with it an image of age.

"I'm calling about the advertisement you have in the Want-Ad Book, about a piano for sale. My name is Elsie Brookings and my children are really anxious for me to get a piano, and I can only afford a used one, and I'm wondering if yours is still available. If it is, we could be in Newton in the morning at whatever time you say is best."

"Oh, my dear girl," the elderly voice said, "It's a splendid idea to have a piano around for the children. I had one in every house I ever lived in. Of course this one is still available. Not many people have called." A pause told Elsie maybe the woman might be checking to see if her last statement was true.

"That's fortunate for me," Elsie said, "but not for you. Are you pressed for money? What kind of a piano is it? How much are you asking for it?"

"Oh, I am not pressed into this deed. It's just some of the ground cleaning I have to do at my age. I'm alone and have no relatives anywhere near here. I sold my home when my husband died, oh, a dozen or more years ago," …pause … pause … "and now I live in an apartment. My

180

name is Edith Jodrey. I know I won't be here forever. It would be lovely to entertain the idea that some children would have use for it, learn to play it, love it just the way I did. A piano always gave me such pleasure. I really think my husband married me because I played the piano ... I was a good at it, I might add."

The pause may have been to get her breath, Elsie thought, before Mrs. Jodrey continued; "I have to admit I am getting a bit excited by this. It's almost exactly like I dreamed it, or thought about it on many occasions. How old are the children? The piano is a Strause upright. It has a lovely tone, a lovely finish. Did I say I asked for $1800 for it? I'll ask $1500 just because it's you and it's a round number."

Elsie was thinking, Shadows and pauses carry messages. I better listen to her. A cousin who worked at a nursing home had once mentioned "sun-downing." Part of the conversation had lingered; "It's like the sun just falls down the other side of a mountain or a behind a big shadow."

Mrs. Jodrey laughed. "It's just my attempt at humor, my dear girl. Did you say how old the children are?"

Elsie could almost see her, a bit befuddled at the phone, a tear in her eye, a happy thought that she could place the piano into a family with children, "We have a girl of 7 and a boy of 5, Pamela and Richard. They have an interest in music. I can tell already, and that gets exciting for me."

"That's splendid, having one of each reaching for the notes. Believe it or not, my sister's name was Pamela and my brother's name was Richard, but we called him Windy most of the time. Pammy and Windy. Isn't that strange to hear it said like that?"

There ensued a long pause, a re-gathering pause. "They're gone now, and my older brother Harold, too. I'm the last of the Hunters. Oh, dear, does that sound terrible, being the last of the Hunters while I'm a Jodrey?"

Briefly, as if a switch had turned, Elsie imagined some joy spanning the elderly woman's features, lighting up the eyes and the quickly-pink cheeks, curving her soft lips, lifting her chin. Elsie also believed her old brow must have suddenly lost some of the indelible marks of care and worry. She thought immediately about sun-downing and sun-rising.

I better try some humor, thought Elsie. "Not at all, Mrs. Jodrey. I'm the first of the new Trotters. Does that sound like I'm tooting the horn too much? The first of the Trotters. Can you see Rockingham Park or Suffolk Downs in there somewhere, or Hialeah Race Track?" The giggle came naturally from Elsie, but she could see the elderly woman, the last of the Hunters, relaxing a bit more as she replied, "Dear heavens, no, but I'm dying to meet you. Bring the children so I can see who will be learning at my old piano as it gets born again."

Her small ecstasy carried through on the phone.

Elsie handed her husband the paper on which she had written Mrs. Jodrey's address in Newton, on Washington Street, with notes of landmarks near her building; "We're behind a huge clump of trees so the number can't be seen from the street. Some of us like it that way, the ones who don't have many visitors. Oh," she said again, the way she rode qualifications, "does that sound too elitist? I didn't mean it that way."

Elsie told Alec what she knew about Mrs. Jodrey, and added, "We have to bring the kids because I think they swung the deal for us, from $1800 down to $1500, get a truck to bring it home in, and some of your buddies to help move the piano. It's a Strause upright, in good shape, looks good and sounds good. So you'll have to marshal up some of your pals. Husky ones. Some blankets. One of those thingamajigs you guys are always talking about when you move a refrigerator for one of the gang. A dolly, is it?"

Alec nodded at each point of the preparations, per order of the woman of the house from the woman of the next house.

"Dell," Alec said later on the phone, "Alec here asking another favor. I need your truck and your muscle in the morning to move a piano we're buying in Newton. Need whoever can come with us. It's in an apartment building, but on the first floor, so it doesn't sound too daunting. We're getting a good buy on it. I checked out comparative prices. Elsie's bringing the kids. Seems they're the ones who locked the deal up for us, from an old lady who's marking her time."

The parade of vehicles, three of them, came down Washington Street from the highway. One truck with Alec and Dell, Elsie in the car with the kids, two pals in a sports car, the top down, the muscles showing on the passengers.

"There it is," Alec said, as he spotted the clump of trees blocking a decent view of a yellow apartment building. "We can run the truck right to the front door. The piano, as the lady said, is on the first floor, first room to the right. Looks easy from here."

Mrs. Jodrey invited all of them into her apartment and stood aside so they could look at the piano. It shone. It had luster. It looked tuned. With a wave of her hand the kindly old woman said to Elsie, "Please play a song for us, see how it sounds to you." She sat primly on the edge of a chair, as if she was sitting down for a concert.

At the first note of Claude Debussy's Clair de Lune, she closed her eyes and kept them closed, her head swaying for long moments, finding places to rest, swayed again, for more than four minutes of the song until Elsie finished her recital for purchase of the piano.

"Oh," Mrs. Jodrey simply said. "Oh," and then, "Still lovely, but I can't explain where I disappeared to or what I did. Simply lovely." Shadows fought for her eyes, took them.

Undoubtedly she had gone someplace and brought back early pieces of her life. "Be sure the children learn the old favorites that will stay with them all their lives." The litany came in a nonmusical rush; "Chopsticks, Twinkle Twinkle Little Star, Mary Had a Little Lamb, Happy Birthday, Away in a Manger, Greensleeves, and of course, your own Clair de Lune."

She stood up and said, "The piano is yours. With my gracious thanks." But shadows were winning a small battle.

The piano, with some little difficulty, was finally in the truck, covered with blankets and a large canvas, and the four men secured it in place.

On parting, Mrs. Jodrey hugged Elsie and the children. I know you will get great enjoyment from it, but I will think of what a gift the children now have."

Elsie said, "Alec will be right back with the check. Thank you very much for a real bargain. We will have a new life with it." She went out the door, ushering the children ahead of her, looking back once to smile at a woman with a long memory.

Mrs. Jodrey, with a sudden start as if waking from a dream that disappeared instantly, looked out the window and saw the vehicles parked in front, the big upright block of darkness tied onto the truck, a fire-engine-red truck. The car carrying the children, with their mother driving, pulled away from the curb. She knew it would be the last she'd ever see of them and she had forgotten their names, oh, so quickly.

The little sports car, almost no taller than a hydrant, also pulled away from the curb. She heard the deep hum of the engine sounding as if it was tunneled in a garage. She heard power, velocity, distance.

One of the bigger men, a giant across the shoulders, climbed into the truck on the driver's side.

For a moment she ignored the thought that fused up in the back of her head.

Then there was a knock at the door. She opened the door for Alec.

"I've got your check here, Mrs. Jodrey. This has been a marvelous morning for my family, my friends, and me." He handed her the check.

With a trembling hand, she accepted the check, looking down sheepishly the while.

Alec, as he turned to go, spun about and said, "I was wondering if there is a bench that goes with the piano."

"Oh," she said again, embarrassment flooding her features, "I am dreadfully sorry for forgetting the bench. One man from a music store answered an earlier ad, maybe six months ago, and didn't want the piano but took the bench. He said he would have to take it with him to evaluate it. He's never called back. At least, not yet." One hand was on her cheek in a manner of punctuation.

An image rose up in Alec demanding an explanation. "Did he look over the bench when he was here?"

"Yes, he did."

Alec saw the image forming. "Did he look inside the bench?"

"Yes, he did. I can see him doing it." She closed her eyes for a few seconds, and repeated, "Yes, he did."

"Did he see anything inside the bench?" Alec almost saw the whole image before she answered.

"Yes, but just a bunch of papers he looked at quickly."

The image was almost complete for Alec. "Do you remember his name, where his place is?"

"No, I can't," she said, "but I remember after he left I found a business card on the floor. It must have fallen from a pocket."

"Do you have the card now, Mrs. Jodrey?" He hoped all the questions did not disturb her.

"If I do, it's in my desk over there." She pointed across the room. "I put little things in one of the cubby holes on the top level. Please look for yourself. I think I've forgotten the names of the children already. Oh,

184

no, there's Pammy and Windy, isn't there?"

Alec let it go, but found a card for the Top Note Music Shop, with the address printed like sheet music notes on the bottom of the card. "May I keep this, Mrs. Jodrey?" He showed her the card.

"Of course," she said. "I have no need of it now." She looked around the room as though she was seeing it for the first time.

Alec jumped into the red truck and said, "Dell, we have a short detour on the way home. Go right out of here and stay on this road heading for Watertown and we look for this address." He held up the card.

Alec entered the shop to face a lone employee, or owner, setting a guitar up on a wall bracket and knew it was a Gibson at first look. Even his $1500 check couldn't buy this guitar, but that revelation did not cut into his errand.

The man presented a musical appearance, suave, bearded but trimmed neatly, sleepy-eyed, had a long face the beard had changed. His blue shirt had an open collar and his sleeveless white sweater was fully unbuttoned.

"Are you Mr. Saunders?" Alec said, as he withdrew a small notepad from his pocket and a ball point pen. He looked up at the Gibson, now a highlight for the whole shop as it hung on the wall. He made an entry in the note pad.

"Yes, I am. Have we met? Can I help you with anything? I see you know your guitars. Have I seen you playing locally?" He too looked at his latest display on the wall ... out of reach of the careless, those without loving hands, the common let-me-try-it-out customer.

Alec looked around the shop. "No, we haven't met, but we have a mutual acquaintance, a Mrs. Jodrey at the other end of the street, way back. You remember her, don't you? An elderly woman who had advertised a Strause piano for sale."

Saunders had flinched, showed a reaction in his jaw, and twisted his mouth in a grimace that rode up one cheek. "No, I don't think I do remember her. If I met her before, it must have been long ago."

"How about six months ago, in her apartment when you carried off her piano bench to evaluate it and never went back, never called her again. Yes, just about six months ago."

"Oh, it must have been worthless. I vaguely remember now. Just worthless."

185

"You do remember what it looked like?"

Saunders did not answer.

Alec jotted on the pad of paper. "How about anything inside the bench? Remember any of that?"

"Junk, from what I can recall. We often get odd material that's stuffed into anything of size. One drum, for God's sake, had notes taped on the inside. A pile of notes. A life story, mind you, of an incendiary creature bound to burn in hell." He laughed, his jaw working again, his whole face. "People scratch up IDs on the sheerest metal surfaces, like on horns, not knowing what they're doing." The face working again, visible tracks working on the big lie.

"All junk that you threw away? Is that right? But you remember what it looked like, Mrs. Jodrey's piano bench?" Alec scribbled again on the pad.

Saunders was coming apart, Alec could see, the telltale jaw in high gear every time he spoke.

At his immediate right side, Alec noticed a decent looking bench. The polished stain looked like that of the Strause piano now in his pal's truck.

He picked up the bench, held it over his head, and said, "Did it look like this one?" His voice carried past Saunders and ran into the back end of the shop, basso profundo all the way, heavy as a threat.

"Yes, it did," Saunders said, and seemed to shiver.

The bench sat upside down on his head, the polished mahogany shining bright as a beacon, as Alec went to the shop door. He could hear the motor purring in the red truck.

He turned once before he left the shop and said, "Thanks for nothing, Saunders. Call the cops if you want, but tell them you're a thief while you're at it."

It was the least he could do for a sweet old lady whose wandering wasn't over yet.

186

ABOUT THE AUTHOR

Tom Sheehan, a 24-time Pushcart Prize nominee, is comfortable writing in several different genres and makes it a point to create each and every day. He's authored the novels *Vigilantes East* and *Death for the Phantom Receiver*. His short story works number *A Collection of Friends*, *From the Quickening*, *Epic Cures*, *and Brief Cases*, *Short Spans* in all of which he manages to uncannily include a very special character, his hometown of Saugus, Massachusetts. His eBook releases are *Murder at the Forum* (an NHL novel of Bruins-Canadiens long rivalry), *Death of a Lottery Foe*, *Death by Punishment*, *An Accountable Death* and *The Westering*, nominated for a National Book Award. Sheehan's poetic ruminations are *Ah, Devon Unbowed*, *The Saugus Book*, *This Rare Earth & Other Flights*, *Reflections from Vinegar Hill* and the eBook *Korean Echoes*, nominated for a Distinguished Military Award.